DEVIL'S BARGAIN

KATHRYN SPARROW

DEDICATION

To B — For making life as crazy as Winthrop's mansion.

ACKNOWLEDGEMENT

So many people helped me make this book possible. I like to thank the following people for their special contributions

Robert for introducing me to characters like Winthrop.

The folks at Critique Circle for your invaluable comments and feedback. This book is so much better for it.

Mychael Black for helping me get this ready for the world to see.

And last but not least, my husband and children for their love, inspiration, and support.

TRADEMARK ACKNOWLEDGEMENT

The author acknowledges the following trademarks for company names and/or products mentioned in this work of fiction:

Google: Google LLC

Wikipedia: The Wikimedia Foundation, Inc

Tang: Mondelēz International

Velcro: Velcro BVBA

Viagra: Pfizer, Inc

Muzak: Mood Media

CHAPTER ONE

Monday, March 27, 5:41 P.M.

Equations danced on the page of Seth Griffin's Astronomy 4410 textbook. He pulled his glasses off and *rubbed* his eyes. Where was his roommate? He and Kevin usually went to dinner around this time, and Seth could use a break. Hanging with Kevin always recharged him, even if his best friend was straight and could never return Seth's well-hidden crush.

A large, manila envelope slid under his dorm room door with a scratchy hiss, catching on the corner of the cheap, blue rug remnant that covered the linoleum floor.

Curious, he placed his laptop and textbook beside him on his bed and rolled to his feet. A couple short steps and he stooped to pick up the envelope and flipped it over. His name, scrawled in fine calligraphy across the front, had smudged with dust. Who would hand-deliver something to his room? Cracking the door, he found the hallway deserted.

He opened the envelope and removed the papers it contained.

The first item was an invitation printed on pristine, white card stock with a picture of a playing card, the King of Hearts, at the top:

The honor of your presence is requested this Wednesday, March 29th, at the Statler Hotel at 7:00 P.M. to discuss your family's unfortunate situation. A business proposition will be presented that should alleviate the current difficulties.

When you arrive, report to the hotel check-in desk.

Dinner will be served.

No RSVP necessary.

Maynard Frederick Winthrop IV

What unfortunate situation? Who the hell was Maynard Frederick Winthrop the Fourth? Seth's chest tightened for a moment. He took a deep breath. No reason to assume the worst.

The next sheet was a signed and notarized paper showing Maynard F. Winthrop owned his parents' mortgage. After that was a document showing the same man owned their second mortgage. Wait, his parents had a second mortgage? His stomach flipped.

The fourth showed he owned their credit card debt. Was that even possible? Could an individual buy another individual's credit card debt? The bile rose in his throat.

The stack went on and on, his student loans, his brother Carl's student loans, car loans, everything. The last piece showed that Winthrop recently purchased ShoreStream Software, the company his dad worked for. His dad had spent a year unemployed, pounding the pavement before he finally landed that job.

A handwritten note on the bottom said: *It's good to hold all the cards.*

Seth rubbed his hand across his stomach, trying to calm the meteor storm inside. What did this man want with him and his family?

Money had been tight, but if these documents were real and accurate, then he had not known even half the difficulties his parents faced.

His education at Cornell stretched them even before Dad lost his job. They hadn't qualified for need-based scholarships and had no savings. Several student loans covered the steep tuition, but the money was still owed someday. And apparently, it was all owed to one man.

Seth lay back on his bed, staring at a mobile of the solar system hanging from his ceiling. He shook his head. *Focus.* First, he needed to scope out the issue. If there were problems with the family finances, his parents would have more information.

After all, this could be an elaborate prank. Would his teammates really screw with him like this? This seemed over the top even for Regi, the freshman prankster who had driven him crazy all season.

Speculating wouldn't help. He needed information first.

After dialing the phone, Seth pushed his glasses tighter on his face and ran his hand through his bushy, brown hair.

"Seth, honey, it's great to hear from you." His mother's voice bubbled out of the phone.

"Hi, Mom." Seth hadn't planned what to say, so the silence stretched.

"To what do I owe this pleasant surprise?" she teased.

He called his parents. Lots. When had been the last time?

He couldn't remember. "What? A guy can't call home?"

"Of course. I just wish you did more."

Why? When she wasted half the conversation making him feel guilty for not calling.

He opened his mouth to say something, hopefully coherent, when his mom spoke.

"Is everything all right?"

An opening. Thank you, Mom. "You tell me."

"What do you mean?" Something was off about his mom's voice. She squeaked by the end. "Things are fine here."

Nope, not buying it. Time to go for the detail. Would she deny it? "Do you know Maynard Winthrop?"

"Um… Why would you ask that?"

Not a denial, a deflection for sure. "He contacted me. He showed me some… documents."

"Documents?" His mother's voice quavered.

"Yeah. Like my student loans belong to him."

"Oh, honey." He imagined his mom, shaking her head with her eyes closed. "We're not sure what happened. He does own your loans."

Seth fell back against his pillow at the head of the bed. "And the mortgage?"

A pause. "And the mortgage."

It was all true? "What about ShoreStream Software?"

"What about it?"

Was Mom purposely being dense? "Does Winthrop own the company?"

"He just bought it, out of the blue. It was a hostile takeover. He cancelled all of the company's planned charitable donations and a few key projects." It was worse than he thought. His mom was babbling. "Your dad says his coworkers are reeling."

"Does Dad still have a job?"

"As far as we know. Mr. Winthrop hasn't made his plans clear. Your dad's put an updated resume online, just in case, but there isn't much out there. In the meantime, no one's seen Winthrop except the former CEO, Ted Hofstra. Ted went to a meeting with Mr. Winthrop and never came back. His office was cleaned out for him, and Winthrop sent an email that he was terminated."

Seth's skin pebbled like tiny, reverse moon craters. Terminated, as in fired, right? "And he has our credit card debt, our car loans."

His mom sighed. "Yes. He does."

"Do you know what he wants? Are we out on the street? Can we declare bankruptcy?" Seth's heart beat faster and faster as he gripped the phone to his ear.

"He sent a letter saying he had a plan. That there was no cause for alarm, yet, but he would be in touch. We haven't heard from him since. We tried to get another loan to pay him off, but our credit is shot. Oh, honey. We didn't want to involve you in this."

"Well, I'm involved now. He wants to meet me for dinner. Who the hell is this guy?"

"I wish I knew. Wait. He wants to have dinner with you?"

"Yes. He does. Did you Google him?"

"Yeah. There wasn't much. He's a bit of a mystery. Did he say why he wants to have dinner with you?" The quaver was back in her voice.

"He said, and I quote, '*A business proposition will be presented that should alleviate the current difficulties.*'"

"When?" Her voice strengthened. "Your dad and I will come up. We'll reason with him."

Part of him wanted to accept and be her little boy again.

Let his parents handle this so he could focus on studying and hanging out with his friends, especially his roommate, Kevin. But he wasn't a little boy anymore. His parents would never see that if he didn't step up. Besides, Winthrop must have had a reason he specifically invited Seth.

"The invitation was sent to me. I think I should go alone," Seth said.

"No." His mother's voice was firm. He knew that voice from a million turned-down requests for cookies. "Who knows what he's going to ask you to do. He's so rich. Maybe he's a mobster. I don't want my son being a drug mule."

That was Mom, always imagining the worst. He was surprised she even knew what a drug mule was.

"Somehow, I doubt that. Look, I think this is the best way. I'm an adult. I can handle this."

"I… I know. But this isn't your problem. We got into this mess. You shouldn't have to fix it."

"It wasn't your fault the economy sucked. I wish I'd known it was this bad. I could have taken a year off from school and gotten a job."

"That's exactly why we didn't tell you. Your education is important. You need this degree to work for NASA."

Seth yearned to explore the stars and would settle for nothing less than working for NASA. Originally, he planned to be a pilot, maybe go to the Air Force Academy to increase his chances of becoming an astronaut, but his need for strong glasses made that particular dream impossible. Not even the latest advances in laser surgery could correct his particular astigmatism.

It didn't matter. As long as he made a contribution, moved the technology forward, he didn't care, (well, mostly), if he actually went to space.

"And your friends on the basketball team. You don't want

to let them down." Her tone changed, more teasing. "Especially not your roommate."

No, Seth certainly didn't want to disappoint Kevin. He would do anything for the man. "Mom, we're just friends. You know he's straight."

"So? He's still your best friend. You don't want to disappoint him. Now, when is the meeting? We're coming."

"No. I'll handle this."

"Son, I heard what your mother said. We're coming up." His dad joined the conversation in that echoey way that meant the line had been switched to speaker phone.

"You two have taken care of me my entire life. I can help here. Let me scope this out and report back. I have to do this."

The sound of the phone being covered by something scratched through. As the minutes passed, images of what Winthrop could want spun through his brain. Could the man be into something illegal like his mom thought? *Holy shit.* Seth had never even had a parking ticket.

"Promise you'll report back?" his dad asked. "Don't agree to anything without us."

"Okay." Seth wasn't sure that was a promise he could keep. "Love you both."

"Love you, too, Son. Be careful," his mom added as the phone disconnected.

His stomach twisted into a knot. Maynard Winthrop would have his dinner guest. What could the man possibly ask him to do? It's not like he had ninja hacking skills. His father was the computer programmer.

Why would Winthrop target his family? Their debt wouldn't make a dent in his bottom line if he had the money to buy a profitable company like ShoreStream. Maybe that was why Winthrop did this. It was nothing to him, but he knew it would ruin them.

Maybe the man was merely inviting him to gloat? Sadistic bastard.

Whatever his motivation, Seth had a bad feeling about what the man had in store for him.

CHAPTER TWO

Monday, March 27, 6:27 P.M.

Seth's heart raced, and his mind would not stop whirling. Who was Winthrop? Without conscious thought, his eyes were drawn to the star charts on his side of the room. Their familiar patterns grounded him. He needed to study hard to earn his dual degrees in Astronomy and Mechanical Engineering, not worry about some eccentric billionaire.

He pulled out his laptop and typed *Maynard Frederick Winthrop IV* into the search engine. The first hit was Wikipedia. The man had his own goddamn Wiki page.

A photo sat on the top right of the page labeled Maynard Winthrop. Three hairs were artfully combed over his bald spot. Dishwater gray eyes looked directly at Seth, stabbing his brain. The man's large jowls and double chin defined the rotund shape of his face. A cigar hung from Winthrop's mouth, a curl of smoke twisting up. For a moment, the smoke seemed to actually move, its stink filling Seth's nostrils. He blinked, and the effect disappeared.

Seth shuddered. The man looked like a comic book villain.

Maynard Frederick Winthrop IV

Little is known about the elusive Mr. Winthrop. Even his date of birth has been kept a secret, although several sources state he was born sometime in February. Nothing is known about his family or upbringing.

What the hell?

Seth shook his head, wondering how this Wiki page had not been taken down or torn to shreds by enthusiastic Wiki users. How did they even know he was a fourth if they didn't know anything about one, two, and three? The pretentious prick probably just wrote it as an affectation. How could so little be known about someone in this day and age? Was he from Mars?

He first became famous during an unbelievable run of luck on the stock market, garnering several billion dollars in profit in a matter of days.

Now wait a minute. How was that even mathematically possible? He must have already had hundreds of millions invested to earn that much, and therefore, he would already have been known by someone.

The Securities and Exchange Commission investigated him for insider trading after this, but insufficient evidence was found to link the man to any of the stocks he purchased and sold.

He'd already been investigated once for something illegal. Insufficient evidence didn't mean innocent.

Mr. Winthrop is reclusive, rarely leaving his compound in upstate New York. No one has been able to get pictures of his house or the property. The spot has been blurred out on Google maps. Visitors to the compound who have been interviewed refused to comment on their time with Mr. Winthrop.

Fuck. That sounded bad. At least Winthrop only asked to meet Seth at the Statler, Cornell's upscale teaching hotel on campus. But the invitation had said to come to the check-in desk. He could only think of one reason Winthrop would invite him to his hotel room. Seth might be gay, but that didn't mean he wanted to have sex with the man.

Mr. Winthrop continues to invest in the market, but only realizes enough to maintain his position as the eighty-second wealthiest person in the world. He engages in a variety of small business ventures. These include buying specific loans of individuals, frequently resulting in those debtors being evicted from their property and their assets sold.

Oh, shit. Seth rubbed one hand on his arm, trying to get some warmth into his suddenly chilled body.

Winthrop had done this before? The page implied some weren't foreclosed on, but what did it take to get that to happen, and was it something he could do?

Could all of this be real? It was like being bombarded by a meteor shower of clichés.

Winthrop couldn't want him for sex. Seth knew he wasn't much to look at. He was lean from basketball, but his bushy hair forever fell in his eyes, and his thick glasses weren't even geek chic. If anything, he would describe himself as adorkable. But why meet at the hotel?

A girlish giggle buffeted Seth's ears like a sonic boom. His head snapped up, his eyes flitting from his laptop to his dorm room door. The paper-thin wood did little to muffle the high-pitched squeal.

The door slid open, causing the piercing, gleeful yipping to get louder. Kevin Fields, Seth's six-foot-three, lightly muscled roommate, moved his arm to encircle a five-foot-ten brunette whose curly hair had been highlighted with streaks of purple. Seth assumed this was Kevin's latest conquest.

Seth clenched his jaw as he snapped the laptop closed and stuffed the papers into the envelope. He was so not ready to discuss this with his roommate, much less his dish du jour. What had Kevin said her name was? Lisa? Lilly? Who could keep track? Kevin changed girls more often than he changed underwear.

The irritating giggling stopped abruptly as Kevin bent his neck and locked his lips with hers.

Seth held in the growl that threatened to emerge. *Not again.* Seth deflated. No matter how many times he saw Kevin with a woman, it still wrenched his heart like it was caught by the gravity from a black hole. *Being in love with a straight guy sucks. At least I've learned to keep my mouth shut so we can be friends.*

"See ya later, Lucy." Kevin straightened from leaning against the door.

"Ouch. My name's Lorie." She drifted away from the door, shoulders slumped.

Kevin's gaze followed her before he turned to his roommate.

Seth frowned. Kevin really could be a dick to women, but he'd never failed to have Seth's back. Like the time Kevin told off a homophobic frat guy. The ass made a rude comment about Seth having his arm around his old boyfriend, Ethan. Too bad that relationship couldn't last.

Steeling himself, Seth pushed his glasses up higher on the bridge of his nose. "Did you and Lorie have fun?" *Why am I asking him this?*

Kevin shrugged. "I guess. We were studying for a prelim in Developmental Biology."

Seth smirked. "What? Biology by Braille?"

Kevin flashed his winning smile and flipped him the bird.

"Maybe."

Seth brushed his shaggy bangs back over his head and went to open his laptop and resume studying when he remembered. Winthrop. Maybe he should ask Kevin if he'd heard of the guy. He shared everything else with Kevin. They practiced basketball together, studied together, and even had double dates together. Sophomore year, they decided to share a double room in Dickson Hall and had stayed in the same room for junior year.

However, his brain froze. Seth stayed silent, unsure how to explain about the unbelievable, surreal situation with Winthrop.

Kevin dropped his backpack on his perfectly made bed. It bounced once and fell backward against the wall adorned with posters of famous athletes and their inspiring quotes. If anyone was going to make it as a sports doctor, Kevin would.

"You look tense." Kevin's lips tipped up. "Let's grab some dinner."

Seth rolled his eyes. Food was Kevin's answer to stress. It was amazing the guy wasn't huge like a hippo. Admiring Kevin's lean, muscled chest, his neatly trimmed brown hair, and his brown eyes that sparkled with motes reminiscent of the Carina Nebula could easily become a full time distraction for Seth.

"I'm surprised you didn't grab dinner with Lorie." Seth tried to keep the snark out of his voice. He had no right to be jealous. Kevin wasn't his and never would be.

Kevin shrugged. "And miss a scintillating conversation with my best bro? No way." He dropped down to sit on the side of his bed with his elbows resting on his knees.

Warmth filled Seth as his heart fluttered. Kevin was straight, but he still cared about Seth. "She doesn't mind?"

"Why would she care? She knew the score." Kevin

crossed his arms over his chest. "She doesn't own me."

Seth shook his head. "No, but you did just nail her."

Tipping his head to the side, Kevin asked, "So?"

"You're such a douche. Do you think with anything other than your dick?"

"Dude, you're so serious. We were just having fun. I probably won't even hang out with her again. I've got my eye on this new girl on the cheer squad. Red curls, huge tits. Jessa or Janet or something like that."

Seth stared at Kevin. He could sympathize with these girls. If he had Kevin for one night, he would want him forever. But Kevin was always on the prowl. "You could try sticking with one."

"I will, when I find the right one. I don't see you with a steady boyfriend."

What could Seth say? Lately, Kevin didn't see him with anyone at all. It had been a while since Seth had even bothered to date. Occasional random hookups to get his rocks off didn't count. No, for something serious, no one matched up to his unavailable roommate.

"So, are we doing dinner or not?"

Seth glanced at his laptop. He still had a ton of studying to do and Maynard Frederick Winthrop the Fourth to worry about, but Kevin's smile beckoned him.

"All right." He stood up and put his coat on, following Kevin to the door.

Before today, Seth's worst problem had been hiding his feelings from his straight roommate. Now Maynard Winthrop, with his fucked up Wiki page, his penchant for buying loans, and his creepy invitation, had taken the number one slot.

CHAPTER THREE

Wednesday, March 29, 3:22 P.M.

Seth stomped out of Upson Hall, completely disgusted by his performance on his System Dynamics Prelim. *Dammit*. He knew this material cold, but his concentration had gone to shit.

His brain had fixated on the meeting later that day with Maynard Frederick Winthrop the Fourth. *Mustn't forget the fourth*. Pretentious prick. Maybe that wasn't fair. He didn't know what Winthrop wanted, but it didn't stop his imagination from creating more and more elaborate scenarios.

If the man planned to ruin his family, foreclose and sell off their house, fire his dad, and kick him and his parents to the street, why didn't he just get on with it? The suspense had Seth's insides knotted and his mind racing at warp speed.

Could Winthrop possibly have a solution that wouldn't involve Seth committing a crime? Maybe he thought Seth's mechanical engineering skills could be used to MacGyver his way into some top secret government facility or to steal some priceless artwork. It was awfully hard to see the stars from a prison cell.

How much did Winthrop really stand to gain? Investing in mining objects in the asteroid belt had a higher probability of increasing Winthrop's fortune than any profit he could obtain from Seth's family's debt.

A horn sounded, and Seth jumped back onto the sidewalk. He had crossed the quad and arrived at Campus Road without even realizing it. He waited for the light, and then crossed and continued walking. It didn't take long for his mind to circle back around to Winthrop.

Winthrop could make it impossible for Seth to continue attending Cornell. His dream of working for NASA would be ruined. Seth pictured his job prospects without a college education. All he could imagine was asking, "Do you want fries with that?"

Seth took a deep breath. He was being overly dramatic, like his mom. He would find a way, but right now, he couldn't see how. He already worked as many hours as he could while still maintaining his course load. Could he really continue at school if his family was out on the street?

But none of that really answered the fundamental question. *What does Winthrop want with me?* Seth couldn't imagine why the man would target his family and want to meet specifically with him.

He stopped and stared at the building in front of him, Willard Straight Hall. Somehow, his body had managed to navigate to the student union without his mind's input. He plodded inside and shuffled down the polished wooden stairs to the dining hall, like he always did after class. He filled his tray with food, some random source of sustenance, and sat alone, tuning out the boisterous diners around him. His stomach roiled as he moved the food around on his plate. Finally, he gave up and scraped it into a nearby garbage can.

Afternoon classes dragged by. His eyes stung, and his mind refused to comprehend the course material. He fell asleep in his Experimental Astronomy lecture.

When he returned to his dorm room, he stripped out of his Cornell T-shirt and jeans, and pulled out the interview suit his parents insisted he have. He smoothed it down with his hand. Maybe he should use the iron his dad had purchased for him.

He pulled on the white-collared shirt with narrow blue pinstripes, and then spent ten minutes attempting to put the knot in the tie in just the right place so the back part wasn't longer than the front. It seemed appropriate that he wore a tie since the damned obnoxious piece of fabric tightened around his neck like a noose. The dinner was really the execution of his dreams and of life as he had lived it.

At least multicolored constellations decorated his tie, pinned with a Halley's Comet tie tack. Winthrop might ruin Seth's life, but the man wouldn't change who Seth was inside.

Or would he? Perhaps Seth would have to make a choice. If he wanted to keep his dreams, would he have to compromise his soul?

During the twenty-minute walk across campus, he tried to clear his mind of the useless, spiraling thoughts that had plagued his day, but his stomach seemed to be filled with an active meteor shower. Perhaps it was best that it was empty.

When he arrived at the Statler, he reported to the check-in desk as instructed. A trill of fear made the lobby spin around him. Why weren't they meeting in the restaurant? Would he be going to the man's room?

He told the redheaded girl behind the desk his name. She looked so young with her hair in a bouncy ponytail and a smattering of freckles across her nose. *Must be a freshman.*

"Just one moment." She studied a computer screen, her

nose crinkling. "Ah, yes." She picked up the telephone and dialed a number. "Mr. Griffin has arrived." She paused. "All right. I'll tell him." She hung up the phone and focused on Seth. "Someone will be down to meet you momentarily. Please have a seat over there." She gestured toward an open corner of the lobby with windows like sheets of slate on two sides.

The space had several couches and chairs arranged into smaller conversation areas, each with a glass and wood coffee table in the middle. Several table lamps gave the night-darkened room a soft glow. Red carpets and ottomans completed the look. The room had an upscale feel with enough red to remind everyone that this was Cornell, the Big Red. Seth perched on a tan couch with red and white striped throw pillows, and waited.

A male voice called out from behind him. "Seth Griffin?"

"That's me." Seth didn't know what he expected, but it wasn't the little person approaching him. He wore a pinstriped, three-piece suit tailored to his three-foot-tall form. His belly had a slight paunch, and his thick, brown hair had been slicked back with a touch of gel that glinted in the light. A golden chain across his vest hinted at a pocket watch or some other ornamental jewelry.

"Mr. Winthrop is waiting. This way." The man headed to the elevators, his short legs covering more ground than Seth expected. He found himself taking long strides, using his full five-foot-eleven-inch height to keep up.

Something in the way the man said *waiting* made Seth's palms moisten and goose bumps dot his arms. He checked his watch. It was only 6:50 P.M., ten minutes early.

Why were they going up to the hotel rooms? There could only be one reason the man would want to meet in such a private space. Seth's chest tightened.

Sex.

Winthrop must want sex. Seth would have to prostitute himself to save his family. But that made no sense. Why would the man spend hundreds of thousands of dollars just to get laid? Granted, Winthrop wasn't all that attractive, but Seth bet there were plenty of men and women who would be happy to satisfy his needs for so much less.

Unless he got off on the power trip. Seth's stomach flipped.

The little man stood on tiptoe to press the top button. After the elevator passed the floor below the top, Seth's nerves went into overdrive. Ants seemed to crawl over his body for a moment before the sensation passed.

The elevator opened into a small lobby with a single door. A label to the side of the door read Royal Flush Suite. A fancy wooden chair with blue upholstery sat to the right of the door. The Statler had only one suite on the top floor? Space was so limited on the Cornell campus; there should have been several smaller suites.

The little man led him through the door into a small sitting room. A large, midnight blue velvet couch with little gold button accents reminiscent of the night sky sat flanked by two satin navy and beige striped chairs. A dark wood coffee table with intricately carved legs stood in the middle.

The table legs resembled cherubim, with little wings, holding bows and arrows. *Bizarre.* Wouldn't the legs be carved like the bell tower or some other Cornell icon? Maybe this was what the rich donors expected when staying in the Statler's penthouse.

"Have a seat," the little man said.

Seth perched on the edge of the couch and stretched his collar. A bead of sweat rolled down his back. The little man knocked on a second door at the back of the room, paused a moment, then opened it and went through, closing it with a quiet click.

Seth tried to stay calm by singing the alphabet song. After seven repetitions, he moved on to reciting the names of celestial bodies he knew. The first Messier object (M1), known as the crab nebula. M2, a Globular Cluster in Aquarius. M3, the Globular Cluster Canes Venatici. When he finished the Messier objects, he moved on to The CMB cold spot, the Eridanus Supervoid, a so-called hole in the universe. Thinking about the icy spot sent a chill through him, raising goose bumps on his arms.

Clearly, Mr. Winthrop was not waiting to see him. Or was he purposely making him wait? How was he going to survive dinner without upchucking like a freshman at a frat party?

He wished he could just leave. Walk out the door, go back down the elevator, and return to his studies. But he had to do this. Had to meet with Winthrop and see what the man wanted. Would the bastard eject his father from his job and launch his family from their home? Seth couldn't let that happen.

He checked his watch. Almost an hour had passed. He stood up and paced around the luxurious room. Off to the side was a large picture window that had a spectacular view of the Cornell campus, all lit up at night. The lights seemed to sparkle, making the campus seem otherworldly and magical in a way that it never had before. He almost smiled. He had lived here for three years, but he could still be caught in the Big Red's spell in a whole new way.

He glanced toward North Campus, knowing Kevin was probably studying in their room. At least, he wanted to think his roommate worked on a problem set or read for a class. Just as likely, Kevin was memorizing the curves of yet another girlfriend. Seth swallowed and tried to purge the image from his mind.

Finally, the door opened, and the little man returned to the room.

"Come. Mr. Winthrop is not a man to be kept waiting."

Seth clamped his mouth shut to prevent a huff of breath from escaping. He followed the little man through the door to a snug dining room with a round table that could seat eight people, although there were only two places set. Two tuxedoed men flanked a door at the far end. And there, seated at the head of the table, the bald man from the Wikipedia entry—Maynard Frederick Winthrop IV.

The little man, his head just barely visible above the table, moved to stand beside his boss. Winthrop had a cell phone at his ear. A feral grin adorned his face. His cigar hung out the side of his mouth. The curl of smoke rising from the cigar smelled like popcorn left in the microwave too long.

Seth resisted the urge to cough. Wasn't smoking prohibited in the hotel?

Winthrop's hair was either very greasy, or styled with way too much gel. And what was the point? The few hairs that had been combed over did nothing to cover the enormous, shiny bald spot. The rest of his hair was cut short and formed a one-inch crescent around the edge. A patch of red marred his head on the top toward the back. Was it a cut or perhaps a rash?

Winthrop reached up and scratched at the spot. "Unacceptable." His high-pitched voice had a strong nasal quality to it. "I'll have it in the morning, or I'll have your head. Quite honestly at this point, I don't care which."

He glanced up at Seth and gestured to the other seat at the table.

Winthrop took a slow, deep breath. "That's better."

The man to the right of the door stepped forward and pulled out the chair for Seth. A ridiculous amount of silverware surrounded the delicate china plate set in front of the seat. Six forks, the first two were tiny, two knives, and two spoons were in the usual places. A nutcracker and a pair of tongs were laid out around the top of the plate. An ornate crystal flute was placed behind and to the right. An elaborately folded napkin perched in the center of the plate. Did they really need all this crap? Stuff like this only existed in the movies.

The man in the tuxedo stepped beside him as he sat, lifted the napkin, and opened it with a snap, laying it gently across his lap while he stared at the man.

"See to it." His host finished his conversation then tapped once on the phone screen and handed it to the little man, who stowed it in an inside pocket of his suit jacket.

Maynard Winthrop was fat, obese really. This was clearly the stomach of a man who ate plentifully and often. He was dressed in a distinctive, charcoal grey three-piece suit that was similar in some ways to the little man's, but the fabric looked finer somehow, with neat hand stitching along the lapel edges. Although every line was designed to accentuate the positives of Winthrop's body, the suit had its work cut out for it.

"Seth Griffin. It's too fabulous to meet you." Winthrop puffed the stogie and then tapped it to deposit some ash in the tray. "Can I call you Seth? Of course, I can." He expelled a stream of smoke as he exhaled. "Thank you for accepting my invitation this evening. I don't often get to dine with such an…" Winthrop surveyed Seth, "attractive young man."

Seth's heart rate sped, and his stomach clenched. Winthrop had him by the short hairs and wanted a personal tour of the area in question. Seth fought to keep the revulsion off his face. He waited a beat to ensure his host was finished speaking before he responded. But what was safe to say?

"You're welcome? Mr. Winthrop, I really don't know why I'm here."

"My boy, please, call me Maynard. I insist. But we'll talk business after we enjoy this special repast I have planned for you." He took out a monocle with a shining gold rim and held it up to his right eye. "Just look at you. All young and strapping. Yes. It's a pleasure to dine with you."

Bile rose in Seth's throat. This was so over the top. Buying his family's debt just to get Seth in his bed seemed beyond insane. What in the name of the Western Spiral Arm was going on?

One of the tuxedoed men stationed around the room stepped forward and pulled a bottle from an intricately cut crystal bucket of ice. He turned to the side and popped the cap, then served Winthrop, who took a sip, nodded, and belched with a grin on his face.

Then the server came around and poured some in the matching, crystal fluted glass in front of Seth.

"I'm not twenty-one yet."

Winthrop's eyebrows rose suggestively. "I won't tell if you won't."

Seth shrugged. What college student hadn't indulged? Although it had been rare for him. He lifted the glass to his lips, and the bubbles tickled under his nose. He took a sip. The slightly bitter liquid slid smoothly down his throat.

"To new endeavors," Winthrop said.

Seth lifted his glass to toast, fearful of what endeavor Winthrop referred to, but also not wanting to insult his host. "To new endeavors."

Maynard snapped his fingers, and a door behind him opened. Two men, also in tuxedos, emerged. With a synchronized flourish, they placed plates in front of Seth and Winthrop.

"Oysters on the half shell. I arranged to have them flown in fresh today from Prince Edward Island."

Seth looked down at his plate as heat rose in his face. Weren't oysters an aphrodisiac? Was this Winthrop's sick attempt at seduction? Seth wished the man would stop this crazy show and just get to the point.

Seth had never tried the slimy looking things. His host

lifted the small fork set at the outer most edge of all the forks and then used it to pry the oyster meat from its shell. He dipped it in a red sauce and then slurped it into his mouth.

"Eat. These are just lovely." Winthrop gestured to Seth's plate.

Seth worried that his stomach would reject the gooey little creatures that were still technically alive. Thank God they didn't move.

Winthrop barked out, "Don't be rude, boy. Eat."

Seth held in a sigh. He needed to get through this meal without insulting his host so he could learn what the man wanted from him and his family. He lifted his fork, mimicking Winthrop's actions, and slurped the little bit of sauced meat into his mouth.

The pleasant, salty flavor mixed with hints of horseradish as he chewed and swallowed. He made sure to eat slowly, not getting ahead of his host. His appetite had returned, and his stomach growled.

As soon as he finished the last one and placed his fork on his plate, the formally-dressed server whisked it away.

Winthrop reclined in his dining room chair, placing his hands on his prominent belly. "So tell me, why double major in Mechanical Engineering and Astronomy?"

Whoa, where did that come from? "I want to work for NASA. I want to design spacecraft."

"A lofty goal. The US government has not been as supportive of NASA as it once was."

"I know. The politicians are stupid and shortsighted." Seth's eyebrows drew down. "Space is the future. The things we've discovered from space exploration have benefitted mankind."

"Do you mean Tang or Velcro?" Winthrop smirked.

"Actually, neither of those things was created by NASA. Water filters, cordless tools, and long-distance telecommunications are a just a few of the technologies that resulted from the space program."

Winthrop shrugged. "At what cost? Twelve billion for a space pen?"

Seth huffed. Winthrop had discovered one of his pet peeves. He knew he should try to move the conversation to his family situation, but he couldn't stop himself from dispelling this urban legend. "Another myth. The space pen was developed by a private company and sold to NASA. Besides, pencils are nasty in zero-g. The lead breaks, and you get dangerous particles floating everywhere."

"You like to argue." Winthrop's head tilted so that he glared down his rotund nose.

Seth snapped his mouth closed. The last thing he needed was to antagonize this man.

The servers brought the second dish, another shelled creature.

"*Escargot*, snails. Served in a garlic herb butter."

It seemed it was going to be a night of firsts for Seth. He again looked to his host, who selected the tongs and another small fork. Using the tongs, he picked up a shell and scooped out the meat inside.

Seth followed suit. He retrieved the snail flesh and plopped it into his mouth. The garlic caressed his tongue, although the meat itself was a bit chewy. He glanced at his host.

Winthrop watched him intently as he chewed. "Do you like the snails?"

Seth wanted to shrug. Butter-flavored rubber really wasn't his idea of a good time, but his host had him captive. *Smile and get through this.* "They're interesting."

"I didn't expect sparkling conversation, but you're even

quieter than I imagined. Why space exploration? Go deeper…."

Seth considered the request. Most people were satisfied with that answer. He put his fork down. "Do you really want to know?"

A broad grin swept across Winthrop's face. "Yes. I really do."

Seth shook his head in surprise that Winthrop seemed to care. Could his answer here affect what Winthrop had planned? "We are trapped on this one little planet. Except for the bottom of the ocean, we've been there, done that. Nothing new. But out there, the possibilities are infinite. The things we find will defy our imaginations."

Winthrop smiled. "Indeed, it is just one small planet. I like you, Seth Griffin."

Was that a good thing? Perhaps it meant he would really help Seth. Or it could mean he wanted to keep him even closer. Either way, as Winthrop pointed out, the man held all the cards, so Seth held his tongue.

The next dish placed before him appeared to contain several chicken wings. Seth was relieved to see something more in his comfort zone. He picked one up, opening his mouth to nibble the meat from the bones before noting that his host was using fork and knife.

His face heated as he placed the wing down on the plate and picked up his fork and knife. He sliced into the meat, although the skin's texture was slightly off. He placed a piece into his mouth, enjoying how tender it was.

"I see you are a devotee of frog's legs. A particular favorite of mine."

Seth had to clamp his mouth shut to prevent himself from spitting out the delicate meat. It wasn't the flavor. It tasted like chicken. It was the surprise. He forced himself to chew and swallow before taking a swig of champagne. He took a deep breath, sampled the asparagus artfully arranged next to the frog's legs, and then continued with the meat.

"You know asparagus is an aphrodisiac. I just couldn't resist including it with this meal."

Seth chose his words carefully. "This feels more like a date than a business meeting. I… don't think… well…"

Winthrop's eyebrows rose as his eyes met Seth's. "Kid, you're not my type."

Whew! Seth's heartbeat slowed. He wouldn't be forced to have sex with the man. Maybe Winthrop really had another way for Seth to pay off the family debt. Other options swirled through his head in a montage of horror. His mom already suggested drug mule, and his mind supplied male prostitute. He could imagine this man in the role of pimp, complete with a hot pink Cadillac and a fedora with an obnoxious feather. That frightened him even more. His heart rate took off like a rocket ship careening into space. Could a fit twenty-year-old have a heart attack? Was his left arm feeling numb?

Taking a deep breath, Seth asked, "Then what is this about?"

Winthrop glared down his nose and frowned. "I said we would dine first and then talk business. Don't anger me."

Seth nodded and dropped his gaze to the food. He took a few more bites of the frog's legs and asparagus. They really were well-prepared and tasty.

I'm eating demented food while a madman plays with my life and my family. But I'm hungry. Weird.

Again, the next plate looked pretty standard. Enchiladas with rice and guacamole. A bowl of chips and salsa was placed before him. However, Seth had learned not to trust his first impressions and looked to his host.

Winthrop giggled. "Rattlesnake and ostrich mole enchiladas." The word mole rhymed with olé.

Seth nodded and took a deep breath. He thought about starting with the rice or chips, but decided to face the crazy head on. He cut a small bite and placed it gently on his tongue.

Heat. Sweat dotted his brow. His tongue burned. Yes, he was a lightweight when it came to spicy food. He took a healthy bite of rice and another sip from his champagne flute, which seemed to be refilled every time he put the glass down.

"I love the interplay of the snake with the ostrich meat. The use of chocolate as a savory instead of a sweet endears this dish to me," Winthrop said, chewing with his mouth open.

Another bite, another wave of heat. Seth nursed the food slowly, wishing he could stand to wolf it down. He wanted this meal over with.

"It's time to cleanse our palates. The intermezzo is a pomegranate sorbet."

Cleanse our palates? How many courses does this meal have?

The cool sweetness was a welcome relief from the burning peppers. Was there some strange ingredient in the sorbet like the other dishes? His host remained silent as he spooned the icy treat into his mouth.

The server who had brought all of Seth's dishes came up to him, holding a piece of cloth. Snapping his wrist to the side, the man unfurled the cloth, revealing a large, deep purple, rounded piece of fabric. The server then leaned in and placed this on Seth's chest, tying it around his neck. He was startled to realize he was wearing a large bib.

"The fabric is a Mulberry silk. Too bad it will be ruined by the end of the meal."

Seth looked up to find his host similarly attired as a platter was placed before him.

"Two-pound Maine lobsters, flown in fresh today, with drawn butter, steamers, and sweet corn on the cob. Bon appétit."

Again, Seth worried the food would have some surprise, disgusting ingredient. If it did, his host would no doubt be delighted to tell him. He picked up the nutcracker and started dismantling the shell that guarded the succulent meat. Everything was delicious, the steamers perfectly prepared, the corn burst with sweetness on his tongue. The tail of the lobster was decadent in its size and richness.

It was a good thing he was wearing the bib because the liquid from the lobster seemed to go everywhere. Winthrop had a clown smile of butter and lobster bits around his lips.

The meal seemed endless. Between sleeping poorly the night before, a stomach full of rich food, and so much champagne, his shoulders slumped and his eyes drooped.

"You look like you're going to fall asleep on this table, boy. That might be amusing, having you at my mercy."

A shot of adrenaline worked through his system, snapping him out of his fugue and urging him to flee. But he had to stay, had to see this through and learn Winthrop's plans for his family.

Another course…How many had there been?

"Pesto Fusilli, with figs and bull testicles."

This time Seth couldn't hold in the spray that shot forth from his mouth. "What? Why?"

"What's wrong? Consuming the sexual organs from other animals is said to make a man virile."

Heat rose in Seth's cheeks. *I thought he didn't want to have sex with me.* Somehow, Seth finished the pasta before him. Like everything else in this meal, it was unusual, but not unpleasant if he could just keep himself from considering the source.

"And now, for the pièce de résistance, chocolate-covered strawberry banana shortcake." Winthrop dabbed at his mouth with his napkin. "There's one thing I don't understand about you. You're gay. You're out. You live in a liberal state. But you rarely hook up. No boyfriends. Nothing. What gives?"

What? Why did Winthrop know he was gay or care?

"Excuse me. I don't see how that's any of your business."

Winthrop's brows climbed. "Believe me, it's my business. Everyone has needs, but you live like a monk."

"I'm a double major across two colleges and a varsity athlete. I don't have time for a boyfriend, and I'm done with hookups."

Winthrop shook his head, a frown marring his face. "That's crazy. There are even a couple guys on your team who have offered to blow you, bottom, top, whatever. But you keep refusing. Even on those away games, alone, in a hotel."

"Look. Enough of this." Seth slammed his hand down on the table. "I came here. I sat through this meal. It's done. You clearly have my family and me over a barrel. Isn't it time to tell me what this is all about?"

"As you wish."

CHAPTER FOUR

Wednesday, March 29, 11:27 P.M.

Winthrop rose from the table with a flourish and gestured for Seth to follow. Someone so intimidating should have been tall, but surprisingly, the squat, rotund man barely crested Seth's shoulders. Would they finally get down to business?

Seth glanced down. Winthrop's shoes had thick soles, increasing his height by several inches. Seth tried not to stare but failed completely. And Winthrop wasn't the shortest man in the room.

The little man, who had escorted Seth to dinner, stepped away from Winthrop's side, opened another door, and then led them down a long hallway. Seth never imagined that the Statler held such a large suite.

Seth shivered even as his face heated. Will this never end?

A staircase led up left. Little man opened a door on the right and gestured for them to go through.

Centered against the back wall stood an impressive mahogany desk. Behind it sat a huge, leather chair with a curved wood-lined top and gold pins attaching the leather to the back and arms. Abstract paintings in muted shades of blue and green adorned the walls, while an intricately woven area rug covered the floor. Two small, wooden chairs, that wouldn't have been out of place in an elementary school classroom, were stationed on the other side of the desk.

Winthrop climbed onto the throne-like piece of furniture, the back of which rose well above his head. "Sit." Winthrop pointed at the seat on the right.

Seth's knees pushed up, and the hard wood pressed against his butt, while the horizontal slats weren't wide enough to support his back. He craned his neck up to meet Winthrop's eyes.

Winthrop clearly had a complex about his height.

Winthrop waved a hand over the envelope on the desk. "I assume you received the duplicate of this."

Seth refrained from saying something snarky, like: *How should I know what's in the envelope?* Or *Would I be here if I hadn't?* Instead, he said, "Yes."

"So I think we can both agree. I'm holding all the cards in this game."

Seth leaned forward a little, his eyes narrowing. "This isn't a game. It's my real life. You've threatened me and my family. I want to know what you want."

Winthrop's mouth cracked into a huge smile as his eyes twinkled. "That's what makes this so exciting."

"I read about you. Is that why you ruin people? For excitement?"

"You read about me? How extraordinary." The peacock presented his tail feathers. "I don't ruin people. I give them choices. I'm going to give you a choice, too."

Here it was, finally, the heart of the matter. At least, he hoped so. Seth swallowed a hint of bile. "What choice?"

"You are direct." Winthrop folded his hands over his substantial stomach and met Seth's gaze with a smirk. "I'm going to give you an opportunity to wipe out your family's entire debt. They would own their house, free and clear, no more money owed. Your student loans would be forgiven, and you'd be given enough money for you to finish college without incurring any more debt. I'll even give your father a promotion at ShoreStream."

Seth sat back in his chair as his stomach dropped. What could Winthrop possibly want from him? A testicle for one of his dinner parties?

Winthrop snickered. "You look like you've seen a ghost. You should see yourself. Your eyes are huge like the full moon, and your face is just as pale. It's adorable."

"I… I…What do you want?"

"It's actually rather simple. You'll spend one week, your upcoming Spring Break, at my mansion in upstate New York. During that week, you'll do whatever I say, meaning…" Winthrop leaned forward and perused Seth from head to toe. "Sexually."

Oh, shit!

"At the end, if you fulfill your end of the bargain, you're free, and your debt is gone, your family is safe. If you refuse, I fire your father, foreclose, and put your family out on the street, etcetera, etcetera."

Seth gasped for air. "That's crazy." Was that his voice? That hysterical, high-pitched squeak? "I thought you said I wasn't your type."

"You're not my type. Few are." Winthrop's face fell, and his eyes focused somewhere over Seth's shoulder for a moment. "The truth is…I like to watch. I'm really a voyeur at heart."

His mind spun into overdrive. Sex with people he didn't know. Would Winthrop ask him to perform with a woman? Seth had been certain of his sexual orientation at age fourteen. At twenty, he wasn't sure he could get it up for a woman. How many partners were they talking about? What if they hurt him, mutilated him? He bet that would thrill Winthrop. His stomach continued to roll and threatened to spill its rich contents.

"Now, boy, I suspect you have all kinds of crazy fears. Let me spell it out. You will not be maimed or marked permanently. You won't be shared like a whore. I merely want to… run you through your paces. So to speak. One partner." Winthrop leered at him. "My choice, of course. A few scenes for my entertainment, and then you're done."

Did one partner make it better? No. And Winthrop still wasn't specifying who, much less the gender. But then Seth considered Winthrop's exact word choice, and little meteors pebbled his skin and drops of sweat rolled down his back.

"Scenes like BDSM? Will I have a safe word?"

Winthrop sat up straight, his eyes wide and his jowl's lifting as he grinned. "Oh ho, you never struck me as someone into the lifestyle."

Seth swallowed. "I'm not. I read a lot."

"So you read it. Perhaps you'd like it." Winthrop winked.

The insane food from dinner was about to decorate Winthrop's desk. "I doubt it. I'm a voyeur as well."

Winthrop laughed. "No BDSM, just sex. I've already chosen the person. And before you panic, a male partner. I have a feeling you're going to like him. You'll learn who when you arrive. If you agree, a limo will be waiting for you after your last class on Friday."

This was insane. How could he even consider this? How could he refuse? Winthrop was willing to spend hundreds of thousands of dollars to watch him have sex. None of this made any sense. Unless… Winthrop screwed him figuratively instead.

"How do I know you'll keep your end of the bargain?"

Winthrop's eyebrows rose as he stared intently at Seth. "Everything will be legal and in writing. If you are still at my mansion at the end of the week, seven days, I sign everything over to you."

"I … I …"

Winthrop snapped his fingers, and the little man gave Seth a card. "Enough questions. I'm a gentleman. Take the night to think about it and call me with your decision in the morning. Erex, show Seth out."

Erex? What kind of name was that? Erex gestured for Seth to follow him.

As they rode the elevator, a shiver passed over Seth.

The lights on the campus buildings and the stars in the night sky sparkled, although they no longer seemed magical. The temperature had dropped considerably, and the wind whipped up East Avenue, cutting him like the impact of thousands of tiny razor-sharp meteors. He zipped up his coat and hunkered down, pushing through the blow. He headed for his dorm on North Campus.

Crossing the Thurston Ave. Bridge, he fought an inappropriate, hysterical urge to chuckle insanely at the high fences that had been installed to prevent the famous Cornell suicides. For once, he could see the allure of ending it all, but that would only make his family's situation worse. They would still lose everything financially, and they would have to deal with his loss as well.

Instead, he considered having sex with an unknown partner. Basically, star in live porn for a week. People did worse. Hell, he'd imagined worse.

What would he tell his parents? They would try to stop him from prostituting himself just to save their house and his father's job. After all, no one would die if he turned Winthrop down.

Although, who knew how long it would take his father to find a position this time? Dreams of NASA would head to the back burner while he searched for work.

He'd have to leave the dorm, leave Kevin, sooner than planned. Was that for the best? Maybe he could get over his crush with some distance.

Maybe it wouldn't be so bad. Winthrop, the bastard, was asking him to… what…have some meaningless sex? What was the big deal? Guys did that all the time.

Dammit! His body, his choice. Winthrop was basically blackmailing him into laying still while someone raped him. Asshole!

There had to be something he could offer instead. Maybe his parents could talk to the man. *Right*. Winthrop had been clear. They had no leverage, nothing to bargain with. They had a mismatched hand to his royal flush. He had to do this.

Would he be able to face his reflection after? A quiver passed through him. This experience was going to change him. He wished he could go back to before he'd heard of Maynard Frederick Winthrop IV. His problems then: tests, making shots in basketball, being in love with his roommate, all seemed so small compared to the astronomical choice he was being asked to make.

It was time to grow up and face the future.

His hand shook as he took out his cell phone. He took a deep breath and exhaled before dialing. "I talked to him. He offered me an internship with a private company he owns. They do space research. He's going to give us time to pay all the money back. Dad's job is safe." The lies rolled off his tongue. "He did all of this to convince me to work for him instead of NASA. I said I'd try it. It doesn't really matter who funds the research."

"You're joking," his mom said with a nervous titter. "That seems a bit extreme."

Seth tried to keep his voice calm and even. "The guy is probably certifiable. A real whack job. But a very wealthy whack job."

"You think he's insane? Are you sure you're safe? He isn't luring you into the job to hurt you?"

"No." *Yes.* "I think it's safe." *Um, not really.* "I just meant… he likes to play games. It was more fun for him to… hire me this way."

His mom let out a relieved breath. "Son, I'm proud of you for handling this."

Why did that make him feel worse?

He hung up and pulled out the little card, dialing as he walked.

"Hey, Seth." Erex's voice spat out of the speaker.

"Tell Mr. Winthrop, I'm in."

CHAPTER
FIVE

Thursday, March 30, 5:42 P.M.

Seth stared down at his plate, barely registering it contained food. Although noisy chatter swirled around him, it had long since faded to white noise. He poked at a meatball, breaking it into pieces.

"Dude, what is going on with you?" Kevin asked for the third time. "You haven't eaten a bite."

Seth glanced across the table at his roommate and shrugged. "It's been a stressful week."

"I know. All my professors wanted to get in one last test or project." Kevin gestured to the large pile of empty plates on his tray. "I really need to learn a better coping technique than eating my body weight." Kevin grinned. "But break starts tomorrow. You're going home, right?"

"Uh, yeah." Seth hated lying to Kevin, but there was no way he was explaining what he was actually going to do over spring break. It was too... something. Embarrassing. Maybe? Mortifying? Cheating? Wait. It couldn't be cheating. Kevin was his friend, not his boyfriend. But that didn't stop his empty stomach from wanting to heave.

"You don't sound excited to be going home. Stay on campus with me." Kevin's one-hundred-thousand lux smile shone on him. "We can chill out, maybe play some ball?"

Any other time, Seth would have launched into orbit over the invitation. "Sorry, my folks are expecting me." Seth moved the cold spaghetti around on his plate with his fork. Why had he bothered to come to the dining hall? Oh, yeah, to spend time with Kevin. "Why are you staying on campus? I thought you were going home."

"My brother and sister got invited to some retreat with church. I guess it's a big deal." Kevin shrugged. "My grandparent's offered to watch my other siblings. So my parents decided to take a last minute vacation. Didn't seem worth it to fly home to an empty house."

Staying here with Kevin would be awesome... Too bad I have no choice.

"I'm heading to the library. I've got a paper to finish." Kevin stood and stretched. A sliver of abs showed between his shirt and jeans.

Seth's pulse quickened as he pretended to check his watch. *Stupid crush.* Kevin would be horrified if he knew. "I've got another prelim to study for."

Seth waved as Kevin set off across campus then went to their room. He emptied his backpack and opened his closet. What does one pack for a week of whoring oneself? His cell chirped.

"Hey, Sweetie," his mom said.

"Hi, Mom." Seth threw himself onto his bed. A wave of tiredness flowed over him.

"Your father and I were disappointed you decided to stay on campus for the week."

"Yeah. I just have too much studying to do."

A moment of silence. "Have you heard anything else from Winthrop?"

His face heated like plasma from the sun. "No, he said he would get me the paperwork after break. Stop worrying."

"It's hard not to. You know me, always imagining the worst."

You have no idea. "Just chill. I got this."

"Love you, son."

"Love you, too, Mom."

Seth's mind spun like a centrifuge. Why would Winthrop promise everything would be with one partner? Would medical test results be presented so the sick, bastard could order them to bareback? He should have stipulated that sex would be with condoms when he had the chance, not that he really had the chance. Winthrop promised he wouldn't be hurt. He hoped that included sexually transmitted diseases.

But what if this was all a ploy to get him to come to Winthrop's compound? He could disappear forever, and no one would know where he was. Seth grabbed a sheet of paper and wrote a note, explaining. He put it in an envelope addressed to his parents and placed it in his top desk drawer.

He really did have his mom's crazy imagination. At least, he hoped so.

On Friday, he grabbed his backpack and slipped his laptop into its bag, in case he found some time to study. He always had schoolwork to do.

True to Winthrop's word, a limo waited outside of his last class. He sped over, head ducked, to where a man, dressed in a black suit and wearing a black chauffer cap, held the door open.

Inside sat Erex, typing a message on his smart phone. Looking up, he gestured to the seat beside him. "I'm here to escort you."

"Okay."

The door closed, and Seth buckled his seat belt even though Erex didn't wear one.

Erex smirked. "Safety first."

The limo drove through the upper College Town exit from Cornell. Seth smoothed his hand over the soft, black leather seats. Beside him sat a few cut crystal glasses and a matching decanter containing an amber liquid. On the side near Erex was a small TV screen.

Erex didn't make any conversation. Seth stared out the window, watching the buildings of Ithaca give way to cows pastured in fields. Traces of snow still dotted the landscape.

It never ceased to amaze Seth how different Ithaca was from the surrounding area. He saw the occasional house, but also a scattering of mobile homes that had so much grass and weeds growing around them, they could not have been mobile for years.

They called Cornell centrally isolated, and it was true. It matched his mood.

Leaning his head back, Seth closed his eyes. Grotesque images appeared. An elderly man popping Viagra before he could ream Seth. A man with his wife watching while she filmed the proceedings. Kevin looking on in… Wait? Why would he think of Kevin?

Desperate to distract himself, he faced Erex. "Have you worked for Mr. Winthrop for a long time?"

Erex turned his head and tilted it up to look into Seth's face. "Yes, most of my life."

"Is he a good boss?"

"He's the best." A genuine smile graced Erex's face and lit his eyes. "He's very effective at getting things done. I only recently got promoted to being one of his personal assistants."

Seth was taken aback by the enthusiasm. "Oh, congratulations."

"Thanks." Erex glanced left and right, as if they were being watched. "You know, he's not evil. This is all going to work out."

"How can you say that?" Seth cringed at the squeak in his voice. "You were there when he laid it all out for me."

Erex shrugged. "I know. It may seem odd. He has his own way of doing things, but it will be for the best."

"Best for whom?" There was that squeak again.

"Ooo… you used whom correctly. The boss will love that. He's a total grammar Nazi. You don't even want to know what he did to the last guy who mixed up affect and effect. It wasn't pretty. But, to answer your question, best for everyone."

Seth stopped himself from shaking his head. "You're lucky to have such faith in your boss."

"He's amazing." Erex appeared almost dreamy-eyed. Did the man have a crush on Winthrop?

"Can you tell me anymore about what's going to happen?"

Erex laughed, but it sounded forced. "Not if I want to continue breathing."

What did that mean? Was the little man kidding, or did he really fear for his life?

After a few hours, the sun set, painting the sky in pinks and oranges. The limo stopped at a ten-foot, black, wrought iron gate, which swung open. The car proceeded through and climbed a hill that reminded him of the steep Libe Slope on the Cornell campus.

Seth sat forward, eager for his first glimpse of the elusive Winthrop estate. The camera on his phone tempted him to snap some photos since the Wiki page about Winthrop said no one had gotten pictures of the compound. He had the feeling he would not be allowed to leave with them.

Just as they crested the hill, a strange buzzing sensation passed through Seth, like one of those electrical stimulation machines in physical therapy. It covered his entire body for a second and then was gone.

He glanced at Erex, but the man hadn't stopped perusing the *Beadwork* magazine he was reading.

Off in the distance, the main house glowed in the twilight as it came into view. Three stories high and painted a medium shade of blue with black trim, it had round, gazebo like porches on each end, connected by a huge front porch that had chairs and a swing. Two towers peeked up from the back of the house, one on each corner.

Seth couldn't imagine living in such a place. It seemed more like a historical hotel.

The limo pulled up into the circular driveway and stopped. A few moments later, the driver opened the door, and Seth stepped out into the deepening twilight.

Glowing fixtures illuminated the front of the house like stars in the night sky. Erex walked toward the granite slab steps leading to the front porch. "Follow me. It's never a good idea to keep him waiting."

Seth grabbed his bags from the car and followed Erex, his heart racing and goose bumps covering his arms. *Let the nightmare begin.*

CHAPTER SIX

Friday, March 31, 7:51 P.M.

Seth followed Erex up the steps to his meeting with Winthrop where he would surrender his right to choose. As he climbed, each step represented how far he was willing to debase himself to save his future, and he couldn't believe how many stairs there were. How did Winthrop climb this and remain so fat? There must be a hidden elevator somewhere.

It had been up one flight to get to the porch. A step up into the house. The two-story foyer had doors on either side with two curved marble staircases leading to a balcony on the second floor. A crystal and brass chandelier, along with numerous matching wall sconces, lit the whole area.

Right on the balcony to a less opulent, more functional staircase. Up two more flights. His muscles burned, and his breathing quickened even though he played varsity basketball.

Erex bounded up the stairs, his breathing even, as he led

44

Seth forward.

A door to the left led to a large, airy space, tainted with the stench of cigar smoke. Dark, wooden rafters criss-crossed the high ceilings, complementing the horizontal paneling on the walls. Several pedestals dotted the area, each with a lit glass box on top containing an artistic object, reminiscent of a museum.

One held a sculpture of a naked woman standing beside an urn with a cloth draped over her arm, Grecian style. A well-endowed statue of a naked man wearing a Greek battle helmet faced her from another pedestal. The statue's left hand gripped a sword. The highly detailed carvings had discolored with age, their creases blackened.

On the far side of the room, near the other wall perhaps twenty feet away, a huge wooden desk dominated the one-foot-tall raised platform it stood upon. *No, Winthrop isn't self-conscious about his height. Not at all.* The engraved desk legs depicted some sort of winged figures.

Behind the desk sat an enormous leather chair with gold studs surrounding the edges. The back of the chair rose three feet above Winthrop's head as he sat like a king on his throne. Once again, the man was dressed impeccably in a white, custom-tailored, three-piece suit. A thick, golden chain stretched over his distended vest, and another hung around his neck, supporting a gold charm shaped like an arrow the size of a crayon.

Maynard Frederick Winthrop IV puffed his cigar, blew out several smoke rings, and then farted.

Now the room reeked from gas as well as the cigar. Seth fought the urge to retch as he met Winthrop's eyes. The man wore a self-satisfied smirk.

Behind Winthrop, two large, stained glass windows showed a muted view of the darkness outside. The lack of lights presented colors that were more shades of black, but the caning in between traced outlines of winged cherubim. This guy did like angels. An oil painting of a playing card, the king of hearts, had been mounted on the wall between the windows.

Winthrop expelled another ring of smoke from his mouth. "Welcome, my boy. So glad you decided to accept my invitation."

Seth fought to keep a scowl from forming but failed. "It's not like I had much choice."

"Now, now. No need to be sullen. We're all going to have a marvelous time."

Erex took up station on the left side of his master's desk, his face impassive. Were he to stand behind it, Seth would not be able to see him.

"Is this the plan?" Seth gestured to the frescos painted on the walls edging the ceiling. Each one more depraved than the last.

Images of groups of people having sex, a man bound and tied over a bench being whipped by a woman while he orally pleasured a man. A woman on the rack, stretched to full, being fucked by a man on top of her. Her mouth opens in what could only be a scream.

"No. I told you, no BDSM. I can tell you wouldn't enjoy it. I save that for people who are interested in such play. For you, I have something simple." He took a puff from his cigar.

Seth raised his eyebrows. *Nothing simple is ever easy.*

A gleeful grin split Winthrop's face. "You're going to have a Spring Break fling, my boy."

"Excuse me?" Seth lifted his head.

"A fling. A week-long love affair. A nice, tawdry one with lots of entertaining sex. Some of which will be scripted by me, of course."

Scripted sex. This sounded more and more like a porno

all the time. "I assume this is filmed and sold for your profit."

"Not at all." Winthrop held his left hand to his chest, his face wearing a *'who me'* look. "Any film will be for my personal enjoyment and for the occasional guest. Nothing will leak to the outside. Surely, your research has shown I can control the flow of information from this compound."

"How do I know you're telling the truth?" *Why am I bothering to ask?*

"My dear, dear Seth. Everything is in writing. I shall lay it out for you." Winthrop pulled out a sheaf of papers and placed it on his desk. "In exchange for a week entertaining me and my guests, I will forgive all debt as detailed here." Maynard gestured with the cigar to a list of each amount Seth's family owed. "See, I've even listed the promised promotion for your father."

The cigar hovered over the paper. A thrill of fear squeezed Seth's chest. What would happen if the ash fell and set fire to the document like a meteor blazing through the sky? Winthrop probably had copies, in triplicate.

"As I told you before, to entertain my guests, you will spend a week with a partner I have selected. You will have your first date with him tonight. Dinner and a movie. Sorry, you won't get to see the whole movie since you'll be making out with him for a good part of it. It's a good thing you've seen it before."

A movie? Was there a media room in this house? More likely, it meant TV from bed. Wait… Winthrop knew what movies he'd seen? How long had this pervert been stalking him?

"Alas, you'll sleep alone tonight to build the sexual tension. No taking care of yourself, either. I want you up and ready in the morning. The week will be filled with fun activities in between sexual encounters with your partner."

Fun activities. A shiver traveled up Seth's spine. What could that mean? He doubted he would find anything Winthrop enjoyed fun.

"Here are the ground rules. At no time during the week may you reveal the reason you are participating in this little adventure. You will fulfill all of my instructions specifying what is to take place in each scene. The rest of the time, you may act as you see fit."

Seth tried not to feel hopeful. Getting to act as he saw fit would give him breaks from the crazy.

"As I promised, you will not have any permanent markings, tattoos, piercings, or be maimed as part of this week. Even if you fail, you will be released hale and whole."

Hale and whole? Who talked like that?

"If at any time before the week is over you refuse my instructions, you will leave immediately, and I will foreclose on all the debt in my possession, and your father will lose his job without a reference. Any questions?"

Seth's heart sped, but he never signed anything without reading it. "May I read the document?"

"Of course, of course. Would you like me to appoint a lawyer to answer any questions about the legalese?"

Any person sent to help him would have no issue lying about the contents to ensure Seth heard what he wanted to hear and not the actual truth. "No, thank you."

"Erex, take Mr. Griffin to the conference room. Bring him back when he is satisfied and ready to sign."

"Yes, Mr. Winthrop."

Seth followed Erex to a door next to the one he had entered. The room reminded him of a boardroom from a movie. Plush chairs surrounded a long table. A glass of water and a faux quill pen at each place. The largest chair at the end of the table could only be for Winthrop.

Seth headed for that chair, but Erex shook his head. "No one sits in the boss's chair."

He sat in one of the other chairs and spent twenty minutes pouring over the pages, reading all of the fine print and looking for loopholes. Erex tapped his foot impatiently.

Clauses promising condoms would be used and videos would not be shared outside of the compound relieved Seth a little. The section on the definition of compliance raised goosebumps on his arms. He had to perform the specific sexual acts Winthrop demanded. These acts were bounded by the caveats of no harm and permanent markings. Despite his best efforts, Seth could find no issues or problematic fine points in the contract.

Erex led him back to the room where Winthrop peered through his monocle at some documents.

Winthrop settled back in his chair and crossed his arms as he cocked his head to the side. "Ah, are you ready to sign, my boy? Excellent."

Seth wanted to snarl, *I'm not your boy*, but held his tongue.

Winthrop handed Seth a large, golden quill pen and pointed to the spot where his signature was required. He signed it quickly, leaving a small spot of ink. Holy crap, the pen had a genuine nib instead of a ballpoint. As he wrote, his signature flared with sparkles and a tingle ran over his skin. He jerked back.

"Holy crap."

Winthrop chuckled but ignored Seth's comment and took the pen. He dipped it in a black marble inkwell, and, with an exaggerated flourish, signed his name, sparkles filling the air. Seth bet a handwriting expert would tell him the man was self-confident to the point of arrogance.

Winthrop snapped his fingers. Erex stepped around the desk and swiftly pressed something against Seth's neck that caused a stinging sensation.

"What the fuck?" Seth pressed his hand to his neck to cover the wounded area.

"Language! Save that for the bedroom. It's merely a subcutaneous communicator. I will hear everything you say, and I will be able to deliver my instructions so only you can hear. Your partner has one as well."

Subcutaneous communicator? I thought those only existed in sci-fi.

Winthrop examined his fingernails. "I wouldn't want to break the tension in the scene by making my interruptions noticeable. Erex, take our guest to his room."

Seth stood and followed Erex to a third door out of the office. How many doors did the room have, and why hadn't he notice this one before? It didn't matter. He was committed now. He hoped he could look himself in the mirror when this was done.

Seth entered a small room with an old-fashioned elevator. *Why did they make me climb the fucking stairs?* The decrepit, 1940s elevator had gates that surrounded the cab like bars on a cage. *Is this thing safe?*

Erex closed the door and gate and grabbed the handle, pulling it all the way to the left. The walls surrounding the elevator slid by as it moved. He carefully kept his hands close at his sides because he was certain there was a dismemberment risk. A cobweb in the upper corner caught his eye as the elevator made its screeching way down. When his shoulder brushed the wall of the elevator, a smear of dust painted it. When was the last time this thing spwas used?

Down three, two, one, and then he was sure they were underground, but the elevator kept descending. How big was the basement in this place? Where was he being taken? His heart pounded.

The elevator squealed to a halt, jarring its passengers. Erex muttered something under his breath and kicked the wall under the lever a few times. The elevator started up again, although the light illuminating it now buzzed and flickered irregularly, occasionally leaving them in darkness for several moments.

Finally, with a jolt, Erex brought the elevator to a halt, not quite level with the floor. The door opening shrieked like metal scraping metal.

Jail cells lined the hallway. Literally, black steel bars. The temperature made Seth shiver and his teeth chatter.

"What's going on?" *This is crazy. I need to get out of here, but I can't.*

Erex walked down the long hall past ten empty, painfully bright cells. The area reeked of urine, blood, and bleach, making Seth's stomach roil. He glanced down a hall to the right. It led to a single, partially open door. The room had been lined with stones, had chains hanging from the walls, and a large table with a roller in the middle. He shuddered as he followed Erex past another ten cells. The last cell on the left sported a white curtain blocking its contents. A guttural moan sounded from within.

Seth shuddered, and his heart raced. "What the hell?"

At the end of the hall, they reached another door. When Erex opened it, Seth sighed in relief. The room looked more like a normal motel room. A queen-size bed was positioned with its headboard centered along one wall.

Across from the bed, a dresser had an ancient TV with two actual dials resting on it. Next to that, a suitcase stand sat followed by a door leading to a bathroom. Seth caught a glimpse of a large tub. A small closet contained some clothes hanging from a bar.

Erex pointed to the closet. "These are for your use this

week, as are the ones in the dresser."

Seth peeked in the closet and opened a drawer of the bureau. The clothes ran the gamut from tuxedo to casual wear to thong underwear. Would he really need all of this? A chill ran down his spine. Probably.

One more closed door on the far wall of the room puzzled him. Before he could question it, Erex said, "Dress for your date, dinner, and a movie. When you're ready, open that door and walk through."

Erex turned and left the way he had come, leaving Seth to ponder what the night had in store.

Dinner and a movie. Seth placed his bag on the suitcase stand and then looked through the closet more thoroughly, considering what to wear for what was essentially a blind date. Part of him thought, *screw it. I'm being coerced. Why should I care what I wear*? The man he was partnered with could be older than his father. He could be fatter than Winthrop. He could be the biggest asshole on the planet. Okay, second biggest since Winthrop was clearly the biggest. Why would he want to dress well for that?

On the other hand, the contract had made it clear that he was to perform for Winthrop. Winthrop said this was a date, and he needed to play the part.

He settled on a medium blue, cotton long sleeve, button-down shirt, a pair of tan khakis, and a pair of brown leather cap toed shoes. Everything fit perfectly. Winthrop had done his homework.

He grabbed a comb from his bag and tried to neaten his unruly bangs but gave up. His bangs had a mind of their own.

He walked over to the indicated door and stood. Deep breath in and out. Another deep breath and then he reached for the knob.

The door swung open easily, spilling a cacophony of sound

into the room. Glasses clinking, silverware scraping plates, the aroma of good beer, and the murmurs of quiet conversations all surrounded him as he stepped into what appeared to be a crowded restaurant.

Seth stood motionless for a moment. *What the fuck?* The man keeps a restaurant in his basement?

The hostess behind a podium looked up at him. "Table for one?"

Seth pressed the heel of his hand to his forehead, blinked his eyes, and stepped forward. "No, I'm supposed to meet someone here. I'm Seth Griffin."

"Mr. Griffin." The hostess smiled, a glint of candlelight flickering off her lip piercing. "We've been expecting you. Welcome to Straight Shot. Your partner is already seated. Mr. Winthrop asked me to tell you that the tab for this meal has already been taken care of. He wants you to enjoy yourself." With a menu in hand, she waved down a row of tables. "This way."

Seth followed the woman past tables filled with laughing patrons toward a quieter back corner. A man sat in the booth with his back to Seth. All Seth could see was neatly trimmed brown hair and a long, lean neck.

The hostess spoke just as he approached. "Your partner is here, Mr. Fields."

Fields? It couldn't be. There must be tons of men with the last name Fields.

Kevin Fields, Seth's roommate, stood, his hand outstretched, but stopped in mid-offer. His mouth hung open, his eyes locked onto Seth's, and his cheeks reddened. "Seth?"

CHAPTER SEVEN

Standing just outside the restaurant booth, Seth couldn't breathe. Heat swamped his senses, and he stared at the man Winthrop had chosen for him to… to have sex with… for the next week. How could Winthrop be such a sick bastard and choose the one man who was his roommate, best friend, and the straight guy Seth had loved for two years?

Seth had feared he would have to *perform* with someone distasteful.

Instead, this was worse. So much worse.

Seth turned, ready to storm out of the restaurant and find Winthrop. Making him perform with the man of his dreams, knowing all along that it was a game. That was a farce he could not allow. He would be forcing himself on Kevin. Back in high school, he had vowed to never lose a friend again just because he was gay. But that little faux pas didn't hold a candle to what he would be making Kevin do.

However, he had no choice. He bet Kevin didn't either. It was the only possible reason the man could be here. What did Winthrop have on him? He turned back to face his roommate.

Kevin's outstretched hand dropped to his side as his mouth snapped shut, but his eyes stayed glued to Seth.

A sheen of cold sweat prickled Seth's hairline and hands. Although noise filled the dining venue, the sound faded away as Seth focused on Kevin. "Why are you here?"

Kevin opened his mouth, but he paused and took a breath. "I got rules, man. I can't answer that."

Kevin had rules? Of course, he did. But, why?

Seth crossed his arms. "Kevin, you—"

The hostess interjected, "Gentlemen, it seems you know each other. Why don't you take a seat, and I'll send your waitress over to get your drink orders. Don't worry about being carded tonight. Mr. Winthrop has taken care of everything."

Of course, Winthrop took care of everything. They were in his fucking basement.

Seth sat across from Kevin and couldn't help gawking as his friend poured over the menu. Yes, they even had a menu with the restaurant name, Straight Shot. Kevin looked hot in a white, pinstriped button-down shirt and a pair of dark tan khakis. It looked like something he would wear when he went out with one of the many girls he'd dated over the last few years.

A rush of heat exploded like a super nova on Seth's face as he realized that tonight he, Seth, was the date.

Seth struggled to word a question that didn't violate the rules. "Do we have the same instructions for the week?"

"I don't know what your instructions are." Kevin smiled and raised an eyebrow.

"You're such a dick."

Kevin chuckled, and then his face fell. He shifted in his seat and glanced away. "Sex. All week. With the person I meet here tonight. Meaning you."

The banter had almost felt normal, and then the reality of the situation collided with Seth. How did Kevin get mixed up with Winthrop? Did he know he would be ordered to go against his orientation?

"I'm sorry."

Kevin's eyes scrunched up in an adorably clueless expression. "Why are you sorry?"

Seth huffed. *Is he going to make me say it?* "For what I, we, have to do. I would never ask this of you."

Kevin frowned. "No?"

Seth tried to school his expression to say, 'I'm not some predator out to debauch straight guys.' "Of course not. You're my best friend."

Kevin's frown deepened as he broke eye contact. "Oh."

What did that mean?

A waitress approached dressed in a black shirt and pants, her brunette hair pulled up in a bun. "Would you like to order some drinks?"

Kevin looked up at the pretty waitress, his usual player smile on his face. "Two beers, whatever you have on tap. That okay, Seth?"

He's ordering for me? I guess it's what he's used to. I thought girls put an end to that shit. "Yeah."

They fell into an awkward silence.

Kevin sat back and tugged at his collar, like it was strangling him.

Seth fiddled with his fork as he desperately tried to think of some topic to introduce, but his brain refused to cooperate.

Instead, his mind spun through images of the things he would do to his roommate. Things he had only dreamed of. He hoped Kevin wouldn't vomit.

"I…"

At the sound of Kevin's voice, Seth startled and looked up.

The candle flickering on the table played shadows across Kevin's glowing cheeks. "Do we have the same instructions tonight?"

Seth shrugged and glanced down at the table, unwilling to see the revulsion in Kevin's eyes. "Dinner and a movie we don't really get to watch. We'll be too busy creating a show of our own." Seth braced himself and peeked up.

Kevin's lips curled up in a halfsmile. "Yeah, that's what he said. Did he inject you, too?" Kevin tapped a small red mark on his neck.

"Yeah, so we can receive instructions."

Seth had dinner with Kevin most nights. They talked about anything and everything. But suddenly he had no idea what to say. Instead, he lifted his menu. Lunch had been a long time ago, but his appetite vanished. In its place, one of his favorite jackoff fantasies ran through his head. One where he was kissing Kevin.

Except tonight, it would be real.

Seth ordered Chicken Marsala over pasta. It seemed like a safe dish. Kevin ordered grilled salmon. The waitress deposited a bowl of rolls and their beers on the table and left.

Seth took a healthy swig of the bitter brew.

Kevin snatched one of the rolls. "I know this is awkward, but it's still me." A smile struggled to rise on his face. "Let's just act normal for now."

Seth's jaw dropped. "Oh. Kay."

"Seriously." Kevin's eyes met Seth's. He took a deep breath. "We're friends. This doesn't change things."

How could this not change things? In high school, he lost a friend when the straight guy found out Seth had a crush on him. Doing this to Kevin was a whole new energy level of bad.

"Dude, calm down. You look like you just ate a lemon. Chill."

Seth took a deep breath. This hurt like hell, and he had no choice. "I guess."

Kevin sat forward. "I thought you were going to spend your break with your folks in Connecticut. What did you tell them?"

"I said I needed to stay on campus to study. Mom was disappointed but supportive. Was this why you told me you were staying in town?"

"No, I was going to stay in town. My plans changed… suddenly."

Seth frowned. He had been distracted this week, but he liked to think he would have noticed if something were up with Kevin. Winthrop must have made his pitch to Kevin at the last minute. Did he buy all his debt and blackmail him? That wouldn't make sense. Kevin's family wasn't wealthy, but his parents were proud that they managed to avoid taking another mortgage on the house his dad had been raised in.

The waitress arrived with two garden salads. Kevin ate while Seth made designs in the salad dressing with his fork.

Kevin shoveled a bite of lettuce into his mouth, chewed, and swallowed. "I know you're stressed, but eat. You've barely touched your food all week. You need to take better care of yourself."

Seth focused on his lettuce. "I've had a lot on my mind with all this." He waved his hand around, encompassing the situation.

Kevin reached out and grabbed Seth's wrist until he made eye contact. "I get that. Eat."

Seth watched Kevin. The softness in his eyes combined with his wry grin sent Seth's heart pattering and his mind spinning. None of this made sense. He nibbled at the lettuce, enjoying the pleasant tang of herbs from the Italian dressing.

Continuing to eat, Kevin snorted. "Remember that time when we went to Joe's Restaurant on a double date?"

Unbidden, Seth's lips curled up at the sides. "Yeah, I had no idea my date was bi."

"The moment we sat down, our dates just stared at each other." Kevin laughed. "Who knew they were exes? And still not over each other?" Kevin's eyes glowed.

Seth's muscles relaxed as he laughed with his best friend. "I heard they got engaged."

"Yeah. This can't be any worse than that."

"True." *At least, the dinner part. Clearly, Kevin is in denial about the rest.*

Because it didn't help to stress about it, Seth focused on the entrees that arrived and the usual things they talked about: classes, the end of junior year. How they were both planning to stay on campus over the summer to take some extra classes. Seth needed the credits so he could graduate on time with the double major. Kevin was trying to get an edge for med school.

Kevin glanced at the list of delectable treats the waitress brought. "Should we splurge and get dessert?"

Even though basketball season had ended, Seth still tried to eat healthy. Not to mention he was pretty full. "No…"

"Yes, live it up." Winthrop's voice echoed through Seth's brain, making him inhale sharply.

Before Seth could let Kevin know what he heard, Kevin rolled his eyes and said, "I guess we're getting dessert."

Seth nodded at Kevin and turned to peruse the list: Mud Pie, Cannoli, Zabalione, New York Style Cheese Cake, Six Layer Chocolate Cake, and Brownie Sundae. "I know you love chocolate. Why don't we split a brownie sundae? I don't think I can finish a dessert by myself."

"I'm a big fan of sharing. So romantic." Winthrop sent with a chuckle.

Seth wanted to be sick. Would everything he and Kevin did be re-interpreted with innuendo?

Kevin stared off in the distance for a moment. "You had me at brownie. You know me too well."

This conversation seemed so normal on the surface.

When the sundae arrived, Seth picked up the long-handled spoon and sword-blocked Kevin's spoon from scooping some of the treat. "That was my bite."

Kevin shook his head, left eyebrow raised. "You did not go there."

Seth lifted his chin. "I did."

"You're on."

Seth and Kevin cackled like loons. So what if they didn't know shit about fencing?

Mid-parry, Kevin stopped, his eyes unfocused for a minute. "Okay." Kevin rolled his eyes. With his hand quivering, he scooped up some ice cream with a healthy heaping of fudge and a chunk of brownie. Then he leaned forward and offered to feed it to Seth.

Before Seth could think, Winthrop's voice sounded in his head. *"Take it."*

Seth opened his mouth while Kevin slipped his spoon in. He closed his lips, grabbing the treat as Kevin slowly slid the spoon out. The intimate gesture unnerved Seth, his heart pounding. He could imagine doing this for real with Kevin, but knew Kevin only acted on orders from the voice in his head.

For a moment, Kevin watched him, his lips parted, and then he snapped his mouth shut and went back to eating the dessert.

Winthrop certainly wasn't shy with instructions. Next up, movie with benefits. Or perhaps, from Kevin's point of view, drawbacks.

When Seth and Kevin walked out the front door of the restaurant-like place where they had dined, Seth expected to be back in his room even though the door looked like it led out to a street.

Instead, they entered a spacious lobby of some sort of theater. Not a modern day theater, but one from times past. The restaurant noises ceased when the door shut, giving way to some Muzak. The tall walls had gold gilt edging and a mural on the ceiling depicting two cherubs, their asses bare, flying almost in a circle, like they were chasing each other through puffy clouds. Each held a bow and arrow. Their big, rosy cheeks flanked huge smiles.

The instrumental Muzak wrapped around Seth as his mind filled in the words of *Friends and Lovers*. His host didn't do subtle.

Kevin walked up to the ticket booth, looking to see what movies were playing.

A young girl, perhaps sixteen, with long dark hair pulled back in a high ponytail with a huge silver and gold sparkly bow, reached out and handed him two tickets. Chewing sounded as she worked a piece of gum. "Here are your tickets, Mr. Fields."

Kevin's eyes widened even as he reached for the tickets. "Excuse me?"

"Mr. Winthrop reserved the entire theater today for you

and Mr. Griffin. He selected the film especially for your evening."

"Oh, thanks." Kevin glanced at the two pieces of printed cardstock in his hand as he wandered back to Seth and showed them to him. *Long-Term Relationship* showed on the slips. "I've never heard of this movie. Have you?"

Seth nodded, frowning. Oh yeah, he knew the movie. Had watched it more than once. Winthrop was sending a very clear message. "Yeah, it's about two gay men who meet when one places an ad in the personals. It's a romantic comedy. It has a lot of… nudity."

Kevin's cheeks glowed red. "So it's like a chickflick for gay guys?"

Hearing chickflick and gay guys in the same sentence didn't compute for Seth. Chickflicks had a girl as the main romantic interest. At least, he thought that was correct. "Really, that's your question?"

Kevin studied the floor. "Uh."

Taking a breath, Seth put a hand on Kevin's shoulder until he looked up. He could only imagine how difficult this would be for his friend. "If it helps, think of it like that."

Kevin smiled. "It helps. I've been to so many chickflicks with so many girls." He shook his head.

Seth did not need the reminder of all of Kevin's girlfriends, dates, and conquests. Tonight, he was the date. *Holy Shit!*

They headed over to the refreshment counter, and each ordered popcorn.

"I'm sorry, gentlemen. Mr. Winthrop was quite specific." The pimply-faced attendant handed them one oversized tub of popcorn to share and an enormous soda with two straws.

Seth's overfull stomach gurgled. "These are huge."

"They're medium." The boy's voice cracked. "The door

to the theater is right through there."

The theater itself continued the old style theme. Seth tried to process how a space this large could be in the basement of Winthrop's mansion, but logic did not seem to apply.

In front sat a stage with a curtain. Tiered seating lined with velvet-cushioned chairs filled the hall. Ornate murals depicting people naked and in various sexual positions decorated the walls. Scratch people, men.

Where was this place? It seemed right up his alley. Kevin, with cheeks brighter than Jupiter's great red spot, stared at one painting of two men. One stood behind the other, his groin grinding into the man's ass as they kissed over his shoulder.

Poor, straight Kevin. Seth wanted to reassure his friend, but then realized that before this was through, he would be part of the problem.

It wasn't fair. Just thinking about kissing Kevin had him half-hard and filled with longing for the man he loved. In opposition, shame permeated him for what he would be forced to do to his best friend.

Kevin led them to seats in the center of the theater, about two-thirds back.

Seth smiled. They always chose this location when they went to the movies together.

As soon as they sat, the lights went down, and the curtain parted, revealing the huge screen.

The clicks of an old style movie projector resounded through the room, followed by a countdown test pattern, 3. 2. 1. Then the credits rolled. Seth had never been to a theater that had no advertisements or movie previews. Winthrop's sponsorship brought privileges, but at a high cost.

As the movie opened with the main character perusing sexually explicit gay photos and clearly jacking off, heat returned to Seth's face. He loved this movie. It wasn't smut. It had a plot, but it had enough hot, naked men to be a fun ride. Now, with Kevin beside him, it seemed more like porn.

Kevin crunched the popcorn beside him. Seth reached in to grab some, and their hands brushed. A jolt of want, like an electric shock, passed through him.

Just from touching hands? I have it bad.

After that, Seth was careful to limit contact. As the story unfolded, Seth grew more and more nervous. His chest tightened, and beads of sweat dotted his neck.

Kevin twitched in his seat, sat still for a moment, and then stretched and put his arm around Seth. Really? People do that? Why had Kevin? He would never have done this before. Perhaps he had instructions from their host.

Seth sat up a little straighter, not wanting to embarrass his friend when the voice sounded in his head.

"Sit back and relax into it. This is a date, boy."

He had his marching orders. He tried to pretend for a moment that this was real. He was here, on a date, with Kevin. *This isn't fair! I get to enjoy this at Kevin's expense.*

Kevin's fingers caressed Seth's neck and twirled in his light brown hair. The sensation sent shivers of pleasure down Seth's spine. He leaned into the enticing touch and froze. Why was Kevin doing that? It must have been another *instruction* from their beloved, interfering, blackmailing host.

The fateful scene happened when the main character thought he had been stood up on Valentine's Day.

"No, don't do that," Kevin whispered.

Seth turned, and his mouth fell open. Kevin was riveted to the screen. *Kevin a softy for romance, who would have thought it?* Certainly not the girls he dated.

"Time to kiss him," Winthrop's voice sounded in his head.

What? They just broke up. Why now? Too bad Winthrop

can't hear my thoughts.

Winthrop answered, *"Because I said so. So pucker up and lay one on him."*

Oh, shit! He can hear my thoughts. No way, must have been a lucky guess.

Seth took a deep breath, let it out slowly, inhaled, and leaned into Kevin, whose eyes were still fixed on the screen, a small frown on his face. Seth reached up, grabbed Kevin's chin, and gave him a smack on the lips.

Kevin stared at Seth with eyes as wide as twin moons.

Irritation filled Winthrop's voice. *"I think you can do better than that."*

How can you even see this? It's dark in here.

"Not your concern. Do it right, or we're done."

Oh, shit. Seth wanted to scream. Winthrop couldn't possibly be hearing his thoughts but... he couldn't be done. He couldn't fail.

Kevin still faced him, eyes wide. As Seth slowly moved in, Kevin's eyes fell closed. His friend's breath rate increased as he tilted his head to the side. Seth tilted in the opposite direction and joined their lips together.

Need shot through him, causing him to hiss in a breath through his nose. Then Kevin's arms were around him, pulling him close.

Seth ignored the armrest jamming into his side and wrapped his arms around Kevin. Kevin's tongue licked along his bottom lip, and Seth's mouth fell open as if it had a mind of its own.

Holy Shit! Kevin's kissing me!

The spot on his back where Kevin held him tingled. The places where their tongues touched sent ever-growing echoes of want through his body, bringing his aroused prick to full mast. Damn, Kevin could kiss.

Some rational part of his mind reminded him that Kevin didn't, couldn't, want this. But they had no choice. So Seth let his little head lead him.

He kissed across Kevin's jaw, his lips abrading on the stubble that grew by the end of a long day. Then down his neck. He licked behind Kevin's ear and was rewarded with a moan.

Kevin's moaning? Why? Then Seth realized—friction was friction. Kevin probably had some story cooked up in his head if he wasn't in full out denial, allowing the sensations to take him.

He reached for Kevin's chest, rubbing his hand across a nipple now tightened. He leaned over, tugging at Kevin's shirt, intending to lick that nub.

"Enough," Winthrop barked.

"What?"

"Tonight is just for making out. You passed the challenge. So stop. We need to save something for tomorrow."

Panting, trying to get his breathing under control, Seth had one thought. *"Cockblocker."*

Winthrop chuckled in his head. *"Watch the rest of the movie."*

Seth pulled away with difficulty. Kevin was already turning, facing forward. Was that a bulge in his pants? When this was all over, Seth had to ask him how that happened.

Or perhaps not. Never speaking of it again would be for the best.

He tried to focus on the movie and the happy ending, but it was hard. Literally, as in his cock was aching with need and desire. *Looks like blue balls tonight.*

The movie ended, and the house lights came up. Seth

stood and walked toward the exit to the theater with Kevin while avoiding his eyes. He wanted to stop, hold Kevin's hands, and kiss him again. *Stupid, stupid, stupid.* He glanced over at Kevin, who seemed lost in his own world.

Stepping out into the lobby, Seth blinked as his eyes adjusted to the brighter light. Waiting there was Erex and another little person. Did Winthrop only employ little people? The man had a serious Napoleon complex.

Erex said, "Seth, come with me. Kevin, go with Phelix."

Winthrop had one more instruction. *"Kiss him good night."*

Seth turned to Kevin, whose eyes widened. Then Seth reached for his friend as Kevin reached for him, their arms colliding in an awkward tangle. A chuckle escaped Seth, and Kevin huffed a laugh. The whole situation. Just ridiculous. But Seth didn't want to delay. Winthrop had given an order. He lunged in quickly and joined his lips with Kevin.

Kevin froze for an endless moment then he wrapped his arms around Seth.

This feels so right.

Seth slid his tongue into Kevin's mouth, and they dueled as Seth became instantly hard. This. This is what he had dreamed about, and it was more than he could have hoped for.

Recoiling, Kevin looked down and away, breathing rapidly.

What am I doing? Kevin doesn't want this.

Seth stepped back.

Kevin walked with Phelix toward the exit. Over his shoulder he called, "G'night," not meeting Seth's eyes.

"Night, Kev." Seth followed Erex to the same door.

CHAPTER EIGHT

Friday, March 31, 10:50 P.M.

Seth followed Erex through the doorway, leaving the movie theater behind but not the memories of Kevin's lips on his. As the door closed behind him, he drew up short. He was back in his room at the mansion? But this was the same door he had used to get to the restaurant. What was going on? Nothing made sense. Or Winthrop's home was more elaborately constructed than he imagined.

His mechanical engineering brain whirled into action, envisioning a system of moving floors and shuffling rooms. Since he felt no motion, it either changed very slowly, or they were careful to only shift rooms he did not currently occupy. However it had been constructed, there was no sign of any tracks or rails inside the room he occupied that could be used to facilitate such motion.

Why? Why would Winthrop do this? Why create this

elaborate architecture? Perhaps the answer was very simple.

Because he could.

"Rest now. You have a busy day ahead of you tomorrow." Erex crossed the room to the other door and exited.

In spite of the comfortable bed, Seth tossed and turned. His mind raced with memories of those hot, wet, smoldering kisses.

Then there was the bulge in Kevin's pants. A straight man should be nauseated, not aroused. Was there any chance Kevin could be bi? Surely, he would have mentioned it during their three years of friendship. That would be too good to be true.

Or perhaps his roommate was just closing his eyes and pretending? That seemed more likely. Seth needed to do everything he could to allow Kevin to keep his sanity intact and support whatever illusion he used to get through the next few days. Winthrop wasn't going to leave it at just kissing. Given the paintings in his office, Seth suspected even he would be forced well outside his comfort zone.

At some point in the night, Seth must have drifted off because the next thing he knew, a pounding at the door startled him awake.

"Hello?"he rasped.

"It's Erex. I have your breakfast."

Go away... "Come in."

Erex entered with a tray full of food holding a bowl of apples, pears, and bananas. A plate of chocolate croissants. A carafe of rich, aromatic coffee and all the fixings. A plate with pancakes, bacon, and scrambled eggs. A glass of freshly squeezed orange juice and a pitcher of ice water. Erex was obviously very strong for a little guy because when Seth stood and took the platter, he stumbled.

At least Winthrop wasn't going to starve him. However, Seth might need to increase his workouts if he still wanted to be in shape by the end of the week.

Seth placed the tray on the dresser. "There is no way I can eat all of this. Would you like some?"

"There's a fridge in the corner. Save the leftovers in case you're hungry later." Erex pointed.

Seth glanced in the corner to find a refrigerator. It was bigger than the one in his dorm room, but smaller than a kitchen would normally have. Why hadn't he noticed it before?

Erex moved toward the door and paused. "After you eat and shower, put on a swimsuit. They're in the dresser."

"Why do I need a swimsuit?"

Erex wrinkled his nose and shook his head. "To go swimming. Mr. Winthrop knew you'd both want some exercise. Just go through that door to meet up with Kevin."

"Okay." Or not. Not really.

The image of Kevin's incredibly fit body in swimwear drifted through his mind. Seth shivered. Given the circumstances, Seth owed it to his best friend to think about anything else. Kevin didn't want this, and Seth respected that.

Seth nibbled at a croissant. The flavor of chocolate caressed his taste buds. He poured himself a cup of coffee and put the rest of the food in the refrigerator. On the one hand, he seemed to be fed at regular intervals and in plentiful quantities. On the other hand, who knew if that would continue? This might be a test and the last food he was given.

The shower was warm, large, and had strong water pressure, with two showerheads in the oversized enclosure. It sat across from a whirlpool tub that was big enough for two.

Seth had a feeling he and Kevin wouldn't be sleeping alone the entire week.

He found the swimsuits, three different colors, all Speedos. A bit more subtlety would be welcome, but this was

Winthrop's kink, so he guessed he would wear whatever the man wanted.

He rejected the red one. Too Lifeguard. The purple tempted, but ultimately, he chose the blue one that matched his eyes. Would Kevin notice?

Stupid. Stupid. Stupid. Of course, Kevin wouldn't notice.

He checked himself in the mirror. At least being on the basketball team kept him trim and in shape, though his abs could have been more defined. For giggles, he flexed his arm, checking his biceps, grunting.

"Seth strong."

Placing his glasses on the dresser, he picked up a pair of goggles from the drawer, adjusting them for size. They turned out to be his prescription. Nice! Winthrop really knew a frightening amount about him.

Stepping into the next room, he blinked several times as the scent of chlorine filled his nostrils. Where there had been a movie theater the night before, now there was an indoor pool. It was shaped like a backward L, and the long side had lane markers on the floor. The short side was labeled twelve feet deep and had both a low and high diving board.

The entire room and pool were tiled in intricate, abstract mosaic patterns of blue, white, and green. He couldn't really tell where the pool officially ended and the deck began as the pool was filled to the brim and some of the water was lapping over the sides. A tall, lifeguard chair stood near the diving boards, its legs covered in about six inches of water from the pool.

Seth stepped onto the deck, his feet splashing the temperate water. A noise on the opposite side of the room drew his attention. Kevin stepped from behind the door.

The room's temperature increased as Seth admired his friend. Kevin stood a touch taller than Seth, with rock hard abs. He wore a green Speedo that left little to the imagination. Seth could just make out the line between hip and groin that had always fascinated him. It promised what was between those legs.

Seth shook himself. Kevin wasn't a piece of meat at a gay club, to be weighed and measured. His best friend deserved respect for his orientation, not ogling as if he was a prospective lover.

Winthrop's voice sounded in his head. *"But he will be your lover. Today. We'll start slow. Have a swim, and then I want you two to jerk each other off in the pool. Kissing and foreplay are required, of course."*

And there it was. Seth's cheeks and neck blazed as he peeked around, checking for cameras. How in the western spiral arm of the Milky Way did Winthrop know what he was thinking? Could that thing they injected into him really transmit his thoughts? Empirical evidence implied that was so.

"Are you listening?" He waited a beat, but no response. Could it all be a coincidence?

He lifted his hand and waved at Kevin, who seemed to pause at the threshold, staring at the water. In a fit of whimsy, Seth adjusted the goggles and performed a shallow racing dive into the four-foot deep end of the crystal clear water.

A slight chill washed over Seth's body as his arms pulled and his legs spread and snapped together in a powerful, underwater breaststroke that moved him up to break the surface. He glided for a moment, and then his arms created the out-forward-in alternating rhythm of freestyle while his legs started kicking in and out, like two sewing needles in perfect opposition.

Using his solid form, he sped through the water, cutting through the currents created by his churning movement. He reached the other side, now ten feet deep, and grabbed the lip of the pool, smiling at Kevin.

Kevin rolled his eyes. "Show off."

"What?"

"Didn't you use to be on a swim team?"

Seth laughed as he held onto the side of the pool. "Yeah, when I was ten. It took too much time away from basketball, and I was never that fast, so I quit."

Kevin creeped through the six inches of water skirting the room to the shallow end of the pool. He clutched the stair rail and placed his foot on the first step.

Seth had never seen Kevin so unsure of himself. "You okay?" Seth called across the pool, his voice echoing in the high-ceilinged room.

"Uh, yeah." But the frown on Kevin's face deepened as the bottom half of his body became submerged.

Seth swam across the pool until he stood face to face with Kevin. "What's wrong?"

Kevin shrugged. "I don't really swim."

"What do you mean, you don't swim? Didn't you pass the required freshman year swim test?"

"Yeah. Barely." Kevin looked away. "When I was done, I crawled out of the pool and lay huffing to catch my breath."

"You? But you're a total athlete. I've seen you run up and down the court like a million times and not even be winded."

"I know. It's not that. I just…" Kevin's face fell, and his shoulders slumped. "I'll show you."

He walked like a man picking his way through the jungle to the end of the pool. Then he squatted down, submerging his shoulders, put his face in the water, and began to flail his arms. Seth stifled the laugh that threatened to erupt. Kevin's freestyle really could be called a crawl. He practically rolled all the way over, every stroke, just to take a breath. His legs kicked occasionally, but really created more drag than forward propulsion.

When Kevin arrived at the other side of the pool, around twenty-five meters away, he grabbed the side, breathing hard.

"Dude… who taught you to swim?"

"No one." Kevin flexed his strong bicep muscles, pulling himself out of the water and onto the deck. "We had a pond in our yard and we used to splash around, but we never took lessons. I watched some videos on YouTube. It didn't look that hard, and I passed the test at Cornell." He walked back to the stairs and slowly re-entered the pool.

Seth smothered a smile. Kevin could be so stubborn. "And it never occurred to you to just take the damn gym class?"

"I didn't need the credits. I had basketball, and I've got physical fitness covered. I run every day and lift weights."

The fine, toned body that was on display for Seth proved Kevin's exercise regime was more than effective. That body was the one he would soon be doing nasty things with. But he needed to focus here.

"Dude, swimming is important. You never know when you're going to be in the water unexpectedly. You run around Beebe Lake every day. You could fall in."

Kevin made a *tsching* sound. "I won't fall in."

Images of the icy path that surrounded the lake in winter flashed through Seth's mind. "No, I'm your friend, and this is important. This summer, I'm signing your ass up for a swim class."

Kevin looked up, his eyes dilated and his mouth opened, presumably to argue. Then his face softened, and he smiled. "Fine. You win, but you suck."

"Too bad. Man, it hurt to watch you. I thought you were gonna flip onto your back a few times."

Kevin shrugged, but his eyes narrowed. "I needed to get

my head out of the water to breathe."

"Don't get defensive. You're a strong athlete. You'll pick it up like that." He snapped his fingers.

Kevin moved closer to Seth. "Douche." Then he splashed Seth.

"You did not just do that."

"What? Afraid of a little water?"

"Me?" He dove under and pulled Kevin's legs out from under him so that he fell back on his ass. The water was only four feet deep, but it still pained him to watch Kevin flail to the surface.

"Oh, yeah. You need to learn to swim. I was going to do some laps to work off all the food I've been eating. You okay on your own?"

"I'll survive. I doubt our host would let me drown."

No, he was sure their host wouldn't. It would spoil his fun. *"You listening, Maynard?"* No response.

Moving to the top of the pool, Seth squatted and pushed off from the wall. Swimming always calmed him when preparing to face a challenge.

He had planned to do fifty laps of crawl, but found himself instead flapping his arms and doing the dolphin kick for butterfly. He was showing off, but didn't know why. It's not like he needed to impress Kevin. They were already friends and attracting him was impossible, but he did it anyway. Four laps of butterfly, four of backstroke. He was glad when that was over. It was his weakest stroke. Four of breaststroke. He enjoyed the bob of his head and the snap of his legs as he swam. Finally, four of freestyle. A proper eight-hundred medley. Assuming this pool was twenty-five meters. It felt like it was around that.

He stood at the end of the pool to take a break and looked over at Kevin. Kevin was moving slowly around in the water.

His arm came up in what looked like a pretend hoop shot, and then he fist pumped the air.

Seth applauded.

Kevin spun around to face him. "You done, asshole?"

The comment was so Kevin that Seth smiled. "No, I want to do another few laps. You looked like you scored."

Kevin shrugged, and his face turned red. "I figured I should at least move around. It's more fun this way."

"Hey, no problem. I bet if you check in that bin over there, you'll find some stuff we can use."

Scrunching his eyes together, Kevin tipped his head to the side. "Like what?"

"I don't know. Kickboards? Floats? Who knows?"

Kevin paused for a moment. "Oh, I thought you meant something else."

"Like what?"

"Nothing."

Seth tilted his head slightly to the side. "I'm going to finish now."

He leaped through the water into a strong freestyle. He tried to lose himself in the strokes, but was surprised his host hadn't interrupted with more instructions. Erex said they could swim for a while, but he knew what was coming. They needed to jack each other off. Just thinking about it sent pulses of need to his dick and filled him with shame.

His body fell into the automatic rhythm of lap swimming. He realized his mistake. This left him way too much time to think. He'd never jacked someone off in a pool. He only had access to public pools with lifeguards and other swimmers. But the idea of doing anything in a pool, especially with Kevin, had been one of his fantasies.

Another flip turn to change direction, and he wondered

how Kevin was feeling. Was he nervous about what lay ahead or just grossed-out? Had he ever gone skinny-dipping in that lake by his house, with a girl, in the moonlight? He could just imagine the play of the moon's beams along Kevin's skin, probably dark with summer tan. The guy could tan. Seth was either pale or burned.

Then he remembered the faceless girl he had probably been fucking out there. Hopefully, he'd been safe and wore a condom. Did the protection work underwater? A growl surged through his chest, knocking him off his rhythm. Ugh. Seth's stomach wrenched. It was just too painful to think about.

After another twenty lengths, his arms were shaking, and he decided to call it quits. He was glad that even though he didn't swim competitively, he had kept up lap swimming a couple days a week. Being in the water refreshed him and usually cleared his mind. Even if today it didn't help.

He stood and peered over at Kevin. He'd found a floating basketball hoop and a ball. He aimed, shot, and scored, then walked carefully through the water to retrieve the ball and set up a different shot.

Seth took a moment and tried to let his heart rate lower, but watching Kevin shoot hoops, practically naked, was revving it up in a whole different way. "You up for a little one-on-one?"

Kevin gave him that confused look, and then threw him the ball.

It wasn't exactly basketball. Dribbling didn't really work in the water. If anything, it resembled soccer with your hands. Seth would fake left and dodge right. Kevin tried to block the shot, but Seth scored. Seth had never been more aware of Kevin's body making contact with his. He had never felt so warm in a pool.

The scoring went back and forth. They were pretty evenly matched, so they didn't bother to keep track. Seth laughed, having made a shot from a particularly tricky angle as Kevin slammed into him, trying to defend.

Their bodies pressed together, and they both breathed heavily from the exertion when Kevin paused a moment, eyes slightly unfocused. He shook his head once, then moved in and claimed Seth's lips with his own.

Seth startled before he realized their host must have given Kevin an instruction. Why didn't he receive one as well? That didn't matter. If he didn't act, the instruction would come, so he went with it. The moment their lips touched, Seth's cock snapped to attention and demanded more.

He leaned in and wrapped his arms around Kevin's athletic, muscular frame, groaning from how right it felt to have him there. He ran his fingers up and down Kevin's back as their tongues connected, dancing. Damn, this came easy. It was as if they had been kissing for a million years.

Kevin's mouth left his first, kissing across his cheekbone and down his neck, nuzzling and licking, making the skin tingle with sensations that seemed directly tied to his prick. A moan echoed in his chest and escaped his lips as his nipples tightened.

Without any conscious thought, Seth's hands slid lower and grabbed Kevin's tight ass, barely covered by the Speedo. The firm, round butt fit perfectly in his palms. He pulled Kevin in tighter against himself, seeking friction for his aroused shaft. Seth couldn't resist looking down to see Kevin's hard cock peeking out of the top of his suit, the cut head purple with need.

"Now would be a good time." Winthrop's smug tone sounded in his head.

"Yes, sir."

This wasn't for pleasure, at least, not his or Kevin's. It was for that sick fuck, Winthrop. He could swear he heard the man cackling in his head.

He moved his hand down toward the waistband of the Speedo. Kevin breathed in sharply and watched Seth's hand descend slowly. He followed Kevin's light treasure trail to the object of his desire.

He reached in and took Kevin in hand, who mewled in response and thrust up into his circling fingers. Seth leaned in to kiss him again as he ran his hand up and down Kevin's hot, throbbing prick.

"Oh, God." Kevin connected their lips, his hips thrusting in time with Seth's hand.

Seth moved to kiss his neck, and Kevin tilted his head to the side, inviting the sensation on his skin. Seth sucked lightly, and Kevin let out such a loud moan of arousal that he sucked harder, wanting to make the sound last.

Kevin's hips thrust faster. Seth knew he had to be close.

"Let go for me," Seth whispered.

Kevin jerked wildly before he stilled, and shots of his spunk flew through the swirling waters.

Kevin bent his head into Seth's neck. Like he was hiding as he panted. Seth felt sick inside. What had he done to his friend?

But Kevin recovered after a moment and reached for Seth's cock. "Time for me to return the favor."

Seth wanted to say, *"Are you sure? You don't have to."* But he did have to. They both had to follow instructions.

Kevin's hand was tentative on Seth's cock. It was probably the first prick Kevin had touched that wasn't his own. Kevin worried his lower lip with his teeth. "Is this okay?"

"Of course. Just do it how you like it. It's easy." Seth placed a hand on Kevin's shoulder to support his wobbly legs.

"You feel the same as me, but different, narrower, longer."

Seth had noticed that. Kevin's cock had been thick and

substantial in his hand. Seth wasn't convinced he was really longer. Kevin was hung. "Would you kiss me? It'll get this done quicker."

Kevin's bottom lip glowed red from his nervous nibbling. "Sure, I'll kiss you," he said, voice cracking. He coughed to clear his throat. "But what's the rush?"

"Don't you want to get this over with?" Seth asked.

"Uh… well." Kevin paused a moment his eyes focusing over Seth's shoulder. "Maynard requires his show."

Duh. It all came down to Winthrop and whatever he held over Kevin.

Then all thought fled as their lips connected and Kevin's hand stroked his cock. A whine of pure desire escaped him, only to be swallowed by Kevin as his tongue consumed Seth.

Thrusting, Seth's hips moved with a will of their own as he sought more. More friction. More contact. *Just more*. His orgasm built quickly as he stutter jerked into Kevin's hands. His balls drew up tight and seemed to inside-out themselves as he emptied into Kevin's hand and the surrounding waters.

His hold on Kevin barely kept him upright. He laid his head against the man's chest. He fought to control his panting breath and listened to the racing of Kevin's heart. Kevin's arms came around him, holding him out of the water until he was able to support himself.

He gave a sheepish smile. What do you say to your straight roommate after he jacks you off, giving you the best orgasm of your life?

"Did I do it right?" Kevin's tentative grin faded quickly.

Can't have him freaking out. Poor guy. "Duh." Seth smiled wide and gestured to the come swirling in the water. "I'm going to hit the shower and wash off this chlorine."

"Sounds like a good idea."

Erex stepped into the room at that moment. "Both of you follow me. The boss had us move Kevin's stuff into your room. You'll be sharing."

Being roommates with Kevin was as natural as breathing. There was just one problem. Seth's room only had one bed. Again, he heard Winthrop's chuckling laugh in his head.

CHAPTER NINE

Saturday, April 1, 10:52 am

Droplets of water slid down Seth's legs as he climbed the pool stairs. Kevin followed close behind, a walking wet dream. Thinking about what they had just done had Seth's prick attempting to revive.

I'm such a pervert.

Seth led Kevin past Erex and into his room. Waving, Erex closed the door.

"Why don't you hit the shower first?" Seth asked.

"Are you kidding me?" Winthrop's mental voice sounded astonished. *"You just had your hand on his cock. Shower together."*

Seth's face burned as Kevin's color rose.

"It sounds like we're showering together," Kevin replied, hanging his head.

"It seems so." Seth wanted to spare his friend. "Should we leave the suits on?"

Kevin's brows raised, and the left side of his mouth quirked up. "Do you really think our host will allow that?"

"Probably not."

Seth stepped into the bathroom and turned on the two showerheads. At least they could both be in a stream of warm water at the same time. He quickly slipped the Speedo off and dropped it in a hamper. He removed the prescription goggles and set them on the bathroom counter. Would he need them again for some other scene Winthrop wanted staged?

Looking through blurry eyes, he stepped into the soothing flow of water. Steam filled the enclosure, further obscuring his vision. Kevin joined him, closing the shower door. Seth turned to his roommate, squinting.

"You can't see a thing, can you?" Kevin asked.

"Uh, I see a blob. Right about there." He moved his hand to circle his roommate's body. He cursed his eyes. Kevin was full frontal to him, but he could barely make out more than general outlines. "I wonder if our host is going to demand another round in the shower."

Was the red on Kevin's body from the hot water or embarrassment?

"I hope not. I need some recovery time." Kevin tilted his head back, wetting his hair.

Seth couldn't help teasing him. "What? A stud like you? I figured you're good for three, four rounds."

Kevin shrugged. "Depends."

"On what?" Seth snorted as he raised his eyebrow.

Kevin stared down and away. "Stuff. Look, just leave it."

"Okay." Duh. Depends on whether he's attracted to the person he's with. Seth's chest felt as empty as the space between galaxies. He didn't have the right fiddly bits for Kevin, and he never would. How could he have forgotten that?

Seth turned his back to Kevin and reached for the bar of soap. What would Winthrop ask them to do in the shower? He dreaded forcing yet another encounter on Kevin. Not to mention the fact that his powerful orgasm left him tender, unsure if he could perform again.

"Sure you could," Winthrop intruded on his thoughts. *"Just look at the inspiration I provided."*

Seth fought the urge to turn and admire Kevin. Not that he could actually see anything. However, just remembering that tight body behind him had his cock firming up.

"See? I told you, but it's okay. I had my fun. I just want you two to get comfortable being intimate."

What does that mean? Why would Winthrop care about that?

"Never you mind. Now turn around and wash his back."

He's reading my mind again. Does he hear everything or just some things? Seth turned, lathering up the soap. He inhaled briefly and was relieved it appeared to be unscented. Many scents triggered Kevin's allergies.

When his hands made contact with Kevin's back, his friend froze for a moment but then relaxed into his touch as he ran his hands along the muscles of Kevin's shoulders and spine.

Kevin spun around to rinse in the left showerhead. "Give me the soap. I'll do you."

The words echoed in Seth's mind, *I'll do you. I'll do you.* He wanted to smack his own forehead. Kevin must have had no idea of his effect on Seth. As he turned, he glanced down. In spite of the fuzzy details, Kevin's cock seemed half-hard.

Winthrop implied that he wasn't going to demand they have sex again immediately. Kevin was getting aroused anyway? What was next? Aliens arriving to take Seth and Kevin for a tour of their planet? Nothing made sense.

The sensation of Kevin's soapy hands stroking his back caused his mind to shut off all speculations and just feel. A moan of delight escaped him before Kevin turned him into the water to rinse.

Seth couldn't meet Kevin's eyes as he left the shower and toweled off.

He searched a few drawers and the closet until he found a red polo shirt and a pair of jeans in his size and sped through dressing, fighting the denim that stuck on his still damp legs. He was running a comb through his hair when Kevin came out, wearing nothing but a towel. With his glasses on now, Seth could see everything. The water droplet making a lazy journey down Kevin's chest. The dark hair sticking every which way. The happy trail leading down under the towel.

Everything.

Kevin surveyed the room. "Do you know where they put my stuff?"

"Yeah, I saw it when I was getting dressed." Seth kept his eyes trained on Kevin's face, forcing himself not to visually feast on the exposed flesh. Just like old times back in their dorm room. "These drawers are yours and so is this half of the closet."

It was strange seeing Kevin's stuff lined up next to his. They each had their own closet in their dorm room. It brought a troubling ache to his heart. Why couldn't this be real? *Because that's life.*

He turned away to give Kevin some privacy.

The minute Kevin finished dressing, a knock sounded at the door. Creepy.

"Come in," Kevin called out.

Erex opened the door. "I've been sent to escort you to

lunch with your host."

Great…What's on the menu this time? Tiger balls?

The two men followed Erex back to the rickety elevator from the night before, but it was different somehow. It looked more *substantial*. Inside, it gleamed with a polished shine.

Seth's head throbbed. Forget the question: how could an elevator change so quickly? Why would Winthrop have an elevator do this? Maybe it was just a coincidence that the elevator had been repaired that day.

They rode to the second floor at a faster pace and followed Erex down a hallway to a large sitting room. A fireplace graced one corner with a fire crackling inside. The scent of wood smoke kissed the air.

Two silky white, Victorian style couches and two matching chairs surrounded a dark wood coffee table. White shelves lined the walls. Some had books, their bindings standing like trees in a multicolored forest. Others contained small statues fashioned in several different media.

"Mr. Winthrop will be joining you shortly. What can I get you to drink?" Erex asked.

"Uh, water?" Kevin glanced over at Seth as he moved to the couch on the right.

"Yeah, water. Please," Seth agreed. He needed to stay hydrated after his workout in the pool.

Erex seemed to look down his nose while looking up at them. How did he do that? "Really? How droll. Are you sure you wouldn't like a glass of wine? We have a lovely Riesling from our vineyard."

Kevin's eyes flared wide. "You have a vineyard?"

Erex straightened to his full three-foot height. "Yes, Mr. Winthrop has a private vineyard here on the property to supply his cellar. Although if you prefer something from California, or France, that can be provided as well."

Kevin shrugged. "No, thanks. Water, please."

Seth nodded.

"Of course. Would you prefer sparkling?"

"No, thanks," Seth said. "Just regular water, you know H$_2$0. They even have it on Europa. With ice, if it's not too much trouble."

Erex sniffed. "As you wish." He half bowed as he left the room.

Kevin sat stiffly on the couch while Seth checked out the books. It was quite an eclectic mix. Everything from Homer's *The Odyssey*, to J.R.R. Tolkien's *The Hobbit*, to Damon Suede's *Hot Head*. Some of the books were clearly antiques, leather-bound.

There was an entire section dedicated to the Bible. Dozens of different translations into a variety of languages. A scroll in Hebrew. And more biblical interpretations than he could ever imagine, including the *Jefferson Bible* and the *Women's Bible*. Mixed in with these were books that sounded like they could be part of the Bible, like the Gospel of Mary and the Gospel of Judas, but Seth had never heard of those. The Book of Mormon sat on the end of the row.

The next set of shelves contained a collection of books detailing the world's religions, including the Qur'an, followed by a section on every mythology he had ever heard of: Greek, Norse, Mayan, Celtic, Cthulu, and many others that were new to him.

Most of the books' creased bindings suggested someone had read them, probably several times given the wear. Who did all of this reading? Winthrop did not strike him as the type to have interest in anything having to do with morality.

The diverse set of statues on the shelves had been created in several mediums with clay, bronze, and stone being the most prevalent. Their subjects ran the gamut. A stone statue of an aroused Satyr proudly displayed his exaggerated, engorged member. Jesus Christ, rendered in clay, washed someone's feet. A bronze Hello Kitty stared vacantly from her twin oval eyes with no mouth present as usual. Where would he get a bronze statue of Hello Kitty and why? Noah's Ark, Babe Ruth, the first harmonic of the L-shaped membrane, a knight in armor… each had a place in the mixed collection. But they all had one thing in common: excellent craftsmanship and attention to detail.

"Anything interesting?" Kevin asked.

Seth startled, having forgotten Kevin's presence. "There seems to be a random mix of stuff. At least he has a copy of *The Hobbit*." He pulled the worn leather-bound book from the shelf and opened it. "Crap! A first edition, signed. It's criminal the way this has been treated." He gingerly set the tome back in its place and went to sit with Kevin. "The more I see here, the more this guy confuses me."

"I know. How do the rooms keep changing?"

Seth leaned back on the couch and crossed his legs. "You noticed that, too."

Kevin watched Seth for a moment, eyebrows climbing, and then flipped him the bird. "Duh."

"Sorry. I've been wracking my brain to think of some design that could shuffle things like that, but I think we would hear something. The cost would be astronomical. A moving pool?"

Kevin shook his head slightly. "There's something very odd about this place. It just seems to make the impossible happen."

Truer words were never spoken. I just jacked off the straight man of my dreams.

The door opened, and Erex returned with a tray containing two bottles labeled Mulshi and two goblets, each with a single, heart-shaped piece of ice. It also contained a bowl with more heart-shaped ice and silver tongs with an elaborate design of Celtic knot work adorning the sides. He placed the tray on the table, poured some water from the bottles into each goblet, and left without a word.

Seth picked up a goblet and sipped the water. A surprising hint of sweetness crossed his tongue, although the bottle didn't indicate that anything had been added. What was Mulshi anyways?

As Kevin lowered his glass, he studied it for a moment. "With these fancy glasses, I feel like we should toast to something."

"Okay, what shall we toast to?" Seth asked.

Kevin met Seth's eyes, a wry half-grin on his face. "Friendship."

"To friendship." The irony of the toast slammed through Seth. Forced to do what he had always dreamed of, at the expense of his best friend.

The glasses clinked, ringing out like bells. The sweet note jarred Seth.

A moment later, the door opened, and in strode Phelix. "Presenting Maynard Frederick Winthrop the Fourth."

Winthrop swept regally into the room, double chin held high, but the sway of his large belly ruined the effect. Once again, the man dressed in an impeccable, dark three-piece suit. The vest stretched to cover his large bulk. A lit cigar hung lazily from his mouth. "Boys, I hope you're having fun. Seth, you're quite the swimmer. It was a pleasure watching you thrust your body through the water with such powerful strokes. Just a joy. And, Kevin, you seemed to enjoy the morning's challenge. At least, the pool boy thought so."

Kevin's skin didn't just turn red. It glowed like a red giant star. Was he embarrassed or possibly angry? Seth couldn't tell.

"This afternoon, I have a special treat for you. I've decided to open my vineyard for a wine tasting to you and some of my other guests. My chefs have been working all morning to prepare complementary food to accompany each of the six varieties of wine we make here at ApisManor."

Seth's stomach twisted. He knew shit about wine.

Kevin was quick to give a polite response. "That's very kind of you, Mr. Winthrop…"

Winthrop's eyes flashed. "Kevin, I told you to call me Maynard."

Kevin shoved his fists into his armpits as his face paled. "Pardon me," he whispered. "That's very kind of you, Maynard. I fear you have gone to a lot of effort that will be lost on me. I don't know much about wine."

Leave it to Kevin to express what Seth thought.

Winthrop's mouth dropped open in an exaggerated way. "How is that possible? You go to Cornell University, home of the famous College of Hotel and Restaurant Management. I believe they offer an excellent class on wines."

"True, but you must be twenty-one to take the class because of legal restrictions. Seth and I are both twenty."

"Well, then, today will be a treat and an education. Follow me, boys."

Winthrop waddled down the right side staircase of the foyer and to the front door of the mansion. Seth braced for the cold that characterized upstate New York in March. However, when the door swung open, warmth streamed in and sunlight bathed his face.

A train of sorts sat parked at the bottom of the porch staircase, although not on a track, with two open-sided cars filled with passengers. For an instant, Seth was terrified that he might recognize someone in the group. He would hate for anyone he knew to be in Winthrop's clutches as well.

Or worse, if they knew him and learned what he was doing here, they might tell his parents. *Guess what? We saw your gay son having sex with his straight roommate to pay off your debt.* His cheeks flamed, but no one looked familiar or even paid much attention to him and Kevin.

Winthrop gestured to them to get inside, and they took the last empty bench at the back of the train. Seth sat on the right, squeezed into the corner to give Kevin plenty of space.

Kevin glanced at him, shrugged, and moved into the left corner.

Winthrop walked to the front of the train-thing, turned, and gave everyone a huge smile, waved, and climbed aboard the engine. He tugged a string twice, and a whistle blared out a toot-toot. Then the engine roared to life, filling the air with sound, and the train rolled forward off the driveway and onto a red brick-lined road.

The smell of spring filled the air, the scents of lilac and honeysuckle swamping Seth's senses. Trees lined both sides of the road, planted in neat rows, covered in light green, new leaves and blossoms. Trellised vines arched over their heads. He suspected they were traveling through a fruit orchard. It shocked him that spring had come so early given the location of the mansion. All was still dark and dreary back in Ithaca with patches of snow littering the ground.

The warm wind on his face soothed him, and he leaned back in his seat. He squelched an urge to move closer to Kevin and lean on his shoulder. What the hell? They'd jacked each other off once, and he wanted to throw all of his boundaries into the wind? What was life going to be like when they returned? Would they be able to move beyond this experience, or would it spell the end of their friendship?

CHAPTER TEN

Saturday, April 1, 12:37 P.M.

Seth's mind spun as the train rolled out of the orchard. The weather was unseasonably warm and pleasant. Global climate change? Kevin sat beside him, lost in his own world of thought. Their friendship was undergoing an unnatural change of its own. This one caused by Maynard Frederick Winthrop IV.

The train approached a large, traditional red barn with white trim, pulling up and parking in front of an arched threshold whose double doors had been propped open. Winthrop dismounted the engine car and walked toward the entry, swinging his arm in an overhand arc to follow.

Kevin and Seth disembarked with the others and headed for the door. Perhaps fifty people, engaged in a variety of conversations, ambled ahead of them.

"I think we're a bit underdressed." Kevin gestured to the

crowd.

Seth glanced ahead and then at himself. Most of the men wore suits, and the women wore cocktail dresses. "I wonder why Maynard didn't give us orders. Maybe he wanted us to standout."

Oh, shit! Would Winthrop force them to *perform* for this group? He implied that they would be entertaining his guests, but Seth assumed that would be via video recordings and not live. Goosebumps ran up his back in spite of the temperate weather.

Kevin trudged beside him, his face set in an impassive mask. Seth couldn't blame him. Having sex in public would be hard enough, but having to do it while going against his orientation seemed like exceeding the speed of light. Just imagining what it would be like if Winthrop gave Seth a female partner made his stomach want to heave.

"Maybe. I can't get a handle on that guy," Kevin said.

The door led to a two-story, open, airy space. Light stained wood planks, showing swirls of their natural grain, covered the floors and walls. Dark brown trusses crisscrossed the ceiling.

Light wood butcher block tables were scattered around the room. Each table held a distinct vintage, small, crystal tasting cups, a large silver bucket with a complex filigree pattern decorating it, small plates, and chafing dishes. A quick count revealed twenty stations in all.

This puzzled Seth at first. Their host had said six wines. But he discovered some of the varieties were repeated, with only the year being different. It made sense in a logical sort of way. Varying weather conditions would affect the crop of grapes and therefore the wine they produced.

As he and Kevin continued exploring, they passed by their host, who spoke with a bearded man with long, blond hair. When Seth passed, he did a double take. The man was stunning, beyond stunning. An Adonis who radiated charisma like the sun radiated light. Seth rubbed the back of his neck, trying to smooth the hair that was suddenly standing on end.

"You old dog. You brought out the '92. That was a great vintage for this wine," the smoking hot blond guy said.

Winthrop placed his hand on the man's shoulder. "I rather thought so."

"What's the occasion? You're pulling out all the stops here."

Winthrop turned and blew a puff of foul-smelling cigar smoke at them. "I'm showing these boys a good time. Seth, Kevin, come meet Mr. Frey."

"Ah, yes. These are your week's entertainment. That was a nice show you put on this morning, boys. Just lovely." Frey took a moment to let his eyes roam up and down both Seth and Kevin. The leer tainted the man's beauty, making him seem less like a sex god and more like a dirty, old man.

Kevin flinched. Seth's hand started to move, drawn by a gravitational pull toward Kevin, but Seth stopped it just in time. The last thing Kevin needed was for Seth to grab his hand, even just to comfort him.

Frey smirked. "I can't wait to see your next performance. The two of you have such chemistry together. How long have you been a couple?"

Seth shook his head, his cheeks blazing. "We're not a couple. Just friends."

"Really? How interesting," Frey drawled. "Perhaps you and I could talk about that together in private." He engulfed Seth's hands between his large palms.

A bitter tang invaded Seth's mouth as the temptation to yank his hands from Mr. Frey's almost overwhelmed him. Fear of offending his host kept him still. Before he could remind Winthrop that he had been promised to a single partner, his host spoke.

"Now, now, Frey." Winthrop wagged a finger in Frey's face. "I won't have you interfering with my fun. I have these boys exclusively for the week."

Frey faced Winthrop, a pouty frown making his visage less handsome and truly creepy. He didn't drop Seth's hand. "But you won't play with them. You just watch. I'll let you watch."

The color drained from Kevin's face, and Seth's stomach twisted like a spiral galaxy.

"Ah, Frey. Don't make me angry." Winthrop's face reddened. His nostrils flared, and his entire body seemed to puff in a way that made Seth sweat and his heart pound. "I'll have you tarred and feathered."

Frey gave an uncomfortable half laugh and loosened his grip on Seth's hand. "You always say that. I dare say your punishments are far more... inventive."

Seth yanked his hand away. *Did Winthrop just help me?* Or perhaps this was more like a farmer who protected his sheep from wolves until it was time for lamb for dinner.

Kevin moved up next to him, glaring at Frey.

Seth spoke through gritted teeth. "It was nice meeting you." He grabbed Kevin's arm and moved him along, the sounds of chuckles following in his wake. "Well, I guess we know Winthrop isn't the only one watching." Seth wanted to find the most remote black hole in the galaxy and throw himself in.

"I think I knew that." Kevin opened his mouth as if he wanted to say more, but snapped it shut.

Why was Kevin here? What did he know that he could not say?

"Ah, ahh. That's for me to know." Winthrop's sneering voice entered Seth's mind.

Seth turned his head, and his eyes lasered in on Winthrop. He was still deep in conversation with Frey. Could Seth have imagined the voice? How could Winthrop be listening, much less sending thoughts without some kind of equipment? Either way, Seth wasn't about to risk the man's wrath. He didn't want to see how inventive the man could be.

Despite the stress, Seth's stomach rumbled. Swimming that morning had given him quite an appetite. He wandered up to the closest station, with Kevin following. They found a chardonnay paired with a creamy mushroom risotto. They each took a plate of the rice and a small cup of wine.

Fruity? Nutty? Okay? Isn't that what people said? Fuck if Seth knew. It tasted like wine. A bit sour, maybe. The risotto's creamy texture contained hints of parmesan.

Seth and Kevin worked their way around the various stations, tasting delicious dishes and sampling each wine.

As they approached a table with another Riesling vintage, Kevin said, "We should skip the food and get totally trashed."

Seth stopped and studied his friend. "Why?"

Kevin gestured to Winthrop. "Give us a chance to forget for a bit."

Seth's heart sank. Kevin wasn't a big drinker, but this week was already pushing him to the edge and it had barely begun. "That might not be a good idea. I can't imagine what Winthrop might have us do when our inhibitions were low."

Another guest passed them, a twenty-something woman, maybe six feet tall, with flowing, blonde tresses, and wearing a short, black cocktail dress. Its form-fitting fabric shimmered as she took a plate of food. If she wasn't a model, she should be. He may not be attracted to women, but he could tell when one was top quality gorgeous. Kevin stood beside him, eyes fixed on her. Seth decided immediately that he didn't like her.

As she strolled off, Kevin shook his head and focused

back on Seth. "Does that really matter?" Kevin said harshly. "He can have us do anything he wants. He doesn't need to get us drunk first." He turned away.

Frowning, Seth moved around Kevin to catch his eyes. "Hey, I'm sorry."

Kevin's lips pressed together, forming a tight line. "Stop saying you're sorry. None of this is your fault."

"But…" Seth's throat thickened.

Kevin shook his head and sighed. "Give it up. It's not. We're doing what we have to do to get through this."

"I know." Seth's heart thumped faster. "I… You're my best friend. That means more to me than anything, and I hate this whole situation." Seth shifted.

"We're good. You're probably right about not getting drunk. Gotta stay sharp. Be prepared for anything."

A burden lightened for Seth. As much as he hated that Kevin had to go through this, there was no one he could count on more.

The model approached a boy, who was perhaps twelve or thirteen years old. He sported a gold hat that looked like a construction worker might wear with wings on either side. After a few moments, she laughed and clapped him on the back.

Seth took another plate of food with the accompanying wine.

As he started to eat, a redheaded man, who appeared close to him in age, introduced himself, "I'm Vincent. I'm glad you guys are here. It took some pressure off me."

"What?" Seth asked.

Vincent's face flushed, making his freckles fade into the color of his skin. "I'm, um, under contract with Maynard as well."

"Oh, why, uh, what, uh?" Was there a question Seth could safely ask?

"I know, don't ask, don't tell. We each have things Maynard requires of us for reasons we can't reveal."

Seth took a deep breath. "Oh. Okay. Have you been here long?"

Vincent's gaze shot over to Winthrop as he cleared his throat. "I have two more days in my week." His voice caught on the word two.

Seth took a moment to study Vincent. He didn't seem to be in distress, except his eyes looked a bit too bright.

"Good luck, man," Kevin said, flashing an encouraging smile. "You're almost through it."

Winthrop called across the room, "Oh, Vincent?"

"Gotta go. The boss is calling." Vincent bee-lined for Winthrop.

Seth turned to Kevin to ask what he thought about Vincent, but was interrupted before he could speak by a black, female little person in a silvery cocktail dress. How many little people did Winthrop employ? Or was this one a guest?

"Which was your favorite?" the woman asked, gesturing around to the various tables.

Seth struggled for an answer when Kevin saved him.

"I liked the 2012 Riesling over there." Kevin pointed to a station that Seth assumed had a Riesling. "The spices from the noodle salad played well off the flavor of the wine."

Seth attempted to keep his mouth shut. Did Kevin know something about wine?

"Ah, a good choice. I was partial to the Cabernet Franc with the rhubarb cheesecake. But I do love a good cheesecake."

Kevin appeared relaxed and natural, as if he discussed wine every day. "That was a nice pairing. I'm so full now."

"I know. Mr. Winthrop is an expert at creating nice pairings."

Kevin coughed, his posture stiffening.

The woman went on. "Perhaps you boys would like to return to your room."

Seth's heart sped. Was this woman inviting them to do something? "I'm not sure our host would appreciate it if we left."

Winthrop appeared behind them as if out of thin air. "Why would I have an issue with that? You boys had a busy day. Did you enjoy the wine?"

Kevin's eyes widened for just a moment before he schooled his expression to one with a pleasant smile. "Thank you. We don't get treated like this often."

"You're welcome." Winthrop took a puff from his stogie and blew a smoke ring. "Listen. I'll have Erex take you back to your room. I know you both brought your laptops so you could do schoolwork. Such dedication. I left the Wi-Fi password on a sticky note on the wall." Winthrop placed a hand on Seth's right shoulder and Kevin's left. "Go relax, have a quiet evening. I'll send down a light supper later. Get a good night's sleep. We have a new, exciting challenge tomorrow."

"Thank you, sir… ah, Maynard," Seth responded.

Erex stepped up to the two of them. "This way, please."

Out in the midafternoon sun, Erex led them to a golf cart and drove them back to the main house. They went in a side entrance and down several flights of stairs, the temperature dropping the lower they went. A thin mist of condensation dampened the walls.

At the bottom of the stairs, he opened a door, and they were back in their room. A sticky note hung on the wall with the password *LotOfLovin2nite*. Both of their laptops had been taken from their bags and were left to charge on two side-by-side desks.

Erex left without a word.

"Winthrop brought in desks for us." Kevin bit his lower lip.

Seth wanted to go over to Kevin and pull his lip out of his teeth, soothe it with his tongue, but knew that wouldn't be welcome. Instead, he tried to focus on the desks. "But how did he get them to fit? It's like the room grew."

Kevin's hand landed on Seth's shoulder. "Maybe this isn't the same room. They keep bringing us in through different doors."

An electric jolt of want shot through Seth from Kevin's hand. "It's possible…"

The sensation pointed out the unfairness of this whole situation. Seth wanted Kevin, but that feeling would never be reciprocated. He sat down at his computer as an excuse to move away from the enticing, forbidden touch.

He opened his laptop and immediately did a spot check of his data and ran virus scanning software. Who knew what Winthrop would do to his computer? But everything came up clean and in order. Of course, that didn't mean much. Winthrop could have access to a new virus. One that wasn't known yet.

On the other hand, if Winthrop wanted to mess with his computer, he already had ample opportunity, so Seth connected to the Wi-Fi. He checked his email. Nothing critical had come in, but he felt strangely comforted knowing he was not completely disconnected from the outside world.

A brief thought crossed his mind that perhaps he could expose Winthrop. Report what he had seen. But the risk seemed too great.

Just because Winthrop's people hadn't messed with his computer didn't mean they wouldn't monitor his outgoing data and perhaps even block it. They controlled his access point to the world, and the consequences of angering Winthrop were severe. His parent's homeless, dropping out of college, the whole nine yards.

"I'm gonna work on a paper for Organic Chemistry I have due after break," Kevin said.

"Sounds good." Seth nodded. "I have some lab notes to write up for Experimental Astronomy."

Working in the room with Kevin felt normal. This was his best friend. The things they had done so far, the things they would do, didn't need to change that. But just remembering Kevin's hand on his cock and the power of his orgasm left him breathless and wanting, and made it difficult to concentrate on his work.

A couple hours passed before Erex arrived with a tray loaded with cheeseburgers and French fries. "This is what you kids eat, right? I even snuck in some sodas. The boss won't be too pleased that I'm feeding you drivel, but I figured you needed a break from the fancy food."

It was a nice effort, although, as an athlete, Seth tried to eat healthier than that. In a way, this junk was more decadent than fancy food.

As he munched on a French fry, he pulled out a problem set due at the end of the break and tried to lose himself in the complex calculations, but his mind kept straying to the bed. The one, king-sized bed. He knew he had to do the right thing, but was not looking forward to it.

Two pairs of pajamas had been laid out on the bed. He assumed his host required them to wear the heart-covered monstrosities. He dressed quickly as Winthrop's chuckle rolled through his head.

Seth took a deep breath. "I'll take the floor."

Kevin's eyes snapped from the bed to Seth. "What? You don't have to."

"It's all right. You take the bed."

"This bed is bigger than our dorm room." Kevin cleared his throat, and his words spewed out. "We can share it."

Poor Kevin. He's trying…

"I know we have to do… stuff this week. But that doesn't mean I…"

Kevin inhaled sharply. "Dude, just get on that side of the bed. I'll stay way over here, on this side, and everything will be fine."

"Uh…" Seth blinked his eyes several times.

"Quit bitchin' and chill. It'll be fine."

Seth lay down as close to the edge as he could, hoping he wouldn't roll off. His cock was painfully aware of Kevin behind him. But he was not that kind of guy. He would do what he had to, but he wasn't going to make this any worse for Kevin.

"Is that what it's like?" Kevin spoke quietly.

Seth gripped the blanket a little tighter, his eyes wide open in the dark. "What's what like?"

"Sex… with another guy?"

"What?" *Did my voice just squeak?*

"Earlier today. Is that what it's like?"

Seth had no idea how to answer. It had never been like that for him. Sure, the moves were the same, except maybe the being in water part, but the way it felt… that was a whole different story. "Why? Is it different with girls?"

"No. Yes." Kevin huffed out a hard breath. "I don't know. Forget I asked."

Seth clenched his jaw. Something was on Kevin's mind. He would talk about it when he was ready and not before. "Okay."

Damn it, and damn Winthrop.

CHAPTER ELEVEN

Seth woke before Kevin. *Thank God. I so don't want him to see my morning wood.* He rolled carefully off the bed to let his friend sleep and slipped into the bathroom and showered. He had just finished dressing in jeans and a red polo shirt when a knock at the door woke Kevin.

Erex staggered into the room, carrying a tray full of star fruit, kiwi, papaya, pomegranate, rice, and several kinds of fish. Two forms of herring filled the air with a hint of vinegar, as well as smoked whitefish and salmon, and several others that Seth couldn't begin to identify. A bowl held an assortment of bagels, and another contained chive cream cheese.

"The boss found out about the dinner I gave you last night and said I needed to be more creative." His lower lip pouted out in a sullen expression.

"This is fine, Erex." Poor guy. Seth hoped Winthrop hadn't

done anything over the top to him for giving them something normal.

Erex bowed and left the room.

Kevin slipped into the bathroom, and the muffled sound of the shower passed through the wall.

Seth waited a few seconds, certain an order would be issued at any moment, but Winthrop sent no instructions to join Kevin. He sighed. Some part of him wished for a command to go and violate his friend's privacy because, even if he couldn't make out all the details, Kevin's body had looked *fine* under the warm spray of water.

What does that say about me? Forget it. Focus on food.

He grabbed a plate and an egg bagel, smearing on the cream cheese and adding some lox. Feeling daring, he took some kiwi and a little of each fish onto his plate. Then he settled down at the table.

Seth averted his gaze when Kevin came out and grabbed clothes to dress. He joined Seth at the table, wearing a pair of ass-hugging jeans and a dark green T-shirt that highlighted his strong chest and wide shoulders. Seth almost swallowed his tongue.

"Do you know what this stuff is?" Kevin pointed to the various fishes on the tray.

"Yeah. That's whitefish."

"Duh, I can see it's white."

"No, dufus. It's called whitefish. It's smoked." Seth pointed to another. "That's pickled herring in cream sauce, and that's smoked salmon. I don't know the others."

"I've had smoked salmon." Kevin huffed. "The others are new." He put a tiny bit of whitefish on his fork and touched it to his tongue before making a face.

Seth couldn't help it. He laughed at the expression of

horror.

Kevin's head swiveled left and he rolled his eyes. "What? You know I don't like fish."

Seth smiled. Bantering with Kevin, he could almost forget the whole bizarre situation. "That doesn't taste anything like the kind of fish we have at school."

"Too bad, I'm not eating it."

"Suit yourself."

Kevin put a full serving of smoked salmon on an everything bagel with some cream cheese and bit into the sandwich.

"You realize that salmon is fish, too."

"Shut up, asshole." Kevin displayed his middle finger. "It's different. I like this."

Seth laughed.

Kevin cut open a papaya. Seth never liked papayas. For some reason, they reminded him of lady parts, and he could never get past that. Unsurprisingly, that wasn't a problem for Kevin as he scooped out the seeds from the center and removed a piece of the juicy flesh with a spoon.

Seth watched as the spoon entered Kevin's mouth, entranced by the way his lips closed over the sweet orange pulp and the spoon slid out. Kevin's eyes closed in appreciation.

"That is the best papaya I've ever eaten. Want some?" He scooped another bite and held it up for Seth.

"No, thank you." *You just can't change who you are. Kevin is perfect for me, but I'm not what he needs.*

Erex returned to fetch them and eyed them over. "Those outfits will do."

Seth met Kevin's gaze and shrugged.

Erex brought them up a long tunnel and into a large, forest-edged field. The open area had been neatly groomed like a football field. Winthrop sat on an immense, throne under a tent that shaded him from the bright morning sunlight. People milled about, talking in small groups.

Seth recognized some from the day before, but not all. At least they were dressed more casually so he didn't feel like a lone star in a sea of black void.

Vincent, the fellow contractee to Winthrop they met yesterday, stood alone, sipping a drink. His face was flushed red although the day was only mildly warm with a soothing, cool breeze. The hand holding the glass shook slightly. Seth tried to wave, but the man seemed lost in Andromeda.

Off to the right, about a basketball court's width away, a large, spitted pig roasted over a firepit. The delicious aroma of broiling meat and wood smoke wafted through the area. Behind the fire pit, a dirt road disappeared into the forest.

To the left of the field, about the length of a basketball court away, stood several targets decorated in concentric circles, white, black, blue, red, with yellow in the center.

A few members of the crowd clapped. Seth turned to see what had caught their attention. Several little people entered the clearing from the dirt road. One pushed a cart stacked with bows in a variety of sizes. A coupled others pulled a huge wagon filled with quivers containing arrows. Cheers rolled across the field.

Did I miss something?

After passing the crowd and arriving around fifty feet away from the targets, each of the little people took a short bow, strung it, and shot at a target. Each of the arrows landed in one of the yellow circles.

The whole action happened faster than a shooting star burned out in the night sky. These folks had serious strength.

Kevin whistled beside him. "That was some shooting."

Winthrop stood. "Honored guests. I have arranged a game of sorts. Many of you know my fondness for the bow. It's an excellent tool with so many uses." Somehow, his voice carried on the wind like he spoke into a bull horn.

Chuckles erupted around the gathering. What was Winthrop talking about? Bows had one use: shooting things.

"For the next hour, my experts," he gestured toward the little shooters, "are at your disposal. You may ask them anything you want." He winked at Seth. "About archery, of course. They will help you refine your technique. Then we'll have a little competition. The winner gets a prize."

"What's the prize?" Mr. Frey called out.

"A fair question. Besides bragging rights for beating the assembled throng." Winthrop's head tipped up, considering. "The winner can select one of my special guests to be pardoned from their burdens to me." Winthrop gestured to Seth and Kevin.

Seth's heart raced, and his head spun. One of them could earn freedom. If he won, he could save Kevin. *Shit! I don't know dick about archery.* Kevin stood beside Seth, nodding and biting his lower lip.

Winthrop pointed out Vincent. He had dressed in jeans and a red T-shirt that said, "Keep Calm and Don't Blink." His mouth hung open.

Then Winthrop indicated an older woman, her face all squished as if she had just eaten a lemon.

After her, Winthrop pointed to a couple of men who stood with their arms around each other.

Finally, Winthrop gestured to a man and a woman. She had some kind of bandaging on her shoulder, and he leaned on crutches.

Winthrop continued, "Everyone is eligible to participate. Perhaps one of you will win freedom for yourself instead of relying on me to fix your problems."

Winthrop's gaze bored into Seth, filled with judgment

about his family's debt.

Fuck you, asshole.

His father had pounded the pavement every day for a year looking for a job, but they had fallen behind. His new job should have ensured they would be able to pay it off, but, of course, Winthrop threatened his father's employment as well.

It wasn't their fault the economy sucked and the housing market had tanked so they couldn't even sell without losing money.

Seth turned to Kevin. Every muscle in his body had stiffened into high alert, and his hands had clenched into fists. What did Winthrop hold over Kevin?

Determination filled Seth. He had to win that contest. If only to prove Winthrop wrong, and then he could free Kevin from whatever hold the man had over him and spare him any more distasteful encounters and humiliation.

"One of us could get free," Kevin said.

Seth nodded. "Do you know anything about archery?"

"Not really, but we're college athletes." Kevin shrugged. "How hard could it be?"

"Really hard. Archery is an Olympic sport, moron."

"So? So is basketball, but I doubt there are any Olympians here. We have to try." Kevin lifted his chin as he straightened and stared right at Seth.

"Of course, we do. Winthrop offered."

I have to do this for Kevin.

Seth and Kevin headed for the group of little people. Before either of them could speak, a little person stepped toward them.

"Hello, boys. I'm Ianthe." Ianthe stood a little over three feet tall. She wore a white, shortsleeve shirt with a picture of a unicorn rearing up and a black skirt. A beaded bracelet wrapped her left wrist. "The boss wants me to work with you. He must think you have a chance."

Does that mean she's gonna increase our chances or decrease them?

She grabbed each of their hands and pulled them until they followed to the pile of bows. Her brown ponytail swished as she walked. "Have you ever shot before?"

"Not since I was eight," Seth answered.

"A few times when I was a kid," Kevin said.

"Right. We'll start from the beginning." She sorted through the bows, muttering to herself. "Both right eye dominant…"

"How do you know we're both right-handed?" Kevin asked.

"The boss told me you were both right-handed. Although that's not important. He also said you're both right eye dominant. That's much more important."

Kevin turned to Seth, eyebrows raised. Seth shrugged in response.

She pulled out a bow that was easily twice her height and held it up to Seth. Nodding, she handed it to him and grabbed another for Kevin. "These are buckthorn long bows. Come on, sweet things, the targets are this way."

Sweet things?

Kevin huffed a laugh, his player smile falling into place. "Sure thing, hot stuff."

Kevin's flirting? Here? Seth messaged his jaw to loosen the muscles. Typical Kevin, always on the prowl, even when assigned to be Seth's *exclusive* partner for a week.

But that was the keyword. Assigned.

As Ianthe tapped the inside of Kevin's leg to get him to widen his stance to shoulder-width, Seth's chest tightened. How dare she put her hands on him?

Rein it in. No more of the crazy.

During Seth's turn to shoot, she made sure the colored feather faced the inside, and then had him draw back to his cheek, look at the target, and release. The wooden arrow spun as it flew through the air, making a *fip-fip* sound. Seth managed to hit the outer ring of the target.

"Not bad, honey." She patted him on the butt. "Your form looks pretty good. Aim just a bit above the bull's-eye."

Honey? Okay.

The next hour both flew by and dragged. On the one hand, Seth needed to learn everything he could about the bow. On the other hand, Ianthe's flirting distracted him. Especially when Kevin responded, bantering back.

Seth nocked another arrow, aimed, and let fly just as Kevin bent down to kiss Ianthe on the cheek. Seth missed the target completely.

"I think you're getting worse," Kevin commented, a shit-eating grin aimed at Seth.

"Seriously? I don't see you hitting the bull's-eye." Seth laughed. Something about giving each other shit about sports brought back the feeling of ribbing each other at basketball practice, back when life was normal.

By the end of the hour, he hit the target every time, although usually one of the outer rings. His bicep burned, and his shoulder ached. He hoped he would be able to keep shooting. Kevin achieved about the same accuracy.

A little woman wearing a black cocktail dress strummed a harp, and the assembled crowd fell silent.

People chose one of the targets and lined up. In the first round, they would each get five shots. The top twenty scorers would continue. Seth and Kevin survived the first round, as did Vincent and the older woman. Vincent's lips pressed together in a tight line, and sweat dotted his brow.

During each round, Seth watched Kevin shoot. In the third round, Kevin bit his lip as he focused on the target. His bicep bulged as he drew back. Eight points. A good shot. But then he hit the outside ring for the next two, adding only two more points to his score.

When his final arrow scored only two points for a total of sixteen, Kevin's stance slumped, and his head dropped. Kevin placed his bow in the bin. "This could have been over."

"I know. I'm so sorry."

Kevin placed a hand on Seth's shoulder. "Not your fault."

"I know." Seth gulped. The sensation of Kevin's hand vibrated through him. "It's not yours, either. We're not archers."

Kevin huffed. "No, but you gave a good showing."

"I got lucky. Should I lose for your ego?" Seth gave Kevin a wry grin.

"Hell, no. Go win this bitch."

"Yes, sir." Seth mock saluted.

Seth made it to the final round, along with Vincent and three other members of the crowd. Vincent knelt down and spoke in quiet tones with the little person who had worked with him earlier. Sweat trickled down his brow, and his eyes were closed as he listened.

Ianthe tugged on Seth's pant leg. "You've done better than I expected. You could win this thing."

"You think so?"

"Probably not, but you do look adorable with the bow and that look of determination on your face."

Seth rolled his eyes. "Thanks for the pep talk."

"Seriously." She grinned at him. "You're getting better with every shot. Just focus."

Kevin rubbed Seth's shoulders. "You can do this."

"Thanks." A soothing sensation penetrated his sore, throbbing shoulders. For a moment, Seth leaned into the touch and allowed Kevin's nimble fingers to un-kink his tired, burning muscles. Why couldn't it always be like this?

The highest score, ten, was awarded for each arrow that struck the innermost part of the yellow circle. The lowest you could get if you at least hit the target was one.

The first person who shot scored an impressive thirty-six. But he got knocked out by the next shooter, who scored forty-two. The third shooter scored thirty-four.

Vincent stepped up to the shooting line. He looked over at Winthrop, who belched and then blew a kiss at Vincent. Vincent shuddered as a drop of sweat ran down the side of his face. He turned to the target, and his brow furrowed. He nodded once, lifted the bow, aimed, and shot.

Bull's-eye. A perfect ten.

His next two shots were just off the mark, earning him a nine each.

He inhaled deeply, aimed, and scored another ten. He needed at least six to tie for first. Aim, shoot, and another excellent shot earned him a nine for an impressive forty-seven points.

Vincent walked over to Seth. "Sorry, man, I can't afford to lose."

"I understand, but neither can I."

Seth had not shot close to a forty-seven the entire day. As he stepped up to the shooting line, he straightened his glasses and focused on what Ianthe had taught him. Feet parallel to the shooting line. Shoulder pointing at the target. Hand behind the bow when holding. Three fingers to pull back to his anchor position.

He took a breath in and let it go slowly like he did when he prepared for a free throw. He took aim and fired. He hit the outer part of the yellow ring for a score of nine points. The crowd cheered while Seth fought to keep calm.

The next arrow hit close to the first, scoring another nine. He needed to step up his game if he wanted to win this. He closed his eyes for a moment and focused, then opened them, aimed, and fired.

A solid thwack sounded as he hit the inner most circle, a ten. He turned to smile at Kevin while the man let out a loud whoop.

"Dude, you're on fire."

Seth shrugged as his cheeks burned. He had great motivation. He was doing this for Kevin.

Another deep breath, another arrow, another ten.

He was now up to thirty-eight points. If he could hit the center again, he would win.

The crowd was silent. Even the wind seemed to cooperate, stilling. He took the bow, nocked the arrow, sighted along the line, and fired.

Thwack.

The final arrow hit the inner red ring, scoring an eight for a total of forty-six.

Seth deflated. He bowed his head. He couldn't save Kevin.

Before he could get into a full-blown pity party, Vincent distracted him from failure by fist pumping the air. The redhead turned to Winthrop's chair.

But it stood empty.

"Over here, boys and girls." Winthrop stood behind the firing line for the end target. A bow dangled loosely from one hand while he puffed his cigar and blew out a heart-shaped smoke ring and farted. Erex held five arrows and stood beside him. "Did I mention? You have to beat me in the final round to gain the prize. Vincent, you had to know nothing is ever that easy."

Vincent's face fell, and his body shook.

Winthrop turned to the target and then took ten steps backward, causing several members of the crowd to gasp.

A terrifying grin split Winthrop's face. "It's too easy, otherwise."

Winthrop took an arrow from Erex, nocked, sighted, and fired. The arrow struck the center of the innermost ring of the target.

A perfect ten.

Four more arrows followed, each splitting the arrow before it.

A perfect score.

The crowd broke into applause as Winthrop swung his arm in front of himself with a flourish and bowed.

"Now, Vincent. I'm so sorry you lost. I provided this entertainment in hopes you could at least tie with me so I could show some mercy. But as many of my guests saw, you failed in your challenge last night."

Vincent stared at Winthrop, his eyes narrowed. "Bastard. No one should be asked to do that."

The bile rose in Seth's throat. Would Winthrop wait until the end of his week of entertainment, and then ask Seth to do something completely reprehensible.

"You knew the rules. You lost."

Winthrop snapped his fingers, and two freakishly large men in suits stepped forward. Seth craned his head back. They had to be at least seven feet tall, and something wasn't quite right with their faces. Like they had been broken and repaired so many times that they no longer appeared human.

Winthrop spoke to the two goons. "Take him to the play room and have fun, boys."

The one on the right rubbed his large, meaty hands together. "Thank you, boss. He's so tasty."

Vincent took a step backward, his head oscillating back and forth. "No, please."

Puffing on his cigar, Winthrop released a smoke ring. "You knew the rules. You signed the contract. This is the payment."

Vincent dropped to his knees. "No, please. I'm sorry. Give me one more chance."

Seth froze, staring at Vincent, unable to look away.

Walking up to Vincent, Winthrop flicked some ashes that landed on the guy's shoulder. "Can't do it. I show mercy, and suddenly no one listens."

The two men grabbed Vincent by the arms, lifting him in the air like he was a doll. His legs stretched, and he kicked his feet as he squirmed in their arms. The one on the left chuckled, leaned in, and punched him in the face.

Seth flinched, and his chest tightened.

Vincent slumped, unconscious. Blood poured from his nose.

"So sorry you all had to see that. I trust my message is clear." Winthrop's gaze lasered in on Seth.

What had Vincent refused to do? Would he be asked to do it? What contract had he signed? He didn't remember any punishment clauses. His body shivered like someone had walked over his grave.

Seth's eyes met Kevin's. His friend's mouth pinched into a thin line, and he nodded once. No matter what, they could not fail.

CHAPTER TWELVE

Sunday, April 2, 11:49 am

As the two brutes dragged Vincent away, Seth fought the urge to vomit. His mind spun, imagining increasingly horrible scenarios of what might happen to Vincent. What the hell did the goon mean when he called Vincent tasty? In a flash, Seth imagined Kevin being carried away instead. Fuck!

What the Hell? Most of the crowd appeared upset but not surprised. Like this was a typical day at the Winthrop mansion.

Little people came out of the forest along the dirt road, pushing wooden carts laden with food. How the hell was Seth supposed to eat after what he just saw?

Winthrop's servants spread blankets and erected tables. A little woman wearing a chef's hat stabbed at the roasted pig with a knife that was longer than her arm, grunting with each stroke. Seth flinched. The picture of a bloody dagger emblazoned across the front of her apron seemed too apropos.

Other little people dressed in black tuxedos and black dresses put out green salad, potato salad, cornbread, baked beans, corn on the cob, sandwich rolls, a huge variety of sauces and condiments, and mashed sweet potatoes.

When it was all set up, Winthrop stood and took a puff on his stogie. "Ladies and gentlemen. My special guests." Winthrop winked at Seth. "I hope you enjoyed my little competition. The conclusion was absolutely exhilarating."

The crowd around Seth applauded politely. Kevin nudged his shoulder and pushed his own clapping hands into Seth's line of sight until Seth joined in. Applauding what just happened to Vincent seemed perverse, but they had to keep in their host's good graces. Now more than ever.

Winthrop nodded to the crowd with a smug look on his face. "Yes. Yes. I deserve it. Now, please, enjoy the lovely repast my servants have set up. *Bon appétit, mes amies.*"

Seth followed Kevin to the buffet line and filled his plate on autopilot. He picked at the cornbread, tasting nothing. His appetite left with Vincent. Damn, no one deserved what Winthrop dished out.

What would Seth and Kevin be asked to do next, and would they be able to do it? He couldn't fail. Too much was riding on this. But, what about Kevin? What if his stakes were lower, and he refused to do something *too gay*?

Kevin also seemed lost in thought as they sat on the blanket together. He shoveled the food into his mouth like it was his last meal. Not a good sign from a stress eater. This gorging beat the time he had four final exams in two days.

After lunch, an area was cleared, and a band struck up some country music. A woman wearing a green dress pulled a man up, and they started dancing. Soon others joined them.

Erex came up next to Seth and Kevin and whispered, "Boss has other plans for you two. Follow me." He led them back to the house and down the same tunnel. But when the door opened, it wasn't the room they had left. Instead, they entered a space that belonged in an hourly hotel, or a bordello.

Seth was almost getting used to doors seeming to move. How was this place made?

In the center of the room stood a large, heart-shaped bed with a royal purple satin sheet that gleamed from flickering candlelight. Sprinkled over the bed was a generous scattering of red rose petals, the aroma filling the room. A scarlet bed ruffle framed the box spring. Enormous purple feathers stuck up to form two rounded pieces, each at one of the curved tops of the heart, for the bed's headboard. A plush, purple carpet covered the floor, and red, satiny wallpaper adorned the walls. Mirrors tiled the ceiling and sparkled with dancing flames from the candle wall sconces. They added a smoky tint to the rose-scented room.

"Time for your next challenge, boys." Winthrop's voice rolled through Seth's head. *"I had this room decorated just for you."*

Seth glanced at Kevin. His friend's face had smoothed into an impassive mask as his eyes met Seth's. Then he shrugged.

"I think it's time for some oral action. Blowjobs to be precise. Show me your stuff, boys, and make it hot." A menacing note entered Winthrop's voice. *"Blow me away, or you know the consequences."*

The color drained from Kevin's face.

"Now strip down and get busy." Winthrop's voice mimicked the harsh crack of a whip.

Seth disrobed, quickly, matter-of-factly. No striptease or seduction like he might consider for an actual lover. This was Kevin. It would be lost on him. Seth didn't have enough curves in the right places. His pair was below and not on his chest.

Kevin turned his back on Seth and stripped in silence.

"Winthrop, you bastard. Why are you making him do this? You are one sickfuck."

Winthrop's laughter filled his head.

Seth followed Kevin onto the bed, crawling toward him. Moving seductively like a predator seeking his prey. He slipped into *that* mode. How many times had he daydreamed about being in this exact position with his best friend, naked and waiting?

But Kevin's expression was blank. This was Seth's straight, best friend. He sat back on his haunches, his face hurting from the frown it formed.

Kevin met Seth's gaze. "What's wrong?"

Seth exhaled a quick breath. "Nothing."

"Bullshit. I know that look. You're overthinking this."

Seth looked away. "What?"

"We're both here for whatever reason. We both know we have to do this. Neither of us made this happen. I didn't make you. You didn't make me."

He didn't make me? Seth wanted to laugh at the absurdity of that concept. All Kevin ever had to do was crook one finger in his direction, and Seth would have been his, heart, body, mind, and soul.

Where had that come from? Kevin didn't want his heart or his body, much less his soul. He couldn't be thinking that way. When this ended, at best, they would go back to being just friends. At worst, Kevin would never speak to him again. No matter what happened, nothing would ever be the same.

Seth forced himself to meet Kevin's gaze. "I know."

"Let's do what we have to. Everything is going to work out."

Maybe Kevin was trying to convince himself. Seth longed to wipe away the fear in Kevin's eyes. He wanted to hold Kevin and make him feel safe, to stand and fight off all the demons. Or just one. Maynard Frederick Winthrop IV.

"We'll get through this…" Seth agreed, but would life ever be the same? He leaned in and kissed Kevin, joining their mouths in that age-old sensual dance.

He put his hand on Kevin's cheek and smoothed it back into Kevin's short brown hair, gripping firmly but gently. He slid his tongue across Kevin's lips, and the man opened to him with a moan rumbling deep in his chest. Kevin's eyes closed. Perhaps he lost himself in some fantasy again. Good. Seth allowed his lids to fall, and he slid into a fantasy of his own. One in an impossible world where Kevin could want this, could want him, of his own freewill.

Not this *farce*.

Kevin's fingers slid up and down his back, leaving tingles of awareness and need in their wake. Seth reached around Kevin and pulled him closer, their bare chests flush against one another.

Seth's erection strained against Kevin's. Kevin's? His friend's cock wasn't just half-hard. It stood at full mast, leaking pre-come and thrusting against him. Their swords in an intimate battle. How could Kevin's illusion not be broken by the reality of what was happening?

Seth didn't have time to ponder as Kevin kissed down his neck and bit into the sensitive flesh at the junction with his shoulder, sending a jolt of need straight to his engorged prick. He threw his head back as a mewl of pleasure escaped his lips. "Oh."

On the ceiling, reflecting back, Kevin kissed down his collarbone and chest toward his nipple. *He probably has plenty of practice with those.* Even knowing that, Seth wasn't prepared for the pointing tongue that flicked out, pleasuring the sensitive bud and making it stand up in a peak of desire. He wrapped his arm around Kevin's head, holding him in place while the talented, hot, wet tongue flicked across the taut nub. The image above mirrored one of Seth's fantasies.

Seth's hips thrust against Kevin's, his shaft desperate for something, anything, he just *needed*.

A warm chuckle rumbled through Kevin's chest as he pulled back. "It's okay. I got you."

Kevin was reassuring him? What was next? Dragons? Sex in the clouds? The utter impossibility of the situation made him want to laugh, but then he remembered that he better get to work on the challenge. Who knew how long Winthrop would wait before interfering? The man seemed content to just watch as long as they stayed within whatever bounds he set.

He bent closer and sealed his lips to Kevin's, swiping his tongue into the warm, wet cavern, but too quickly, Kevin pulled away and pushed him onto his back.

Then Kevin continued his journey south. He nuzzled Seth's belly button, eliciting a little giggle from him. "Ticklish?"

"A little."

A smile touched Kevin's lips, and his eyes twinkled. "Good to know."

Now that really had Seth worried. Kevin knowing where he was ticklish seemed like giving Kryptonite to Lex Luthor. When he least expected it, in the locker room, or elsewhere…

All thought fled as Kevin kept moving lower, and then his tongue shot out and licked Seth's throbbing prick, before engulfing it.

"Holy shit."

Kevin's eyes shot up. "Did I hurt you?"

Seth stared, mesmerized by the twin views of Kevin's face at his groin live and in the mirror. "What? How?"

"Oh, I've just… never done this before."

And Seth returned to the guilt. Here Kevin was running

the show when Seth should have been trying to make it as easy as possible. Get it done fast so Kevin could compartmentalize this whole experience away.

"No, you did it just right."

A slight smile graced Kevin's face as he dove in again, surrounding Seth's prick with hot, moist pressure.

At first, Seth couldn't believe how intuitive Kevin was. The man hit every hot spot, bringing him higher and higher, until Kevin gagged a bit and pulled off.

His grin was sheepish now. "You're really big."

Something about the look on Kevin's face, his lips swollen from sucking, shiny with saliva, and the way he said big really punched Seth's ticket. He almost came on the spot.

"You don't have to take the whole thing in your mouth. Just wrap your hand around the base and move it as you… you know." Seth's face burned like the sun. When had he become shy about sex, about talking dirty? Oh, yeah, since he was asked to do it with his straight best friend. "I have an idea."

Seth encouraged Kevin to swing his legs around so they were head-to-toe, on their sides.

"I guess gay guys do sixty-nine, too." Kevin gave a cheeky grin.

"Honey, we invented sixty-nine." Why had he called Kevin honey? Before he could think too much about that, he leaned in and took Kevin's large cock into his mouth and sucked him to the root, deep throating him in one move.

Kevin's strangled gasp ramped him up even more as he worked his throat muscles, swallowing around the head.

A guttural grunt escaped Kevin as he lowered his head, taking Seth in his mouth.

Now came the best part. The hard part. Each working the other while engulfed in ecstasy. Trying to keep the rhythm while sensations attacked at the center of his need. But Seth was determined to make this great for Kevin. The best blowjob he ever had. He doubted any girl could suck cock like he could. They just didn't have the necessary frame of reference to know how it felt.

He used every trick in his arsenal. He hummed, he licked, swirling his tongue around the head, teasing the sensitive spot underneath. He bobbed his head, trying not to stop and lose himself in the sensations between his thighs, but it was hard, so hard.

He reached out and tickled Kevin's balls, working his way from the front to behind them, and then pushed on his perineum.

Kevin leaped and gave a muffled, full-mouthed yelp as Seth thrust over and over into his mouth. It was only a few moments more before Kevin pulled off Seth, let out a loud groan of pleasure, and shot his load straight into Seth's waiting mouth.

Seth kept swallowing as stream after stream of hot spunk exploded out of Kevin. He made sure not to miss a drop.

"That was… that was… oh, my God." Kevin panted.

"Glad you liked it."

"I did. But I'm nothing if not a solicitous partner." Kevin lowered his head and took in Seth, bobbing now in a steady rhythm.

Seth placed his hands on Kevin's head. He didn't want to control the action, just support it. Every third stroke, Kevin twisted his hand as he sunk on Seth's prick.

Seeing Kevin bobbing there with his own eyes and reflected in the mirror sent tremors of need straight to his cock and sack. Seth could feel the orgasm growing inside him, building, his balls drawing up tight. It grew to monstrous proportions before exploding from him, filling Kevin's mouth.

Should he have warned Kevin that he was close so he could jack him to climax? Probably, but he had been utterly lost in the sensations surrounding his shaft.

Slipping off with a wet pop, a dribble of come slid out of the corner of Kevin's mouth. Damn if that didn't look sexy.

Kevin shook his head as his eyes fell closed. "I guess I figured it out."

Seth huffed out a laugh. "Uh… yup."

Kevin crawled around and settled his head on Seth's shoulder.

"Nice work, boys. That was lovely to watch."

The elation from post-orgasmic bliss crashed around Seth. This had all been for Winthrop.

"Get decent. Erex will be in to escort you back to your room. Put on the tuxedos. Dinner is formal tonight."

Seth sighed and tried to edge off the bed, but Kevin grabbed him and held him in place.

"Can't we just have a few minutes to… I don't know, bask in the glow? Girls love that shit."

"You're right, Kevin. I'll have Erex knock. You have until then."

Of course, Kevin related all of this back to girls, but who would have thought Kevin was a cuddler? He usually loved 'em and left them, getting home before bedtime. Seth could count on one hand the number of times Kevin stayed out all night.

Still, Seth wasn't objecting to snuggling. He slipped his arm around Kevin and pulled him close. Kevin's breath played across his chest. This would be a lovely memory when they were free from Winthrop and things returned to normal.

That was really going to suck.

Winthrop told them to wear tuxedos that night. Kevin

would look hot in a tuxedo, but Seth could only imagine what their host had in store for them.

CHAPTER
THIRTEEN

Saturday, October 4, 7:42 P.M., Senior Year High School

Spending Saturday night in Stacy's basement seemed like a good idea, but now all of his friends were gathered in a circle, focusing on Seth.

"Truth or dare?" Stacy asked.

Seth's heart raced. Which would be more difficult? Answering a question truthfully? Or doing some messed-up dare his devious high school buddies invented? They already knew he was gay, so truth seemed much safer.

"Truth."

Stacy's eyes lost focus for a moment. "Who do you have a crush on?"

Oh, shit! Seth had never planned to tell his friend Zack about crushing on him, but here he was, sitting next to Seth. Laughing.

Seth tried to sound nonchalant. "What makes you think I have a crush?" That squeak meant epic fail.

"Clearly an attempt to avoid." Stacy smirked. "Answer the question."

How bad could the truth be? Zack knew he was gay. It wasn't as if he would attack his friend or something.

"Zack."

The room went quiet. Deathly still even. Then the laughter started.

"I knew it!" Stacey crowed, clapping her hands.

Zack stood and headed straight for the door.

Shit! "Zack, wait!"

Zack paused and turned to look back at Seth, but his face…

Kevin *stared back at him, eyes filled with disgust.*

* * *

Sunday, April 2, 2:59 P.M.

Seth's eyes snapped open as he awoke to a knock on the door. His heart pounded like a meteor shower pelting the moon. He hated any reminder of that day with his friends, the last time Zack had ever spoken to him.

"Get decent, boys. You have two minutes before I come in." Erex's voice sounded through the door.

Kevin had nestled into Seth while they dozed in postcoital bliss. Although it felt good to have his best friend and roommate in his arms as his lover, the dream reminded him of the reality. As right as this felt, this was temporary.

When the week ended, everything would return to the way it, was or even worse, Seth would lose his best friend just like he'd lost Zack back in high school.

However, this experience was cracking the hard shell he had erected around his heart. He needed to repair it quickly, or he would be vulnerable to serious heartbreak he should have avoided. He knew better than to be in love with a straight man.

Kevin smoothed a hair off Seth's forehead, rolled to his feet, and slipped on just his underwear and pants. "Might as well. We have to go back to our room to change anyways."

"Good point." Seth did the same. "We're decent, Erex."

The door opened, and Erex, dressed in a gray suit, perfectly tailored to his three-foot frame, beckoned them to follow. A white-walled hallway replaced the gently sloping concrete tunnel. How did they do that?

At the end of the hall, Erex opened another door into Seth's room, now their room.

"You have a couple hours before dinner. I don't think you want to go smelling like sex. Not with this crowd. So shower up. The tuxes are in the closet, cufflinks and such are in the top drawer. Be ready at five o'clock."

Seth's cheeks flared like a super nova as he entered the room with Kevin following behind.

"You shower first. I'm gonna check my email." Seth waited to see if their host interfered, hoping he spared Kevin this time. When no orders came, he fought his inappropriate disappointment.

Kevin shrugged and headed into the bathroom while Seth opened his laptop.

This situation—he shook his head—the only word to describe this situation was intolerable. He glimpsed a perfect life with his closest friend as his lover. If only it could go on forever. Forget school, forget debt, forget Maynard Frederick Winthrop IV.

This. He wanted this until entropy won and the universe

went dark.

He pulled up his email and skimmed through the subjects. All boringly normal, mundane. The real world had revolved without them. His buddy, Mark, sent inappropriate pictures that were funny as hell. His mom forwarded an Internet joke that was older than he was. No, he did not need his penis enlarged, thank you very much.

Seth took a deep breath and focused on his heart. *You can't have this. It's not real.* His eyes stung, but he pushed it away. When this was over, he would go trawling and find a guy as hot as Kevin and have mind-blowing sex to make him forget.

Except he knew it wouldn't be mind-blowing. It might satisfy for a moment, but it wouldn't even scratch the surface of what he felt when he was with Kevin.

"I'm done. Your turn," Kevin said.

Seth almost leaped out of his chair. "Dude, watch the ninja skills."

"Sorry, it's hard to turn off." Kevin smirked and clapped him on the back. A guy clap.

No tender kisses from a lover.

Seth stepped into the shower and tried to let the warm water wash away the memories, the feelings, everything… let the pounding stream empty him out and leave him clean.

It was only three-thirty when he left the bathroom. He slipped on some briefs and a pair of shorts and sat on the floor. He would lose himself in a calisthenics routine. Shit! He should have done that first and then showered. Oh, well… He needed something to keep him from thinking about Kevin and work off the insane amount of food they had been consuming.

* * *

Sunday, April 2, 5:00 P.M.

Erex arrived precisely as the clock in the room changed to five. "Finish up. It's time to go, boys." He pulled a smartphone out of his pocket and tapped at the screen.

Both men had donned the Oxxford tuxedos that had been provided for them. Seth's fit as if it had been tailored for his exact measurements. The warm material flowed over his skin, softer than the fur behind a cat's ear. When he found the cufflinks, he stared for a long moment and then burst into laughter. Little silver arrows.

"What?" Kevin futzed with his tie.

"Winthrop really likes arrows." Seth waved the cufflinks at Kevin. "Nothing phallic about that."

"Uh-huh… At least he isn't obsessed with swords."

They cracked up together. Once Seth started, he couldn't stop. All the stress. All the ridiculousness. It just bubbled up inside and erupted from him. Tears streamed down his face, and he bent over, hands on his knees. Finally, he held his nose to get the chortles under control.

After a couple of deep breaths, he faced Kevin, who was red-faced and smiling. Glancing down at his friend, he almost swallowed his tongue. *Oh, my God!* The clean lines of the solid black tuxedo emphasized Kevin's wide shoulders and lean chest to perfection.

A vision of Kevin's wedding day flashed in his head. The man waiting at the end of the aisle for the luckiest lady in the universe to join him. His parents seated in the front aisle, his oldest brother beside him. The minister looking up at the coming bride in satisfaction. And Kevin looking down the aisle with the broadest grin on his face. The perfect image of the happy groom.

In his head, Seth turned and scanned the seats. He had to

be there somewhere. Why wasn't he one of the ushers standing with his best friend?

There he was, dressed in a morning coat, walking down the aisle with his mother and father. Kevin was looking right into his eyes. *Bliss*.

He shook his head. What the hell? He was not going to marry Kevin. That was just absurd! But, for a moment, he had been happier than he had ever been in his entire life.

Erex tapped his watch. "We'd better go. The boss doesn't like to be kept waiting."

They followed Erex out of the room and down the hall, this time to a fancy elevator with gold embellishments and an ornate crystal call button. Seth shook his head. This week was right out of *Harry Potter* or some other magical, mystical, impossible book.

The elevator door opened to reveal a bench along the back wall of the elevator cabin, covered in deep red velvet cushions. Leather crimson squares trimmed in gold rope adorned the walls.

They arrived at a room decorated in red and gold accents. A large double staircase with gold banisters up to a second-floor balcony graced one wall. Several groupings of couches and chairs made up conversation areas. The whole room reminded Seth of a hotel lobby. Was there any venue their host hadn't bothered to recreate in his funhouse mansion?

Erex led them past other tuxedoed men standing in small groups or sitting in conversation areas. Flames danced in a large central fireplace, sending a mild scent of wood smoke through the air. They crossed the lobby and stopped at a table outside double doors.

"Go ahead and find your names," Erex said.

A group of folded cards stood like army tents. Seth looked in the G's for Griffin, but Kevin found the card first:

Messrs. Kevin Fields and Seth Griffin

Of course, their names were on the same card. On the Inside, Table Number One was printed in the same font.

"Feel free to mingle with the other guests until dinner is called," Erex said as he left.

As Seth surveyed the lobby, it quickly became apparent that there were no women present. Just an unrelenting sea of black tuxedos. Although several men had donned formal ethnic dress from a variety of countries. One man wore full Scottish regalia, including a kilt. Another man wore a formal, traditional Japanese kimono. The gray underpart peeked out from a light blue overdress of some kind. A man wearing a black, brown, and white West African Dashiki spoke with a man whose head was adorned with a white Arabic kufiya, held in place with a black `iqal. His robes shone with gold threads.

A few of the men stood paired off, holding hands. The two young men from the archery contest that morning, whom Winthrop had indicated were also here to entertain, came up to them, their hands clasped together.

The shorter of the two, a blond man said, "I'm Jeff. This is Todd. I guess you're in the same boat we are."

Kevin shook his hand. "Looks like we are. I'm Kevin. This is Seth."

Todd's red curls flounced around his face. "You two been together long?"

Seth wanted to spare Kevin any embarrassment. "We're just friends."

Kevin stared at Seth for a moment before nodding, a frown on his face.

Why is Kevin frowning? Are we not friends anymore?

"Oh, sorry. Todd and I have been together for three years now. When this is over, we're getting married."

Todd grinned and looked at Jeff. "Yeah, and my standards for an elegant wedding have so been raised. Look at this place. I wonder if Maynard would let us have it here."

Jeff's face grew somber. "He probably would, but I'm not sure we could afford his price."

Seth's stomach sank. Why were these men here? What debt did they owe to Winthrop?

The strum of a large harp flowed through the room.

"May I have your attention, please?" Erex stood on one side of the second-floor balcony. His voice carried throughout the cavernous space. "I'd like to direct your attention to the top of the stairs." He gestured to the center where the curved double staircase led down. "Presenting your host for the evening, Mr. Maynard Frederick Winthrop the Fourth."

Winthrop strutted onto the landing, decked out in a pristine, solid white tuxedo. A wisp of smoke rose from the cigar hanging from his mouth.

The crowd broke out in applause as Winthrop sketched a curtsy-like bow. The strands combed over his bald spot lifted and dangled as he bent at the neck and waist. Seth was fascinated as they flipped back into place, framing a large, black mole he hadn't noticed before. The thing looked big enough to be cancerous. How had he missed it?

Seth glanced at Kevin, who shook his head with narrowed eyes that fell closed. He took a deep breath, and his expression went blank.

Winthrop continued his stately entrance, regally descending the stairs and waving like Queen Elizabeth II while the crowd applauded him as if he was a rockstar.

Seth and Kevin clapped politely as he swept up to them.

"Shall we enter?" Winthrop smirked.

"Uh," Seth responded.

Kevin grinned. "Of course." Seth wasn't fooled. Kevin may have been smiling, but he was not happy.

They followed Winthrop in and up to a long table at the front of the room. It stood on a long platform, like the head table at a wedding. Yet another large, throne held the center location. Winthrop never missed an opportunity to aggrandize himself. Six white silk seats on either side of the gilded monstrosity all faced the room. A number one placard stood in the middle. A white tablecloth draped the table with a decorative green tulle swag in front that seemed to sparkle as if lit from within. Lush ivy lined the table's edge with small lights interspersed like glowing flowers.

Winthrop came to the throne at the center place and beckoned Seth and Kevin to sit beside him on the right.

The other men found their tables, which surrounded a large dance floor. A band on the opposite side to the head table played a quiet jazz tune as people found their places.

Winthrop turned to Seth and Kevin. "I have quite a special meal planned this evening. A real treat."

Seth's stomach dropped, his appetite fleeing for deep space.

"I could eat." Kevin's face showed an impassive mask Seth knew all too well: Kevin's stress face.

Phelix, the little person who had worked with Kevin their first night at the mansion, cleared his throat, bringing Seth's attention down and to his left. "Mr. Winthrop, what would you like to drink?"

"My usual." Winthrop's eyes sparkled.

What? The blood of his victims? Seth shuddered.

"Mr. Seth? Mr. Kevin? A drink?"

"Water for Seth and me."

He's ordering for me again. I should order something

else, except I really do want water.

Seth wasn't surprised when a large, cold, glass bottle of sparkling water was brought to them. This time, the name Borsec appeared on the label in blue above a picture of green mountains. Waiters also filled their wine glasses.

Winthrop leaned in close to Seth, the smell of rancid smoke permeating his breath. "Boys, I've arranged a special menu just for you. Foods from around the world. Every continent is represented."

Seth's first thought was not Antarctica. No one lived there.

Winthrop clapped Seth on the back. "Even Antarctica. We had some squid flown in fresh. We'll let our sushi chef prepare it, but just like penguins, we'll enjoy it raw."

Huh? Why do I keep forgetting he can hear my thoughts? Or at least sometimes he seems to, and other times he doesn't. I can't guard my thoughts all the time. Seth resisted rolling his eyes at the gleeful look on Winthrop's rotund face.

"Go, it's set up buffet style over there. We are table number one, no waiting." Winthrop gestured to the right wall.

Erex tapped Seth's elbow. "Come."

Kevin and Seth followed Erex to the long row of tables crammed with chafing dishes, plates, and bowls of various foods. Little placards accompanied each item, detailing its name and country of origin. The foods were roughly organized by continent.

Ceviche, whatever that was, made with Chilean sea bass. The bowl contained white bits of fleshy, raw meat mixed with some kind of juice and spices.

Roast goat from Ghana. Foie gras from France. Kevin took a chunk of the brown glob.

The promised sushi of squid native to Antarctica. Balmain bug tail from Australia. It looked like lobster, but the word bug was very off-putting. Pork satay from Thailand. Seth took several skewers—he loved satay—although he never had it made with pork.

The list of foods went on and on. Forget food from every continent. This was food from every country. Hundreds of dishes filled the tables. Relief passed through him when he arrived at the section for North America. Some good old southern fried chicken looked cooked to perfection and was complemented by corn bread. He skipped the mashed potatoes in favor of the poutine from Canada.

Seth promised himself he would do double laps when this was over and he returned to normality. A world without exotic food—and without Kevin in his arms. Just like that, his stomach turned, and his appetite fled for Mayall's Object. Once again, Winthrop had drawn him into his distorted fantasy world.

Seth and Kevin followed Erex back to the table. The little man placed his full plate in front of Winthrop. Of course, Winthrop wouldn't serve himself. He might risk burning off a calorie from the meal.

Winthrop surveyed Seth's plate. "You didn't try any of the more interesting dishes."

Seth shrugged. "Maybe on my second pass."

"You don't know what you're missing. *Kimchee*, fried caterpillars, and *ful medames* are just a few of my favorites." Winthrop pointed to each of the items as he said it. "I could order you to try this stuff."

Seth tried not to stare as Winthrop speared his fork into a crispy caterpillar and raised it to his mouth, then chewed and swallowed with delight.

"Here." Winthrop speared another caterpillar and raised his fork to Seth's mouth.

Seth fought the bile back in his throat as he pulled the creature into his mouth. A mild flavor of chili powder caressed his tongue as he crunched down and swallowed.

"How was it?" Kevin asked.

Seth swallowed. "Not bad. Tasty."

"Here, Seth. Feed one to Kevin." Winthrop handed Seth a fork with another speared little creature.

Seth gulped and took the fork. When he faced Kevin, their eyes met. Seth wanted to spare Kevin this, protect him from each and every indignity at the hands of Winthrop, but as usual, he had no choice.

Kevin's lips parted as Seth pushed the fork into his mouth. Then those delicious lips closed and slid down the length of the tines, pulling the caterpillar in. Kevin's gaze never left Seth's. The intense expression sent skitters of electricity through Seth's body, awakening his cock.

Chewing, Kevin smiled. "Wow… uh. It's okay."

"This from the guy who wouldn't eat smoked fish." Seth couldn't tear his gaze away from Kevin.

"Shut up, you." Kevin's grin turned goofy.

"Good boys, you can eat your food now," Winthrop interrupted.

Seth jumped. The universe had belonged to him and Kevin for those fleeting moments. He'd forgotten the man was there. He turned to his own plate. Winthrop certainly liked to push boundaries. The ones between Seth and Kevin were crumbling under the assault.

As the meal wore on and the staff continued to pour the wine generously, the room got rowdier. Once the main meal was completed, the band's volume increased, and the singer invited people onto the dance floor.

Kevin's eyes grew wide as saucers as couples of men took to the floor. Seth smiled. Poor straight boy. But so far, this was tame compared to what went on in gay clubs. However, as the beat flowed, Seth recognized the song, and it sounded a little too true to be just a cover band. He studied the lead singer carefully and gasped. Bouncy black curls framed the man's face. It really was Darren Criss. Seth had tried several times to get tickets to his concerts, but they generally sold out in like seven seconds.

"Kevin, it's Darren Criss."

As Kevin focused on the stage, his jaw dropped open. "Holy shit."

Winthrop leaned in to them. "I always get what I want. I'm glad you approve of the band. Go dance, boys."

Seth followed Kevin to the floor. On the one hand, it was a fast song, so he didn't have to touch Kevin. On the other hand, the crowd was well-lubricated and getting a little crazy. Nothing new, but he imagined Kevin wouldn't appreciate having some guy grinding into his ass.

The song ended as they got to the floor, and ironically, a slow song began, *Not Alone*.

Kevin turned, his expression strange, unreadable. "Uh, how do we do this?"

Seth fought the urge to smile and faced Kevin. "You just do what you usually do, and I'll adjust."

Kevin's eyes lit. "So you're the girl."

"Sure. I'll be the girl, but I better not hear it later, asshole."

Seth reached up and put his hands around Kevin's neck, just like a girl at the prom, and tried to let Kevin lead as they swayed their hips from side to side. Criss crooned out the romantic words. Seth felt a sudden urge to lay his head on Kevin's chest. To take a moment and pretend this was real. His head moved without his permission, and Kevin's arms tightened around him.

Seth never remembered feeling so warm and safe as he did at that moment, held by Kevin. Damn Winthrop for making him wish for things he couldn't have.

"It's all right, Seth."

Seth looked up into Kevin's smiling eyes. "What?"

"I felt you get all tense. It's all going to be all right."

"How can you say that? How are we going to look at each other when this is over?"

Kevin's lips fell, and his eyes sparkled with longing. "I suppose you're right. It doesn't have to be that way. We can get through this. Otherwise, Winthrop wins."

Seth took a few deep breaths. Kevin wanted things to go back to the way they were. He wouldn't hold all of this against Seth. "You're… You're right. I just worry."

"I know. I'm used to it." Kevin softened the words with a chuckle.

When the song ended, they returned to their seats.

Both doors from the main kitchen flew open at once, and several little people servers streamed out, trays held above their head, putting them at about eye level for the seated guests. Each tray was filled with individual, flaming baked Alaskas.

Seth marveled that they could get so many of the quick-burning confections to flame simultaneously, giving the entire room a blue, flickering glow. A hush of oohs and ahhs spread around the room, and the scent of smoking sugar wafted about, almost hiding the nasty smell from another of Winthrop's cigars.

Erex placed a flaming portion in front of Winthrop and then Seth and Kevin. The flames burned out moments later, leaving a neatly singed, delectable treat that looked like a snowdrift on the side of the road in Ithaca.

How can we still be eating? At least he'd worked out this afternoon to burn some of the calories.

After dessert, the band ramped up again. This time, any

inhibitions the dancers felt seemed to have melted away. Men were openly grinding against each other, sometimes in groups of three or four. Others, still seated at tables, were engaged in various stages of making out. In one corner, covered in shadow, Seth could hear the sounds of flesh slapping flesh and muffled groans.

Winthrop's gaze darted around the room with obvious delight. "Ah, the next round of entertainment has begun."

Jeff and Todd stopped by the table to invite them dancing. "Come on, dudes, this is an epic party."

Kevin stared at the couple with eyes as wide as the full moon and red painting his cheeks. Seth had to…do what…get him out of there, protect him.

"I think we'll pass."

Jeff opened his mouth, presumably to argue, when Erex arrived at Seth's elbow.

"Come with me. I'll take you back to your room."

Holding his breath, Seth looked to Winthrop, who nodded.

Seth sighed in relief. Things were getting crazy. Even crazier than the gay clubs he had been in. Would a full-out orgy occur? He and Kevin followed closely behind Erex out of the ballroom doors and back to the elevator.

Kevin sighed. "Is that normal?"

Before Seth could answer that he had never seen anything quite like that, Erex answered.

"The boss knows how to throw a party. He said it was okay for me to get you out of there once the real fun began."

Seth exhaled slowly. Winthrop wasn't going to require them to participate in…whatever that was. An image of Kevin engaging in… He shook his head. No. Not going there.

Would he have stayed and enjoyed the party if Kevin had been his real lover? A little public display of affection wouldn't hurt. It might have been fun. But Kevin wasn't his lover. They were friends, that's it. And Seth wasn't going to consider doing anything they didn't have to. He loved Kevin, so he wanted to protect him from as much as he could. What did Winthrop hold over Kevin to get him to do this?

Seth wasn't ready to sleep when they returned to the room, so he went to his computer and opened it, intending to check his email and surf the web.

He had just finished reading a note from his mom when Kevin's hand landed on his shoulder. He turned to face his friend and couldn't read the look in Kevin's eyes. Nervous? Excited? Something.

"Something became clear to me tonight," Kevin said in a soft tone.

"What's that?" Chills travelled up Seth's spine.

"I don't know what the hell I'm doing."

"What?"

"That was a gay party." Kevin shifted from one foot to the other. "Everyone there was gay except maybe Winthrop, and who the hell knows what he is. The dancing, the everything… it wasn't like parties with girls."

Seth sighed. "I have news for you. I've never been to a party like that. I'm not saying they can't happen since it just did, but who cares?"

"Me. We don't know what Winthrop is going to demand next. What if he hadn't let us leave? What if he expected us to act like them? I'd be screwed." Kevin turned bright red like a radish. "I mean… if we get ordered to do something and I hesitate because I'm out of my league, we could fail. I can't let anything…" Kevin stopped. "I can't fail."

"Neither of us can." *It's so unfair that I can't protect him from this.* "What do you want to do about it?"

Kevin flushed again. "Well… I'm sorry to ask, but could

you teach me?"

Seth's mind filled with images of Kevin and the things his friend wanted to learn, and his shaft stiffened like a rocket ship ready to break orbit. "Uh…"

CHAPTER FOURTEEN

Standing in the middle of their room, Kevin widened his eyes. "Please?" He looked appealing in just pajama bottoms, his six-pack readily visible. "It would be practice."

Bzzt. Seth's brain short-circuited. "Practice?"

Kevin nibbled his lower lip. "Yeah."

"Like what?"

Kevin's face reddened. "Dancing… maybe making out. I feel so lost with all of this. I don't even know if I'm doing it right."

He wanted to practice making out? It made no sense.

Seth had to spare his friend. "You've been doing just fine. It's not like I can fake my reactions."

The blush on Kevin's cheeks glowed like the sun. "I know. And I know it's weird to ask you to do this with me, but you're the only one I've got. We have to do this together. I'm sorry."

143

Seth's breath quickened. "Are you sure you want to do this… extra?"

Kevin shrugged and met Seth's eyes before nodding. "Yeah, besides, I bet the sick fuck records us, even in here. Maybe it'll give him a thrill. Earn us some goodwill. He clearly likes to watch us together."

"He's probably way too busy with the party, but if this will help you…. What kind of dancing did you want to do?"

"Er… uh… that, um, grinding thing, like *Dirty Dancing* or something."

"Oh, that." Blink. Blink. Holy Shit. "Sure."

Seth opened the music on his computer. He wasn't a big dancer, but he had learned a few moves in the clubs. He skimmed through the list and settled on "Scream and Shout" with Will.i.am and Britney Spears, a great song for dancing.

As the rocking beat began, Seth walked over to Kevin, who stood in the open area in their room. The space seemed bigger than he remembered. At least they would have room to move.

Would Kevin be more comfortable in the front or the back? Probably the back, but could he really teach from the front? No, Seth needed to be in the back. At least, that's what he told himself.

He moved behind Kevin and slid in close to his exposed, strong, and muscular back. Seth still wore the tux pants and shirt, although he had shed the jacket and tie. He reached for the first button of his shirt, skin-to-skin contact would make this even better. He froze. This was to help Kevin, not molest him.

Kevin waited, facing away from Seth, who leaned in. Just a couple inches shorter than Kevin, Seth's nose was almost in Kevin's neck. The aroma of sweat and Kevin filled his nostrils, waking his cock up further.

He put his hands on Kevin's hips and felt the man stiffen.

"Relax. It's okay. This is all about moving fluidly." He rocked his own hips and applied gentle pressure to Kevin's to get him swinging to the music. He kept it simple at first, just side-to-side, not moving closer but not giving Kevin any more space, either.

When Kevin seemed more relaxed, Seth moved in closer and closer until his cock brushed Kevin's firm backside. The friction, the motion, caused blood to rush south. He moved his arms to circle Kevin and rubbed his hands up and down Kevin's chest.

He was doing this for Kevin, right? Yeah, right. Shimmying against Kevin filled him with need.

After a bit, Kevin seemed to get the hang of the movements, swinging in tempo to the beats. To spare him, Seth started to offer to switch places, but instead, Kevin ground his ass back against Seth's engorged shaft. All rational thought fled Seth's brain for the next galaxy.

Seth thrust in, and now the real *dancing* began as he undulated against Kevin. Kevin ground back, just like they had seen others doing earlier on the dance floor. It was practically obscene, an imitation of the sex act.

Seth reveled in it.

Kevin turned his head to the side, and Seth's instinct took over. He leaned in, rising up on his toes, and joined their mouths like they had been doing this for years. Everything felt so in sync. So right. Kevin spun around to face Seth and deepened the kiss.

The song ended, and "I Could be the One" with Avicii vs Nicky Romero came on. Seth cringed. He would never have chosen that song. It expressed too much of what he felt for Kevin, but could never have.

His tongue in Kevin's mouth, his body flush with Kevin's

as they swayed, his own staff at full mast. It was hard not to dream.

Was there a chance this wasn't all abhorrent to Kevin? The full frontal action made Kevin's interest abundantly clear as their hard shafts pressed together. Kevin grabbed his ass and pulled them closer.

Holy Shit.

The song changed to Fergie's "A Little Party Never Killed Nobody."

Kevin's tongue invaded his mouth and became his new reality as the two men bumped and ground against one another.

Seth didn't know what was happening, and he didn't care. He needed this man. All the careful walls he had built up over the last three years were crashing down. He wanted Kevin, wanted him more than anyone, anything.

Who knew what the end of this week would bring, much less tomorrow? But Kevin was here, now, in his arms, and so hard. Their tongues clashed, and Seth panted as Kevin swallowed his very breath, everything he was.

The bed beckoned, so inviting, but what if that broke the spell? Instead, he let his hands fall to Kevin's delectable ass and crushed their groins together.

He feasted on the man's lips and tongue and made grinding friction. So much friction. Something wonderful and monstrous built inside of him. Growing, gaining power. His balls ached with the need to succumb as he thrust. He took a handful of that perfect ass he had admired whenever Kevin wasn't looking, thrust their cocks together, and let go, unleashing it all, his orgasm tearing through him, making him soar to the stars.

Kevin thrust a couple more times and stilled, calling out, "Seth," as he reached his own pleasure.

Panting from the exertion, and shocks of pleasure

sweeping over him, Seth gazed at Kevin. The man's eyes had closed, and a tear escaped his right eye.

Shame stormed over Seth like a meteor shower. What had he done? He just rubbed off on Kevin. So what if Kevin hadn't complained? So what if Kevin had asked for them to "practice?" Whatever the hell that really meant.

He ducked his head and shuffled over to the computer to stop the music.

"I'm gonna hit the shower," Kevin muttered behind him. Was that disappointment in his voice or disgust?

The door shut before Seth turned. His briefs stuck to him, hot and… gross. He knew now that he was one sick fuck because he had loved every moment in Kevin's arms and never wanted it to end. His orgasms this week kept getting better and better. He never knew he could come like that.

And it would all come crashing down around him.

When Kevin stepped out of the shower, Seth couldn't meet his gaze. Seth slipped in and let the water run for a long time. Washing away the sweat and sin. Not sin from being with a man. He had long ago come to terms with those who preached hate in the name of God.

No, the sin was that Kevin wasn't willing. Not really. Just because Kevin came didn't mean he wanted any of this. Seth's chest twisted.

He pounded his fist against the tile. The wetness on his face really was just the shower, right?

When he finally got out of the shower, a pathetic, waterlogged prune, Kevin was already in bed, his back to where Seth would sleep, eyes closed. Seth pretended Kevin slept to save him from talking about any of this.

Seth slipped into pajamas, shut the lights off, and curled up in the fetal position on his side of the bed.

What had he done? How much worse was it going to get?

CHAPTER
FIFTEEN

Monday, April 3, 7:41 am

The sound of tapping keys woke Seth. He opened his eyes slowly to find Kevin working on his computer. He stretched and realized this wasn't their dorm room. Then the memories flooded in.

Winthrop.

Last night.

Practicing with Kevin.

I should say something.

Seth opened his mouth, but nothing came out. He padded into the bathroom and brushed his teeth.

I really should say something.

Another fail. What could Seth say that wouldn't embarrass Kevin and probably ruin their friendship?

Seth headed for the dresser to get some clothes and

glanced at Kevin, who quickly averted his eyes.

Has he been staring at me?

A knock sounded at the door. "Breakfast," Erex called out.

Seth let him in, finding he carried another ridiculously enormous tray filled with breads, croissants, bagels, crackers, jams, peanut butter, and a bottle labeled Vegemite. Seth sighed. Another new food to try.

"Buck up, Seth. The boss is in a good mood. He said to dress casual." Erex left the room.

Kevin moved to the table and loaded a plate with enough food to fill a black hole. He was stress eating again. Seth wanted to help.

"Kev. Leave some for me."

"Douche." Kevin's eyes remained focused on the table. "There's more than enough."

"I know. But..." What could Seth say? He grabbed a plate and spread a little Vegemite on a piece of toast. Winthrop seemed intent on making him try everything on the planet. The smooth paste slid across his taste buds. *Bitter.* He took some bread and made a peanut butter and jelly sandwich.

Kevin stared into deep space as he shoveled food into his mouth. He probably didn't taste a bite.

As Seth dressed, he glanced at Kevin every so often. Sometimes, he caught Kevin staring at him. Other times, Kevin appeared lost in thought. What happened to their easy conversation and comradery? Once this week was over, would anything be left of their friendship?

After breakfast, Erex took them up in the elevator that had changed once again. This time, it was back to rickety like the first day. Seth's heart pounded as it ascended, moaning and whining.

Finally, Erex opened the gate and stepped out and into Winthrop's office.

It looked much the way Seth remembered. The desk on a platform, the bow and arrow on the wall flanked by two brilliant, stained glass windows. Each depicted a cherub, its little naked butt showing as it flew through a glowing blue sky, a bow in hand, with a nocked arrow. Depictions of ivy vines twined around the edges of each window. The two cherubs faced each other. It all seemed to make more sense now given Winthrop's expertise in archery.

"Come in, boys, come in. Have a seat." Winthrop gestured toward two hard-backed chairs set before his desk but off the platform. "Your initiative last night pleased me no end. Really hot stuff, boys." Winthrop puffed his stogie.

So Winthrop had watched, and they were going to talk about it. Seth shifted in his seat and studied his hands. So much for sparing Kevin any embarrassment or Seth forgetting his guilt.

"If you guys keep that level of enthusiasm for the rest of the week, then I will have gotten my money's worth." Winthrop winked.

Out of the corner of his eye, Seth saw Kevin tense and clenches his fists. What did Winthrop hold over Kevin?

"In fact, I was so impressed, I decided to knock a day off your contract. You boys can go home on Thursday."

Seth slumped in his chair. What day was it now? Monday. Thursday still seemed farther away than another galaxy.

"I guess I'll have to find someone else to play out my Minotaur fantasy." Winthrop took a pull off his cigar.

Seth shuddered at how casually Winthrop dropped in that he would do this to others. That he had scenarios planned with a Minotaur no less. He would need a really tall actor to play that role.

"Thank you, Mr. Win… Maynard," Seth said.

Winthrop beamed when Seth switched to his first name.

"You're welcome, Seth. I'm a reasonable guy. I bet we can all be friends."

I doubt it.

"I've got your next challenge for you. So far, you guys have performed well, so it's time to kick it up a notch."

Seth's insides quaked. What could that mean?

"I want you to rim each other."

Seth cringed. He had only done that once. It had been for his boyfriend last year, although the relationship ended soon after. The intimacy of the act ensured he had not done it during a casual hookup. When he glanced at Kevin, Seth's face tightened.

Kevin blinked at Winthrop, his eyebrows raised. "What does it mean to rim each other?"

"Rimming?" Winthrop's gaze lasered in on Seth. "Ask Seth. He knows."

Damn! Not only did he have to do it, he had to explain it to his straight friend. He braced himself for a look of disgust. "Rimming is… well… it's."

Kevin huffed. "Just say it, Seth."

"Using your tongue to pleasure the anus."

Kevin froze for a moment.

Seth could see the wheels turning.

"You mean you lick someone's ass?" Kevin shot out.

Seth wanted to hide his face, preferably in Andromeda. "Yeah."

"Ohhh. Kay." Kevin drew out the syllables. His eyebrows climbed to his hairline.

"It actually feels really good." Seth looked away from

Kevin to find Winthrop smirking. Of course, that sick bastard was enjoying the show. Seth huffed a breath and focused on Kevin.

"You've rimmed someone?" Kevin's cheeks flushed, and his lips pinched together. That look on his face… that had to be disgust.

Seth swallowed. "Yeah."

Kevin's brows drew down, and his eyes narrowed. "Who?"

"Does it matter?"

"Yes… No… I don't know." Kevin shook his head.

What did all of that even mean? Why would Kevin care?

"It was Ethan. We were together for a while, so we tried it. It feels good." Seth shrugged. "You know things with Ethan didn't end well." How could they end well? Ethan all but accused him of being in love with Kevin.

Kevin took a beat and seemed to calm his breathing. "Yeah, man. Sorry."

Winthrop spoke, startling Seth, who had almost forgotten he was there. "I've got a very special venue planned for this challenge. I think Seth will find it to be a special treat. Erex, escort the boys."

"Yes, boss."

Kevin and Seth followed Erex out of the office and down a hall to another elevator. This one looked very modern and functional. No embellishments. Just pure stainless steel.

Erex stood on tip toes, but could not reach the top button. "Help me out?"

"This one?" Kevin pointed to the top button.

"Yes, please."

There were a hundred buttons on the panel, which made no sense. The mansion could not be more than three stories tall. Even if you counted all of the basement levels, how many could there be? Dante only counted nine layers of hell. Besides, the panel indicated they were on level three.

The doors closed, and the elevator ascended, gaining speed rapidly. Seth's stomach flipped from the fast acceleration. Periodically, his ears popped, and the temperature fell. At first, he focused on the strangeness of the ride. How could they be going up in an elevator, from the top floor of a mansion? The time between floors seemed to be astronomically long and increasing with each floor.

His brain got caught up in circles trying to imagine how all of this was even possible. In a fit of illogic, it shut down. System overload.

The time continued to wear on, and inevitably, his brain rebooted and headed straight for the task at hand. Rimming. He imagined rimming Kevin. Would Kevin enjoy it? Nerves were nerves. The sensation was pleasurable, although everyone had different hot spots. In a flight of fancy, he pictured Kevin howling in pleasure as he licked him. Wouldn't that be nice? Certainly, it would make all of this easier. However, knowing his luck, Kevin would just be disgusted by the whole thing. Another crazy thing gay men did to each other. Did hetero couples do it, too?

Seth's body tensed. He wanted to get this challenge over with, but the elevator didn't stop. It just kept going up and up and up.

Kevin stood at the other side of the elevator, lost in thought. Steeling himself for the challenge ahead?

Erex whistled the score from *The Little Mermaid*. After a while, Seth started humming along.

Finally, the bell dinged, the number one hundred showed on the digital read out. The doors swept open to a small metal room. A large, double door was on the opposite wall with a giant button beside it.

"Just press the button to get out of the airlock," Erex instructed.

Airlock?

Kevin stepped forward and shivered when he crossed the threshold of the elevator. Seth understood why as soon as he moved across. A feeling like electrical tingles passed through him.

Then his entire body lifted off the ground, slowly floating away from the elevator. He looked up to see that Kevin was a little higher.

That's when he noticed the hand and toeholds strategically stationed around the room.

How was this possible? There was only one way to simulate realistic zero G on Earth. It involved an airplane and lasted less than a minute at a time. He had spent more than a minute just considering this.

Sustained weightlessness could only be achieved in space. He knew this.

Unless... unless Winthrop knew a way. Some new, revolutionary technology that could have this effect? Then why the farce with the fake elevator? Was he trying to convince them they were somehow in space? What was really more plausible, an elevator to space, rooted in upstate New York, or a game-changing technology that could effectively simulate zero G for extended periods of time, that no one knew about?

Both were utterly impossible.

Kevin grabbed one of the handholds and worked his way over to the button by the door. Floating perpendicular to it, he slapped it with his hand.

The double doors slid open with a swish reminiscent of a low-budget Science Fiction film.

He grabbed a handhold and propelled himself into the large, rectangular, two-story room. One entire wall consisted of man-sized panes of glass separated by thin strips of metal, affording the view of his dreams.

Space.

The view was of space and not just some random spot. Front and center, covering half the view, sat Earth.

Seth's mouth fell open, and his heart raced.

Earth, all blue and green and white, swirling clouds.

Earth. Only a select group of people had ever witnessed this first-hand with their own eyes.

Earth. His home planet. A place he'd never expected to leave. In all his dreams of working for NASA, he never expected to get off the planet with eyesight like his. There were too few missions, the selection process too rigorous, the cost too high. He never expected to be in space. But here he was.

He swallowed as rational thought tried to take over. Winthrop wasn't just an eccentric billionaire. He was a magician, an illusionist of the highest skill. Or he employed such a person.

How could he possibly be in space?

Could the glass really be screens, projecting an image? But the weightlessness felt so real. Just as he had read, a lightness, an effortless floating, the feeling was amazing. How?

"Never you mind how. Just enjoy the ride."

Winthrop. The sudden discombobulation of his entire worldview had momentarily made him forget about Winthrop and challenges. Rimming.

"I wanted to give you somewhere unusual to take this next step. I trust this qualifies."

"Uh… Uh…" Seth could only stutter.

"Play around for a bit, boys. This is a once-in-a-lifetime experience that few are able to have. You are in space. View your world and enjoy."

"I don't know how this is possible." Seth's voice was a reverent whisper. "It must be fake, but we don't have the tech to do that." Seth shook his head slowly in awe.

"I don't know either, but let's enjoy it." Kevin pushed off and did a forward roll in the air, whooping in delight.

Seth tried to do the same, pushed too hard, and ended up ricocheting off the walls of the large room until he managed to snag a handhold near the windows.

The view mesmerized him. Below, North America stretched, colored in greens and browns. White swirls and eddies obscured part of Canada and dotted the rest of the continent. South America's large green top peaked out from the curve of the Earth. And the ocean, surrounding the land, in deep blue. A perfect marble on a black background.

His breathing quickened. *Unforgettable.* Whether it was real or not, it amazed him.

He pushed off slower this time, but he aimed poorly, colliding with Kevin, who flung his arms around Seth, catching him mid-room. Momentum pushed them along a third path, but at a slow, easy, steady pace.

"Got ya." Kevin's tender smile lit his eyes. "I can't believe this. My mind just won't process it. Maybe we'll meet fairies next."

Seth almost made a comment about Kevin knowing one big fairy, himself, but he held his tongue as reality came crashing around him, even as he floated in space. They had to have sex again, rim each other, for the entertainment of an increasingly bizarre man.

Then Kevin's mouth was on his. At least one of them seemed to remember why they were here and what they had to do. It was his last thought before his little brain took over, and all he could do was feel warm lips pressed to his, and a hot, wet tongue sliding to meet his own.

His arms came around Kevin, the momentum knocking them into a lazy spin while their legs locked together. Seth never thought of himself as a sex addict. He had a normal, healthy sex drive, but he came twice yesterday, hard, earth-shatteringly hard, and already his prick was up and ready for action.

Kevin. It had to be because of Kevin. The man was crazy hot in so many ways. His easy charm, his rocking body, his quick mind. Seth had always been attracted to the whole package, but had closed his love away. Hidden it deep inside so he could stay best friends with the attractive, straight man.

But with each kiss, each swipe of his tongue, each intimate nibble, the walls were falling, plunging to the ground. He was falling for Kevin faster than terminal velocity. That could only mean one thing. At the end of the week, his heart would hit harder than any of the mind-blowing orgasms and smash into a million pieces.

He gasped, in need, in fear, and then he pushed it all aside and lost himself in the sensations. Kevin pressed against him, their tongues dueling for supremacy. A battle they both won just by joining. His hands soothed Kevin's back.

The weightlessness increased the unreality. No up or down, he spun with Kevin like the two stars in a binary system.

Kevin yanked at Seth's T-shirt. Seth lifted his arms as the material slid up his chest and then shot away as Kevin flung it across the room. His pants and the rest of his clothes soon followed. Then Kevin's mouth moved on his chest, his tongue tormenting Seth's nipple with licks, his teeth with perfect nibbles, just the right amount of pain/pleasure to send need ripping toward his groin.

Skin, he needed skin. He was going to do this. Again. He was going to forget all about the immorality of what he was doing to his best friend and let himself savor the moment. Capture it along with the other memories for the lonely road ahead without Kevin in his arms.

He tore Kevin's T-shirt up and off, sending it who knew where as it winged around the room. Then he attacked Kevin's button and fly, hauling his pants down. He had to see that delicious prick, taste it. Now.

Kevin helped, toeing off his shoes and socks, sending them spinning away, and Seth used Kevin's body as literal handholds to slide down the perfect abs and face the object of his desires, his dreams.

He anchored himself by grabbing Kevin's hips and then engulfed that smooth, hot spike of steel in his mouth.

Kevin threw back his head, moaning and sending them spinning slowly, ass overhead. "Ungh."

Seth used his hands to push and pull Kevin in and out of his mouth while the man mewled and moaned. Kevin's hands gripped his hair and gave a tug.

"Stop. You have to stop, or I'm gonna come, and we haven't fulfilled the challenge yet."

The challenge.

It all came crashing in on Seth. The challenge. Rimming. Not lovemaking. None of this was voluntary.

He spun Kevin around and pushed him toward the wall, grabbing onto his feet to get pulled along. "Grab the handhold and hang on."

Kevin managed to reach out and snag a handle before momentum failed them, and then looked over his shoulder at Seth.

Seth took a deep breath. He needed to show Kevin how this was done.

He pulled himself up Kevin's body, gliding until he arrived at Kevin's goddamn perfect ass. Tight glutes greeted him, and he reached out and grabbed a handful, kissing.

Slowly, he spread the two cheeks, exposing a tight, virgin pucker. Every muscle in Kevin's body went rigid.

"Relax. It's okay. I got you. Just forget everything and let the sensations take you."

Seth hoped it would work, and it seemed to, as Kevin's body became more pliable and less like a tree trunk.

Leaning in, Seth inhaled the scent of musk and sweat and Kevin. Perfect. His tongue shot out once to circle the pretty pucker, and the sound of a sharply indrawn breath echoed around the room.

"Shit."

Seth hoped not.

He started slowly, gently moving in a circle around the opening as the muscles fluttered along his tongue. A strangled moan escaped Kevin, and Seth took that as encouragement to continue. He thrust his tongue against the opening now as Kevin writhed in his hands.

"Oh."

When Kevin's hips started thrusting as if he had no control, Seth reached around and grabbed the engorged, throbbing prick. He set up a rhythm between his tongue and his hand, jacking Kevin and thrusting his tongue against his pucker, every third or so stroke. He dropped his tongue down to lick Kevin's balls, which were quickly drawing up tight against his body.

Seth slurped up a bit of escaping saliva and renewed his assault on Kevin's clearly sensitive pucker.

"Oh, oh, God. Oh, God. Seth!" Kevin cried out as ribbons of come shot from his aroused member, spattering the metallic white wall with his pleasure.

Seth kept going, working him through the orgasm until he had milked out every last drop.

Kevin shuddered and panted, his body slicked with sweat. "I never imagined anything like that. Holy mother."

"I bet it would work with girls, too."

"Maybe, but it seems like half the girls I date have noses that are more sensitive than dogs. I can't imagine them getting anywhere near there without complaining." Kevin's face glowed as he admitted that. He wasn't embarrassed about having his ass licked, but he was talking about girls? "I think it's my turn now. I have an idea."

Kevin reached out, and Seth took his hand. Kevin propelled him toward the top of the glass, where he snagged a handhold.

"Face the windows."

Had Kevin finally decided they had to be windows? That this was all real and not some drug-induced hallucination? It didn't matter. Seth followed Kevin's instructions, bracing himself with both hands as he looked down on the planet below him.

Hands spread him, a pause, and then a tongue swiped up his crease, sending waves of sensation directly to his cock.

"Like that?"

"Uh, yeah. Definitely like that." It felt so good, his brain shutdown, making coherent speech practically impossible.

The tongue played with first one ball, then the other, then back up his crease, circling around the opening.

Seth's head fell forward between his arms until his forehead rested on the glass. His eyes were filled with the beauty and grandeur of planet Earth in its shining glory. A thought tickled his mind. Could a large enough telescope see into this window? He would certainly be giving a show: his hard cock flapping around in zero G while his lover licked his hole.

At least, it would look like that to any observer except the evil Winthrop, who knew exactly what he was putting them through. The thought was almost enough to make him lose his hard-on, but fingers tickling his balls and hot breath and a tongue lapping at his pucker fixed that right up.

Both hands on his ass now, spreading him wide as the tongue speared into his hole, penetrating just a little.

"Holy… oh."

The tongue thrust forward, in and out, fucking his hole, making him want so much more. He wanted that big cock between Kevin's legs penetrating him, rubbing against his sweet spot and making him come, sending his brain to oblivion, making him forget money, challenges, and despotic, small men.

One group of clouds below made a spiral pattern, just like the galaxy their planet inhabited. Another looked like a giant boomerang. Now wasn't that prophetic. What had he thrown this week that would come back to haunt him?

But the sensation was too much to keep up that line of thought. Waves of pleasure washed over him, sending jolts of excitement to his now leaking prick.

The orange of the sun reflected over the edge of the world on his right, the play of colors and tongue mixing together in his brain, making a beautiful sunrise, the beginning of something beautiful and full of promise.

Then Kevin's hand was on his cock, tugging, swiping up pre-come, sliding down, all in rhythm with his thrusting tongue.

That was all it took. His balls seemed to inside out themselves in an attempt to send every ounce of his pleasure out, painting the window in white lines. The pleasure was so intense, he let go of the handhold and drifted away, his shudders causing him to spin.

Then Kevin grabbed Seth and held him tightly while

he panted through the last throws of pleasure. Kevin's hand stroked through his bushy hair, and he could swear he heard Kevin saying, "I got you," in a voice that was barely a whisper.

Seth looked up at Kevin. Moisture collected at the edge of his eyes, but his face was tender, almost loving.

Seth reached up and rubbed his hand along Kevin's jawbone, a light rasp of stubble already starting to grow.

"Nice job, boys. You two really are a delight to do business with. Erex is on his way. I suggest you get dressed."

Kevin and Seth sprang apart, each bumping into the opposite wall. Seth grabbed a handhold and worked his way around to gather his floating clothes. For one sock, he had to push off, grab it in the air, then he couldn't resist flipping with a grin before catching a handhold on the other side.

They dressed quickly, if a bit awkwardly, unaccustomed to zero G.

"Erex is in the elevator."

Kevin pushed the button by the doors to open the airlock, and there waited the elevator, doors open, and a knowing smirk on Erex's face.

Seth took one last look out the window at the planet he called home. Filled with a sense of awe, he watched for a moment. Would he ever make it here again?

He crossed back into the elevator, another wave of electric shocklets passing over his body. He had chosen to push himself in floating, a clear mistake as he crashed to the ground, the wind knocked out of him as gravity reasserted its reign.

That was another oddity. What caused the abrupt change?

Kevin appeared to learn from Seth's experience as he positioned himself before stepping through. Even so, his legs buckled, and he fell on his ass. How long had they been in zero G?

The two stayed on the floor, exhausted and resting, as the elevator began its descent. Seth endured a few queasy minutes of dropping as the elevator accelerated before his stomach adjusted to the motion.

Sitting next to him on the floor, Kevin nudged him with his shoulder. "That was amazing. You did it, Seth. You got there."

Did he really? Was he in space? It almost didn't matter. It had been an awesome experience. "Yeah. It was even more beautiful than I imagined."

"And zero G was crazy." Kevin's head fell back against the wall.

"Yeah, it was perfect."

All Seth could think about was how perfect it had been, all of it, not just space, but the time making love to Kevin. Except that part, possibly all of it, was a lie. When they returned to school, Seth knew his life was going to change. He couldn't go back to what they had, but there was no forward either. What was he going to do?

CHAPTER
SIXTEEN

Monday, April 3, 12:24 P.M.

Kevin and Seth sat at a table together in the corner of the main ballroom, away from the other guests. They ate from a lavish brunch buffet with an omelet station that included lobster, caviar, six different varieties of mushrooms, and many other fillings. Peanut butter cup pancakes, Eggs Benedict, and fresh fruit from all over the world were just a few of the delectable offerings.

With so much luxury, it was a shame Seth's appetite had fled. This entire experience could have been a dream come true. Instead, his friendship with Kevin was about to go supernova.

Kevin stared at the wall to his left. He shoveled food from his heaping plate into his mouth, chewed, swallowed, and repeated, seemingly without regard to what he was eating.

Watching Kevin implode, knowing he was the cause, wormed its way through Seth like a parasite. He needed to take

Kevin's pain away like he needed to explore space.

Seth leaned forward, pitching his voice low. "I'm probably the last person you want to talk to, but I'm here and I'll listen. I know this isn't your choice. You won't offend me."

Kevin looked up, his expression dark, his lips pressed together in a thin line.

Seth's chest tightened. Of course, Kevin wouldn't appreciate a chance to talk because clearly Seth was the problem.

The couple from the night before, Todd and Jeff, came by about halfway through the meal and joined them. They had black circles under their eyes.

Jeff inhaled the aroma of his coffee before taking a hefty sip and sighing.

"Late night?" Seth asked.

"Night never really ended. What a party. Freakin' amazing." Todd sipped his coffee. "Lost track of you guys."

Seth pushed the food around his plate with his fork. "We bugged out early."

An older gentleman stopped by the table. His skin was dark, and gray streaked his short, tightly curled hair. "Lovely performance today, boys." His accent hinted at an African nationality.

"Uh, thanks?" Seth's entire body heated like it was the slow-roasted pig on a spit from the day before. After that, he noticed many people glancing their way and talking quietly. How many of these people had watched him and Kevin rim each other? Too many. He prayed none of these people worked for NASA.

Kevin glanced at the man, his cheeks the color of Mars and his eyes twin moons.

"It's not so bad." Jeff patted his shoulder, a wry grin on

his face. "There are worse challenges."

"You saw us, too?" Seth squeaked.

Kevin stilled for a moment, eyes locked on his dish. Then he resumed shoveling food into his mouth, not looking up from his plate.

"Yeah." At least Jeff had the decency to blush.

Seth shook his head. "Are we gonna see your challenges, too?"

"Doubtful. Ours aren't that kind of challenge." Todd leaned back in his chair.

Seth poked at a home fry with his fork. "What do you have to do?"

A half-smile graced Jeff's face. "We're not allowed to talk about it."

"Of course." Seth shifted in his chair.

That bastard Winthrop had them all sewn up tight. No one could say shit to anyone. His imagination filled with images of what a sick fuck like Winthrop would do to people he had over a barrel. Pain? Images of a medieval dungeon filled his head. Maybe a round on the rack or just being caned. Or perhaps the illegal things he feared when he was first approached. Safe cracking, hacking into some company to steal their tech. Who the hell knew?

Speak of the devil. The balding sicko swept into the room as Seth gave up on eating, his stomach too strung out. The man sat at a table set for one on another raised dais. It amused him with a sort of grim satisfaction to see Winthrop so self-conscious about his height. Two of his little people servants ran back and forth from the buffet, serving him food, lighting yet another cigar, keeping his wine glass full. Seth couldn't help noticing how the man consumed with gusto.

Kevin glanced at Winthrop then refocused on his plate, his shoulders hunched.

There must be something I can do to help him. What does that sick fuck have over Kevin?

Winthrop stood, and Erex clanged a fork against a glass until the room quieted.

"I have a special treat for everyone today. In honor of my special guests, Kevin and Seth, who gave us all such lovely entertainment this morning." Winthrop paused and saluted Kevin and Seth. "Delightful boys. Truly a treat. Join me in a round of applause."

The room filled with polite clapping while Winthrop gloated.

Winthrop continued, "I have prevailed upon my good friend, Mr. H., for a special favor." Winthrop gestured over to a table set off in a corner where a tall, pale man sat, wearing a gray business suit. The man waved, but a frown marred his face. The crowd applauded politely, if somewhat subdued.

Seth's skin pebbled when he looked at the man.

Winthrop continued, "We are going to have an old-fashioned basketball game. Mr. H. has brought some special players for team Hominidae, and I've gone to great effort to collect some excellent opponents to play on Team Teros. I was somewhat limited by the constraints of the game. The need for hands and all."

Many in the crowd laughed and applauded.

Seth glanced around. What did Winthrop mean?

Looking directly at them, Winthrop held his hand palm up. "Seth, Kevin, tell me you'll play."

Seth looked at Kevin, whose eyes closed for a long moment. His friend had been through enough, now they wanted more? No fucking way. Seth stood to reply.

Kevin spoke quickly. "Sure, I'll play. Standard rules?"

Winthrop bowed in Kevin's direction. "Of course."

Kevin's eyes pleaded with Seth. "You in?"

Seth sighed. He had a bad feeling about Winthrop's definition of an old-fashioned basketball game. "Yeah, I'm in."

"Excellent. Ladies and gentlemen, a round of applause for our two athletes." Winthrop smirked as he gestured toward Seth and Kevin with his cigar. "Erex, show them where the team is suiting up."

Erex led them down yet another hall, this one with signed portraits of famous athletes. One of Babe Ruth, with a personalized message to Winthrop, caught Seth's eye. How was that even possible? Tom Brady, Michael Jordan, Wayne Gretzky, LeBron James, Jackie Robinson, Dan Marino, Pele, Muhammad Ali, the list just went on and on. All made out to Maynard Frederick Winthrop IV. Could he really have met all of these people? The collection must have been worth a fortune, perhaps several fortunes.

At the end of the hall, Erex opened a door that led into a locker room. A bunch of very tall men were dressing in a set of red jerseys with Hominidae printed on the front. Erex led them to two lockers, each labeled with their last names, Griffin and Fields. Inside were red jerseys with their names on the back. Winthrop was nothing if not confident.

Looking around at the other players, many seemed familiar in that impossible way that Seth was coming to associate with everything Winthrop did. Seth scanned the names of his teammates, Robertson, Chamberlain, Bird, *Bird?* He looked over the man with Bird on his back and lost his breath. The man looked just like Larry Bird. Not even Larry Bird, Team President of the Indiana Pacers. No, Larry Bird back when he was first drafted in 1979.

Kevin turned to him. He shook his head once slowly, smiling.

Another shirt said Russell. Seth's mouth dropped open. Standing before him was one of his personal idols, Bill Russell, centerpiece of the Celtics dynasty. Young again, in his prime, laughing with someone whose shirt said Schommer.

Had Winthrop found look-alikes? What were the chances that these guys would even be able to play?

Another look-alike approached in a suit, and Seth's heart almost stopped. Before him was Coach Red Auerbach of the Celtics. Alive and well, with a clipboard in hand. "Okay, we have a game to play, and the competition is fierce, literally. I'm going to do a roll call just to make sure I have you all straight. Abdul-Jabbar, Bird, Chamberlain, Fields, Griffin, Jordan, Page, Robertson, Russell, Schommer."

Each man indicated his presence, and Seth's neck hurt from swiveling around and gawking.

Kareem Abdul-Jabbar, Larry Bird, Wilt Chamberlain, Michael Jordan, Oscar Robertson, and Bill Russell. Six names that should be said with awe and reverence. Giants of the game. All standing before him, young and in their prime. Not old men. Not in the ground. Here. The last two names were unfamiliar. Perhaps others in a challenge for Winthrop. And Red Auerbach, back from the grave.

Not possible, not possible, not possible.

Seth's room in high school had been decorated with pictures of these men, and they didn't look like imposters.

Impossible!

"We lucked out today. They got David Tobey to referee."

Seth had no idea who that was. He looked at Kevin, whose wide eyes looked ready to pop out of his head as he shrugged.

The coach spent the next few minutes talking to them, explaining the game plan. Seriously, a genuine, Red Auerbach game plan.

Holy Shit!

The plan did involve Kevin and Seth on the bench more

than the others, but given how dizzy and off-balance he felt, perhaps that was for the best.

Then they hit the court to warm up.

Any doubt that these guys could play evaporated. Look-alikes with skill. Seth wanted to just stop and watch the amazing show as they did layup drills.

But the shocks weren't over. The other team took the court, and Seth's brain ignited and launched into space.

Their players didn't appear to be human.

CHAPTER SEVENTEEN

Monday, April 3, 2:57 P.M.

The seats around the basketball court filled with hundreds of people, presumably Winthrop's guests. Seth scanned the sea of faces and picked out Jeff and Todd to the right of center court in the middle of the crowd.

Winthrop sat on a balcony at one end of the court, like a Roman emperor preparing to enjoy a gladiatorial slaughter, with a turkey leg in one hand and a cigar in the other. *Nothing phallic there.*

A deep voice boomed from loud speakers around the arena. "Ladies and gentlemen. Welcome to a classic rivalry. The red Hominidae at the blue Teros."

Seth and Kevin moved to the team bench and faced the court.

"Introducing tonight's Home Team." The sound reverberated around the crowded room. "Winthrop's blue

Teros."

The audience burst into applause, hooting and shouting.

Seth turned to the entrance for the opposing team's locker room. That familiar tingle of excitement tightened his chest.

As the announcer blared, "Cyclops," an eight-foot-tall—words left Seth—one-eyed creature, in a blue jersey, jogged across the court and bowed to Winthrop before heading to the Teros team bench.

"Minotaur," echoed loudly from the sound system. A huge man lumbered in, swinging his bull's head from side to side and flinging snot from his nose. His Jersey had a zipper up the back. He, too, paid obeisance to the fat man.

No way.

Winthrop had a sexual fantasy involving that thing! A droplet of sweat trickled down Seth's face. Kevin stared at the beast and squeezed Seth's shoulder.

"Medusa." A gorgon entered, pacing fluidly across the court, her snake hair hissing and writhing in all directions. Her eyes were covered with some kind of mirrored protective gear. *To prevent her from turning competitors to stone?* She curtsied deeply while each of her snakes curled in a bow.

These had to be people in costumes, but not just any costumes. They were supreme, top-of-the-line, Hollywood would drool, professional costumes. Winthrop never did anything halfway.

Those outfits had to be hotter than Hell.

The announcer listed off the rest of the Teros' one-by-one. Satyr, Harpy, Siren riding on a powered wheel platform, Golem, Cherub with wings sticking out the back of his jersey, Vampire, and Yeti. Each made their entrance, giving Winthrop his due.

Robertson clapped Seth on the back. "Don't worry, I've been up against these guys before. They're big, but the ref keeps them in line."

Seth stared at Robertson. This had to be the strangest moment of his life. Considering he had sex in space that morning, that was saying something. He had seen these men play on the NBA channel. He had even attended a game when he was young with his dad where Michael Jordan played. But that had been MJ at the end of his career. This man moved like Michael in his prime.

The costumes didn't slow the competition. Seth marveled at the small details. The way Medusa's sweat rolled down her face as she dribbled the ball, but never touched the green makeup. The way the Cherub's wings fluttered as his chubby baby legs ran down the court. Legs like that shouldn't be able to support weight, yet and how he was managing to dribble the ball, it was almost as tall as he was.

Seth decided to suspend disbelief and enjoy the game. Great players from history vs. mythical monsters, gotcha.

The sound of sneakers squeaking on hardwood and the smell of sweat washed over him, reminding him of a hundred other games played with Kevin. His best friend was right there, next to him, radiating excitement. He wanted to grab Kevin's hand but settled for punching him in the arm as MJ made a particularly skillful layup after evading the siren.

When Auerbach called Kevin into the game, Seth's heart leaped into his throat.

Watching his best friend play amid the skill and brute force terrified Seth. The first time the yeti slammed into Kevin, knocking him to the floor, Seth stood to run to him before Larry Bird helped him up.

Although Kevin limped to the foul line, he turned to Seth and saluted, a grin on his face. He lined up the shot, and with a knock on the rim, the ball fell through the hoop. He aimed the second shot and scored again for team Hominidae.

Kevin resumed playing, his leg seeming fine, but Seth wanted him out of there. Away from the vampire who looked hungry, away from the gorgeous gagged siren who found a way to press in close, even on her wheeled platform.

That was *his* man!

But Kevin wasn't his. He had to say it over and over. Kevin wasn't his. This was all because of Winthrop. Someday, Kevin would meet Ms. Right, get married, have two-point-two children, a white picket fence, and a dog named Rover. He would have the perfect life as a doctor, with a perfect wife on his arm, living somewhere in the middle of America.

Seth hated that nameless, faceless woman. Jealousy reeled through him, knocking him around. Kevin would never really be his. He would have to settle for memories of his tongue on the perfect ass, the perfect cock. How was he going to go back to the way things were?

Coach Auerbach waved Kevin out and signaled Seth to go in. He ran into the game, and immediately, Wilt Chamberlain passed him the ball. He dribbled down the court when Minotaur swept by him, stealing the ball. He turned to chase when Minotaur attempted a shot from the three that was blocked by Kareem Abdul-Jabbar.

Seth's heart pounded, and his muscles burned as he orbited the ball. A quick pass from Robertson to Jordan resulted in a score for the Hominidae.

Golem dribbled the ball up the court with a speed one would never expect from stone. A pass to Vampire and the Teros had another two points.

Seth handled the ball a few more times, learning quickly to pass it on before it was stolen by the Teros.

After about five minutes, Coach Auerbach called him out and sent Bill Russell to replace him on the court. Panting, he sat next to Kevin.

"Fuck. That was amazing. It felt so real." Seth struggled to catch his breath.

Kevin patted his back. "I know. Better than a video game in VR."

Seth smiled at Kevin and turned his focus back to his team.

At half-time, the Teros were up by three points. The other players filed into the locker room, hot and sweaty. Seth had a few serious teenage fantasies about some of these guys, but he couldn't appreciate seeing them in person with Kevin there. How could he even consider the others? Kevin may not really want him, but that didn't change what they were doing this week and how it affected Seth.

He was saving up. Treasuring each twisted experience, building a fantasy that he once had everything he could ever want. It was going to have to sustain him for the rest of his life.

His only hope was that eventually, he would move on and meet someone even half as perfect as Kevin would be for him... but gay.

Coach Auerbach distracted him from his thoughts. "You know what we have that our opponents don't? We love this game, and that's what's going to make the difference."

Seth focused on the pep talk being given by his coaching idol. Too bad he would never be able to tell anyone about this... except Kevin. His best friend sat beside him, drinking in the words of the basketball legend.

The team took position on the court for the second half.

"Hominidae ball." The announcer's voice filled the room.

Wilt Chamberlain inbounded it to Bill Russell, and the action began again. As usual, the Hominidae now aimed for the opposite basket. Seth could almost forget the weirdness of famous players and monsters. Everything really was like a typical game. From the announcer booming the number of each Teros player that scored, to the increasing tempo music that played when the Hominidae raced the shot clock.

The tide turned in the game, Larry Bird scoring another three points followed by a quick recovery of the ball by Oscar Robertson, leading to another two points.

The coach for the Teros, a bear of a man, picked up a large bull whip and flicked his wrist. The loud crack echoed across the court as the yeti howled in pain. The coach sent the yeti in for the Cyclops, who came out for similar treatment.

Holy shit! You don't treat... beings like that, whether they are people in costumes or mythical creatures.

Whipping the players seemed ineffective. Instead, the yeti barreled into Kareem Abdul-Jabbar, leading to yet another foul. Consummate professionals, the Hominidae played clean through the desperate aggression of the Teros.

As the clock ran down, Seth held his breath. The Teros had the ball, the Hominidae were up by one. Medusa dribbled the ball and went in for a layup. Bill Russell blocked the ball, and the buzzer rang.

The final score: Hominidae eighty-four, Teros eighty-three.

When the game ended, Winthrop stood and spoke to the assembled crowd. "Teros. I'm disappointed in you."

Yeti whimpered, and Vampire turned even paler.

"You know the penalty for loss." Winthrop snapped his fingers twice, and a group of little people surrounded the huge monsters.

Penalty for loss? Winthrop never said anything about that. Seth's stomach dropped like a satellite falling from orbit.

"Hominidae, you are dismissed with my thanks for a job well done. You have each earned the reward you were promised. Seth and Kevin, you've earned a night off. No more challenges today. Go... how do you kids say it... 'chill out.'"

Seth exhaled. *No more crazy today.* Erex materialized at Seth's elbow as if by magic, gesturing for them to follow him.

They left the court and went down another hall, descended a few flights of stairs, and arrived back at their room.

"I'll bring down dinner in about an hour." Erex pulled the door shut as he left.

After taking turns showering, Kevin headed to his computer, so Seth decided to check his email and surf a bit. Dinner came, and they ate in silence. Thoughts about the game spun through his head. How did Winthrop do that? Where did he find those players? Every time he glanced at Kevin, hoping to discuss the game, Seth was met with his friend staring at his plate, frowning. The weight of everything they had done settled on Seth's shoulders.

Seth needed to get out, take a walk, clear his head. He had been in Kevin's company constantly for three days. Not that he wasn't normally in Kevin's company. He liked being there, but his mind was so messed up, he just needed some alone time to sort things out. If he could only leave the room.

"I'll send Erex." Winthrop's voice sounded in his head.

And there it was, again. Winthrop could somehow hear his thoughts. At least, sometimes. That tech alone had to be worth millions. Why hadn't the man created products to market the discovery? How had he kept an elevator to space a secret and why? How did the mansion keep reconfiguring itself like some kind of Rubik's cube? Was Seth really starting to believe this wasn't all smoke and mirrors?

Erex arrived.

"I'm going to take a walk. I need some air," Seth said.

Kevin didn't respond, just waved. Why would he care where Seth went? They weren't dating. They weren't a couple.

Erex led him up a short flight of steps and out of a basement bulkhead. How did the house keep changing? When they emerged, the sun was just setting, the sky painted in orange and pink bands swirling across the partially cloudy sky. Seth inhaled the crisp spring air, now cooling as the sun set.

"Can I walk alone?"

"Sure, I'll meet you back here."

"Okay."

Seth set off through a landscaped yard toward a forest in the distance. The trees stood like stick figures, spring leaves still to come. He found a path through the trees and followed. A bird chirped from a high branch. Seth's feet ruffled leaves as he passed, a whisper of whooshing sounds.

What was he going to do? Everything was messed up, changed. He was having sexual encounters with Kevin, and his carefully guarded feelings were sprouting like the leaves soon would this spring. Growing into something beautiful, something wonderful.

But winter was coming, too.

The light faded, and Seth turned around on the path, picking his way back carefully to make sure he didn't trip on a root.

By the time he had reached a towering maple, the feelings were a bit more manageable, more numb, because none of this was his choice. Not the situation, not the feelings, and definitely not the resolution. There was nothing he could do. He would have to put his feelings for Kevin away, or lose him entirely.

Would his friend be able to do the same? Would he be able to forgive Seth for what they had done? Seth was gay, and this was Heaven to him. It had to be Hell for Kevin. He vowed to help his friend. Maybe he should get him into trauma counseling. Was all of this like rape? Winthrop was screwing them both by proxy.

Erex was waiting when he returned to the bulkhead. "I

was about to send out a search party. I should have given you a flashlight."

"It's a bright night, and I have good night vision, even if I need these." Seth tapped his glasses.

Seth took one last look at the gibbous moon that had provided the light for his journey. He admired the million stars in the sky. Enjoying the view from an area not saturated with light pollution. He even saw the bands of the Milky Way. He followed Erex back to the room and let himself in with a wave to the small man.

The room was empty.

Seth's head swiveled from side to side, but Kevin was definitely not in the room. He didn't know what he expected, but his heart raced a little faster. Where was Kevin?

The bathroom door stood ajar, but the light shone from inside. Could Kevin be in there?

He peeked around the corner and found his best friend, sitting in an empty bathtub. His head was bowed, his knees drawn up, his elbows resting on his knees. He still wore jeans and a T-shirt, but his feet were bare.

His body shook, like shivers, or tears being held in.

Oh, shit.

"Kevin, man, you okay?"

Kevin tipped his head back, his normally smiling face drawn, dark circles under bloodshot eyes. Seth checked to see if some injury had occurred.

"Kevin, can you talk? What's going on?"

"I… I need… it's all messed up." Kevin wiped one eye with the heel of his hand.

Seth dropped to his knees by the tub. He wanted to reach out and grab Kevin's hand, give him support. But he suspected his touch was not what Kevin needed right now.

"It's okay. It's all going to be okay. We did what we had to do."

"I know. I never… but he," Kevin pointed between his legs, "didn't seem to mind."

"It's okay. Friction is friction. Anyone would respond. It doesn't mean anything. Don't sweat it."

Kevin looked up at Seth, his eyes inscrutable. "Really? It doesn't mean anything?"

"Of course not. When this is over, we'll go back to school." Seth steeled himself to utter the words Kevin needed to hear no matter how much they hurt Seth. "You'll screw that girl, Linda, Lisa, whatever her name was, and this will all just be a bad dream. You'll find that perfect girl, get married, have kids, everything you ever wanted. We give up our dreams, and he wins."

Kevin peered up at Seth, eyes wide. "Wh—what about you?"

"I'm a gay guy. We hook up all the time. It's nothing, just sex." He wanted Kevin to feel safe with him even though everything he was saying was total bullshit. Kevin needed to know that Seth had no expectations that Kevin had somehow switched teams.

Shoulders slumping, Kevin deflated. "Just sex?" he whispered.

What was that look in Kevin's eyes? Disbelief? "Yeah, no big deal."

"But, dude, you don't hook up. Barely ever. You rarely date."

That was true. It was hard to date when the man of your dreams was right there and unattainable.

"Hooking up doesn't exactly have a long shelf life, and I figure you don't want to hear about that shit." A white lie to keep his friend from figuring out the truth.

Kevin slowly shook his head. "So you get lots?"

"Gay guys, we get it all the time. As long as you use a condom, no worries, it's all good."

Kevin's voice dropped to a whisper. "Oh."

"Come on, it's getting late." Well, not exactly, it was only around eight o'clock. "You look wrecked. Let's get some shut-eye." He was careful not to say get into bed.

"I guess."

"A good night's sleep and everything will make more sense in the morning."

Kevin let Seth pull him to standing and followed Seth to his own side of the bed. Seth pulled back the covers and helped Kevin get in, fully clothed. There was no way he was undressing him and risk that being seen as a threat.

He tucked Kevin in like a small child. "G'night, Kev."

"G'night."

He turned off all the lights and quickly changed into pajamas. He slipped into his side of the bed.

His best friend, the person he loved, was hurting, and he caused it, or at least part of it. He wanted so much to help him and felt so helpless.

Damn Winthrop.

CHAPTER EIGHTEEN

Tuesday, April 4, 7:53 am

Seth struggled to open sleep-encrusted eyes. He moaned and slapped the nightstand, looking to press snooze. Despite his attempts to silence the noise, the pounding on the door continued.

Kevin groaned and pulled his pillow over his head.

Seth had tossed and turned all night. What would Winthrop make them do today? More importantly, what would those acts do to his best friend's psyche?

His chest tightened. The next logical step for Winthrop's challenges was for him and Kevin to have anal intercourse. He liked anal. Liked it a lot. In any position. Kevin would probably have no problem topping, it wasn't that different. But would he be able to bottom or would he freak out?

Seth had heard some straight boys liked anal play with their girlfriends, but some didn't. Winthrop loved to push people. Make them do things they would never consider. He would definitely make Kevin bottom.

Laughter sounded in his head. *"I like you. We think alike. Of course, I will. Today, in fact. Now get out of bed and let Erex in."*

Oh, my stars. Anal. With Kevin. Today. Seth rolled, stumbling as his feet hit the floor. Disgust rumbled through his empty stomach. How could he have anything in common with Winthrop?

He opened the door to find Erex holding a breakfast tray filled with warm pastries, muffins, and a carafe of aromatic coffee, the scent a complex mix of deep roast and chocolate. Erex placed it on the desk and then swung a backpack off his shoulder.

"This has some extra supplies you'll need for today. Wear bathing suits."

"Back in the pool?" Kevin clenched his teeth as he swung his legs out of bed.

"No, different venue. Wear sunscreen. It's in the bag."

Sunscreen? It was early April in upstate New York. Where were they going that they would need sunscreen?

"Eat up and get ready. I'll be back in an hour to escort you."

Seth took a peek in the bag, finding the promised sunscreen, two large, fluffy towels with bright red hearts on a white background. Tacky. Two shovels and pails, the type little kids used to play in a sandbox. Nestled in the bottom of the bag sat condoms and lube, waterproof. Everything they needed for the next challenge. Bizarre.

At some point during his perusal, Kevin had headed for the shower, the streaming water sounding like a quiet rainstorm. Seth headed for the bathroom door. One step. Two. Then he stopped. He fought the urge to go in there, put his arms around

Kevin, and lay his head on the man's back. Ask if he was okay. But he had to resist. It was getting harder to resist. His walls lay shattered around him. Wreckage everywhere he stepped. Would he ever be able to get past this pain?

Kevin shuffled out of the shower, mumbling, "Morning." His head was still bowed, but he didn't seem quite as defeated. Hopefully, sleep had done its magic.

Seth showered quickly and came out to find Kevin already suited up in a purple Speedo and eating a *Mille-feuille*, a bit of the white icing sticking to his lips.

Must not lick sweetness.

Instead, he put on a matching purple Speedo.

How delightful, we're twins.

He donned his glasses and slipped the prescription goggles in the backpack.

Erex arrived as they finished eating. Kevin grabbed the pack, and they followed Erex out the door, down a hall, and through a small room. Erex opened another door and…

Light. Bright, blazing sunlight. Heat.

He and Kevin stepped out of the room onto hot sand, hopping foot to foot.

"Oh, sorry," said Erex. He tossed flip-flops on the sand. "Almost forgot."

Turning to pick up the sandals, Kevin gasped. The door wasn't attached to anything. It floated like the entrance to the holo-deck on Star Trek.

The burning sand forced Seth to focus on slipping the footwear on his feet.

How could they have stepped through a door in upstate New York onto a beach? How was any of this week possible? Seth's logical engineering mind reported a system error and refused to think about the problem any further. Whether it was special effects, a working transporter, or fae magic didn't matter anymore. He was here, and it felt real.

The sand stretched to either side of them, as far as the eye could see. The water lapped in gentle waves, sparkling in the warm sun, painted in shades of aquamarine. A mild breeze soothed Seth's glowing skin.

Seth looked up and down the beach, noting that there were no other people. The beach was theirs.

"This is a private island that Mr. Winthrop owns in the Caribbean," Erex said.

Kevin gave a hollow laugh.

Erex placed a cooler on the sand. "Lunch, snacks, and drinks inside. The boss says to relax and have fun for a while. He'll let you know when the challenge begins."

Erex stepped back through the door, and Seth heard it close as he looked off into the distance. When he turned around, the door had vanished leaving only sand leading to a palm tree jungle.

"Shit. We're stuck here."

"What does it matter? We're stuck until Winthrop's done with us. At least it's nice here." Kevin grabbed the cooler and walked up the beach to a small wooden hut. He placed the cooler in the shade and grabbed the sunscreen from the backpack.

Squeezing some into his hand, Kevin rubbed it along his chest and six-pack abs. Seth watched out of the corner of his eye as those long, skilled fingers massaged the white liquid into his skin.

"Uh… could I use some?" Seth asked.

"Sure." Kevin took another squirt and tossed him the bottle.

Seth worked on his arms, legs, and torso, while continuing

to monitor Kevin doing the same. The man really was a work of art, from his lightly muscled arms to his muscular calves. Folks called them Cornell calves. They came from walking the hill by the library, Libe slope, and the rest of the hilly campus.

"Do my back." Kevin turned his back to Seth.

Tingles travelled up Seth's skin. Kevin would allow this touch? Why not? Before this week, he wouldn't have thought anything amiss at helping his friend with sunscreen. Now? His world had been flipped on its axis.

Seth rubbed the cold, white goo onto Kevin's smooth, strong back. Kevin wasn't a muscle head, but his back was lean without an ounce of fat. Staying fit for basketball had some perks.

When he was done, he handed the bottle to Kevin. "Do me?"

Did I really just say that?

He turned around and held his hair off his neck to let Kevin get access. Kevin's hands were smooth on his skin, rubbing back and forth, up and down, ensuring that every inch was covered. Seth's prick tried to take notice, but he shushed it in his head. That would come soon enough.

Kevin grabbed the backpack, stowing the sunscreen, and headed down the beach, closer to the water. The sound of the surf and the occasional seagull shared the air with the popping sound of his flip-flops.

Seth inhaled the scent of salt in the air. He remembered his childhood, swimming in Long Island Sound on the beaches along the shore of Connecticut. Jumping in waves, running along sand bars. The ocean there looked nothing like this. The water was dark, a blue-black, with white foam at the breakers. The crisp surf cooled his body from the summer heat.

Seth followed Kevin to the water. "Can I have the backpack?"

Kevin handed it to him, and he pulled out the buckets and towels. He laid his towel out then grabbed a bucket and searched for seashells. Another wave of childhood passed over him as he collected the tiny remains of sea creatures.

He left the starfish alone, uncertain if they were still alive, and gathered a variety of shells. Most were shades of tan with brown accents, dots, stripes, a few had brighter highlights, pinks, and purples. Most were small, but he found one huge conch shell. The kind you hold to your ear and hear the ocean.

Fifteen minutes later, he realized he had worked his way up the beach and was surprised to discover Kevin ten paces behind him on a similar search, his bucket about half-full.

Green tropical foliage and palm trees surrounded the edge of the beach. This might be the most beautiful place in the world.

Kevin faced the water. "It's amazing here. I don't know how he did it. I know we can't be here, but it feels so real."

"I know. Nothing makes sense this week."

"Truer words..." Kevin paused, took a deep breath. "Sorry I lost it last night. It's all..."

"It's okay. You know we're in this together. I'm here for you."

A slow smile spread across Kevin's face while his hands trembled. "I know. It helps."

"Yeah?" For some reason, that was the best news Seth had heard all week.

"Yeah." Kevin ducked his head and rubbed his neck while clearing his throat. "More than I can say."

"I wish I knew why you were here. I..."

"Uh-uh Seth. That would be telling and spoil my fun," Winthrop growled.

"Sorry, I can't say." Kevin clenched his fists at his side.

"I heard." Seth tapped his head. "At least I can be here for you."

Kevin patted Seth on the shoulder.

Without words, they turned and fell into step together, walking back to the towels. A weight Seth hadn't realized he carried had lifted from his shoulders. Kevin seemed to be doing better and didn't blame Seth, even though Seth blamed himself. Would Kevin even be here if Winthrop hadn't targeted his own debt? Or was Kevin Winthrop's first choice, and Seth was along for the ride?

They placed their buckets near the towels in the sand, and then Kevin whooped, "Race ya," and took off running for the turquoise waters.

Seth stared with a smile on his face. Kevin always found the fun in situations.

Kevin ran several steps until the water was almost up to his knees and turned to face Seth, a huge smile split his face. "Slow poke."

Seth dropped his glasses on the towel and grabbed the prescription goggles, adjusting them so he could see. "Slow? I'll show you." Seth blew past Kevin, running until the water deepened, and then he dove in, the salty taste splashing his tongue. He definitely wasn't swimming in Connecticut. The water was warm, almost a bath, and soothed his sun-heated skin. He surfaced a few feet beyond Kevin, standing chest deep.

"Gets deep out here fast."

"I'll take your word for it."

That's right, Kevin can't swim.

"It's okay. The current isn't very strong. No surfing here."

"You've been in for like one minute. How do you know it won't get stronger?" Kevin had a point. "No lifeguards either."

Seth knew he should be cautious, but somehow, he knew nothing bad would happen. Winthrop, for all his being a total dick, would not let his playthings get hurt. He felt certain if either of them were in trouble, the cavalry would come galloping over the hill or perhaps riding in on jet skis. Seth shook his head, chuckling. When was the last time he had such flights of fancy? He was an engineer, a scientist, facts, figures, equations were his view of the world.

For that matter, had he ever stopped to just look at the stars before he came here? He hadn't even visited the campus observatory, too busy with problem sets and basketball practice. He made a promise to himself to remedy that. He didn't want to gain an understanding of the skies above at the cost of losing the wonder.

"It's okay, come on." Seth held out his hand. What possessed him?

Kevin approached slowly through the water and took Seth's hand, grasping it firmly, like a lifeline.

"See, it's not so bad."

Kevin's smile slipped, but slowly returned. They stood in the water, holding hands, like it was the most natural thing in the world.

Together like this, Seth felt powerful. Strong. They could do anything as a team. He could taste just how great they would be. Did Kevin feel it?

The gentle waves moved around them, rocking them. A few small colorful fish played at their feet. Seth dug his toes into the fine waterlogged sand and turned his face to the sun.

As usual, it had been a cold, snowy winter in Ithaca. Anyone who could, headed south for Spring Break. He grinned. He was south, too. Probably, farther than most who were getting drunk in Florida.

He opened his eyes to see Kevin, basking in the warm

glow from above, a gentle smile gracing his face, his eyes shut.

Seth wished he had a camera to capture that perfect moment. Dark hair, light skin, and bliss. He studied it for a moment, committing it to memory.

"Kiss him."

CHAPTER NINETEEN

Tuesday, April 4, 10:14 am

"Kiss him," Winthrop instructed Seth.

The warm salty water lapped around Seth's chest as he gazed at Kevin standing in front of him. For once, Seth appreciated the direction. It gave him permission to do exactly what he had been longing to do. He reached up, placed his hand on Kevin's cheek, and pulled their faces together.

Kevin's gaze bored into Seth's as he leaned in, meeting Seth halfway. Kevin's eyes fell closed as their lips joined.

Heaven—Kevin tasted marvelous as his lips moved against Seth's. Salt, a hint of sunscreen, and that unique flavor that was all Kevin.

The water flowed around them as he pushed his tongue against Kevin's lips, seeking entrance. Kevin opened to him like a wormhole allowing access to the most exotic regions of outer space.

Seth slid his tongue alongside Kevin's while his friend's arms came around him. He held Seth tightly as their mouths joined, and they explored each other's hot, wet caverns.

Letting the water support his weight, he bent his legs and wrapped them around Kevin. Their hard shafts pressed together, not completely separated by the thin fabric of their Speedos.

Kevin moaned as he grabbed Seth's ass, encouraging him to thrust. Seth threw his head back, grinding while Kevin assaulted his neck with lips and tongue, sending ripples down his spine and straight to his cock and balls.

Thank God for Winthrop. The thought came unbidden into his mind and was quite disturbing. Almost enough for him to lose his erection.

Winthrop's obnoxious laugh rolled through Seth's head. *"I don't know about God, but don't lose focus now. It's time for your challenge. You're going to top him. But I think you knew that."*

Of course, he knew, but he would stress over that later. Right now, Kevin's hand was on Seth's nipple, doing wicked things with his fingers. Damn. His erection sprung back to full mast, ready for action.

Seth pulled back, panting. "Stop. I'm gonna blow soon, and we have to get the condoms."

Kevin stared at Seth for a moment, and his face went blank. He shivered once, then nodded.

"Come on." Kevin released Seth's ass, allowing him to stand. Kevin tugged his hand and pulled him toward the beach. He dropped Seth's hand when the surf was lapping at their feet and ran, grabbing the lube and the condoms. He returned to Seth and tossed them in the sand, just out of the water. Then he fell to his knees and reached for Seth's hand, pulling him into the surf.

"Eager much?"

Kevin looked at him, then away. When he turned back, his pupils were dilated, and his voice quavered. "Maybe. Maybe nervous, a little."

It felt like cold water had splashed Seth in the face instead of the gentle lapping of the warm, salty sea. Kevin was about to be topped for the first time, and he knew it. He had probably never pictured being topped. Might even find it a bit repulsive. He could just imagine Kevin's first reaction.

Ewww, butt sex.

Seth stopped, his hands fell to his sides. Every muscle in his body froze, his prick went soft, lifeless. "I can't do this."

Panic and something more difficult to identify showed on Kevin's face. "It's okay."

Seth's head seemed to turn of its own volition, back and forth. "I can't. Not to you. You're my best friend…"

"It's okay." His voice so gentle, Kevin stroked a hand along Seth's cheek. "We need to do this. We *have* to do this."

"But you …"

A small grin tugged up Kevin's lips. "It is what it is. Just show me how. I never…" Kevin amazed Seth. He didn't dwell on things, he moved forward.

"Are you sure?"

"Yes. I want us to do this… now." Kevin rolled his eyes. "Come and, uh…take me."

A smile bloomed on Seth's lips as he held in a chuckle. "Who says that? Are you kidding?"

"Maybe." Kevin's smile widened, and the tension broke.

"Come here." Seth wrapped his arms around Kevin and pulled them together and down so they lay half in the surf, lips joined, tongues dancing, caressing.

The breaking waves tickled along his skin as Seth took

possession of Kevin's mouth, exploring every inch. He ran his hands along Kevin's back as his hip dug down into the powder soft sand. His hands drifted lower, cupping Kevin's ass, pulling him closer.

He had to top Kevin. There were no choices here. He vowed he would do everything in his power to make it the best experience he could for his friend.

He kissed his way down Kevin's jaw, loving the light stubble brushing his lips. He licked and nibbled down Kevin's neck and headed for a nipple. Nip, kiss, lick, the tiny nub hardened from the attention, and Kevin's head fell back as he moaned.

Seth continued his odyssey down Kevin's stomach, nuzzling his treasure trail and finally arriving at his destination. The object of his desire.

Kevin's prick extended out the top of the Speedo. Seth pulled back the wet bathing suit, Kevin's cock popped out, a drip of pre-come at the tip. He stutter slid Kevin's suit down his legs. While Kevin kicked the suit off, Seth stuck out his tongue and lapped up the fluid, made extra salty from their swim in the ocean.

He lowered his head and engulfed Kevin in one smooth motion, nuzzling in his pubic hair. Nothing beat the feeling of a hard shaft in his mouth and down his throat. He bobbed in a smooth rhythm and reveled in Kevin's mewls of pleasure.

Now came the delicate part. He worked slowly, bringing his fingers up Kevin's thigh, pushing lightly to spread his legs.

Kevin tensed, but Seth redoubled his efforts, bobbing faster on Kevin's cock, and the man soon relaxed. Seth reached up to tickle his balls and press on the perineum just behind. Tickle, tickle, swipe, tickle, tickle, swipe. After a few iterations, he reached further up into Kevin's trench. Just a touch. Tickle, tickle, touch.

With each touch, Seth spread Kevin's cheeks a little further, and after a few times, he laid his index finger along the crease, the pad just touching Kevin's virgin pucker.

Kevin startled a moment and then relaxed. Seth felt very much like someone gentling a wild animal, and he hated it. Because once the animal trusted him, he was going to gut him with his dagger.

He tapped at the opening and circled it, getting the muscles there used to his touch. They quivered against his finger in response.

He pulled off Kevin's cock. "This doesn't have to hurt, but you are going to need to relax and let it happen. Bear down when I push in, it helps open things up."

Kevin's face, already flushed from the pleasure of the blowjob, glowed even brighter. "Okay."

Seth poured lube on Kevin's crack and slicked up his hand. Then he licked Kevin's cock from root to tip and engulfed it from above while pushing with his finger against Kevin's hole.

The muscles tensed, resisted, but Kevin started to take deep breaths. In through the nose, out through the mouth, just like their coach taught them to get focused and in the zone for a game. Kevin's muscles loosened as Seth's finger pushed in to the first knuckle.

Kevin hissed a breath, and Seth stopped moving and waited.

"It's okay. I'm okay. Keep going. *Please.*"

Please? He must mean he needed to fulfill the requirements for Winthrop.

Seth pushed in a little further to Kevin's scorching, tight channel. He couldn't help it. He imagined what his prick would feel like in a few minutes, and the desire to rush filled him. However, he forced himself to keep to his slow pace, even if it seemed like a ship at sub-light speed could reach

Andromeda faster.

His finger was into the second knuckle now. Kevin's ring clamped down and relaxed, clamped and relaxed.

Seth slid in and out, opening the passage.

"You know, you're a lot bigger than a finger," Kevin said in a dry tone.

"Right, hot shot. This is just the beginning."

He pushed a second finger in with the next thrust, spreading them to increase the opening. He had done this before, prepared a lover, but half of them wanted it fast and hard. He would be inside by now. All of them had previous experience and most of all, not just consent to allow this, but an actual desire to participate.

Not Kevin. Still, the man was doing an admirable job of staying calm.

He pushed his fingers in deeper, searching, searching, until Kevin's hips thrust forward suddenly.

"Holy. What the fuck was that?" Kevin called out.

Seth's heart pattered. "Was it okay?"

"Are you nuts?" Kevin gazed at Seth down the length of his chest. "That was fucking fantastic."

"Prostate. Not just for uncomfortable doctor exams. We call it the sweet spot."

"Shit. Is that why guys do anal?"

Seth crooked his finger again. "Pretty much, well, there are some other perks, but that's a good one."

"Christ." Kevin moaned.

Seth added some more lube and a third finger. He aimed for that spot, making Kevin jump and curse again. Kevin's swollen, red prick leaked pre-come.

Seth withdrew his fingers and grabbed a condom. "Flip over, hands and knees."

"What? Why?"

"It's easier in that position."

"But I want to… okay."

Seth wanted to ask what Kevin was going to say, but he was already flipped and positioned.

Seth slicked his cock and ran his hand down Kevin's spine. Then he lined up his crown with Kevin's hole. Even through the condom, he could feel Kevin's opening quivering, just waiting for the intrusion.

"Bear down now." Seth rested his hands on Kevin's hips and pushed forward slowly, savoring this moment that he thought would never be possible. His eyes fixed on his cock as the head popped past the guardian ring of muscle, and he stopped, letting Kevin adjust to the feeling of this latest invader.

"What are you waiting for?"

Seth grinned. "Impatient." Breaching his lover's inner depths inch by inch, he slid deeper.

He paused at the thought. Kevin wasn't his lover. The irony of that wasn't lost as he bottomed out balls deep in the man's ass. Kevin was his friend, but maybe, for a moment he could pretend.

Seth gripped Kevin's hips harder, steadying himself, as the warm salt water lapped around his legs, baptizing their actions with its own personal benediction.

"You okay?" Seth asked.

"Yeah, just move." Kevin's breath came in fluttery pants. "Do it."

Seth started a slow thrust and pull, coming almost all the way out before rocking his hips forward. Then he took aim and slammed in.

Kevin howled.

Seth's heart raced as Kevin's passage rippled around his cock. Please, God, let that not be a scream from pain. "Did I get it?"

"Get what?" Kevin panted.

"Your sweet spot."

Kevin glared over his shoulder at Seth, his eyes blazing. "Fuck, yeah. Do it again."

"As you wish." Seth fought the urge to smile at the horrible quote from *The Princess Bride.*

Feeling a little more secure that Kevin was getting something out of this, Seth pulled out and pistoned in to Kevin's channel. Maybe Kevin's future girlfriend would need a strap-on.

Little moans and whimpers escaped Kevin. "Oh, God, yeah. Fuck me."

Seth's hips snapped in a strong rhythm. He tried not to think about how Kevin would be sore later. Maybe he could convince him to soak in that big tub back at their room.

He knew this wasn't for love, but he couldn't resist. He needed more. He pulled Kevin to a kneeling position and twisted his head to join their lips in a wet, sloppy kiss, while he continued to pound into Kevin's channel.

Seth reached around Kevin's body and wrapped his fingers around the man's steel spike and pushed him to thrust into the circle his fingers made with each pounding stroke into his backside.

Kevin's head fell back onto Seth's shoulder, and Kevin let out a loud strangled moan before he stiffened. His come shot out of him like shooting stars in a meteor shower, and his channel gripped Seth, clenching and unclenching in time with each spurt.

Seth thrust a few more times, and then he stilled. His eyes rolled into the back of his head as he filled the condom.

He must have lost it for a moment because, the next thing he knew, his panting breath was slowing. His head leaned forward on Kevin's sweat-slicked shoulder.

Cognizant that his friend would be tender, he eased himself out of Kevin's ass, holding the condom in place. Then he skinned it off and tied it, tossing it up the beach out of the way of the surf.

He encouraged Kevin to lay on his side in the sand, the water lapping his legs. He was pleased when Kevin opened his arms and engulfed him, pulling him close. Kevin ran his fingers through Seth's hair while Seth rested his head on Kevin's arm. Seth's eyes fell closed as the warmth from Kevin's body and the sun overhead soothed him.

The waves gently surged over his legs in a lulling rhythm while a seagull called out overhead.

"I get the fuss now." Kevin's voice was just a whisper.

Seth's eyes popped open, but he stared at Kevin's chest. "Really? I'm glad."

"Do you… Have you… done this?"

"Fucked? Yeah." Seth was surprised at the question. Kevin knew he wasn't a monk.

Kevin coughed, the motion of his chest pushing lightly on Seth's head. "No, been the um… receiving partner?"

Seth didn't know whether to be amused or embarrassed. This was not a topic he ever expected to discuss with Kevin, but the man was his best friend. They could talk about anything. If Kevin needed to know this…"Oh, yeah. I do both, but I usually bottom."

Seth lifted his head and glanced up at Kevin, whose head lolled back in the sand. His eyes were closed, and his face relaxed.

"Okay. 'S'good?" Kevin's voice was somewhat slurred, like he was half-asleep.

Seth smiled. Kevin looked so sweet this way, relaxed, sated. His chest swelled at the thought that he had put that expression on Kevin's face. "Yeah, real good," Seth said.

"Do some men just do one or the other?"

What was this, anal sex 101? Why would Kevin need to know this? Maybe he was thinking about a strap-on for his next girlfriend.

"Some men are tops only, others bottom. Some switch. It's all a matter of preference. How your body's wired. What nerves fire when."

"That makes sense."

They lay there until the sun and the little shells digging into their sides grew uncomfortable. Then they ran into the water to rinse off their bits and pieces.

They dressed in the Speedos, not knowing when, or how for that matter, Erex would arrive, and headed to the little shack where they left the cooler.

Bottles of water with condensation dotting the sides and sandwiches awaited them. They sat on the towels, soaking up the rays and munching the food.

"Time to head back, boys."

Seth's head shot up at the sound of Erex's voice.

They turned to see the open door had appeared, floating in the middle of the beach. Kevin huffed, and Seth shared the sentiment. One day, he wanted to retire on a beach just like this, with Kevin at his side. He sighed. There was no happy ending for them. Kevin would find his perfect girl and leave Seth behind.

They gathered their stuff, including the used condom. Nothing would mar the beautiful sand when they left.

Following Erex through the door, they arrived back at their room. The bed had been made, and clothes were laid out, including thick pants and sheepskin-lined leather jackets.

"Get showered and changed, boys. The boss has a special surprise for you." Erex gestured to the bathroom, his eyes sparkling.

Seth's heart sped. That couldn't be good.

CHAPTER TWENTY

Tuesday, April 4, 12:47 P.M.

Seth inspected the clothes on the bed: sturdy jeans, a sheepskin-lined leather jacket, a long-sleeve shirt, a pair of thick socks, a pair of warm boots, sunglasses, and a lined helmet. Most peculiar, all the garments had switches labeled heat. The sunglasses were the sports type that had a strap to keep them on. Seth's pair was, once again, prescription.

"Where could we be going now?" Kevin tilted his head.

Seth shrugged. "Skiing? The Arctic Circle?"

"I can't figure this guy out." Kevin shook his head. "This morning, we're in a tropical paradise. Now we're going to a winter wonderland?"

Seth shrugged again and smiled. "Well, at least we get to rinse off first. I've got sand in places it has no business being."

Seth ducked into the bathroom. Hopefully, Winthrop

wouldn't be giving any orders for a while. He wasn't sure he was ready to perform again.

While Kevin showered, Seth suited up, or tried to. He hated putting on jeans when his skin was damp. They stuck, and he had to shimmy into them.

When he was dressed, a bead of sweat rolled down his back, and he hadn't even turned any of the switches on yet.

As if by magic, once they were ready, a knock sounded at the door. Erex had returned. "Follow me, guys." His eyes lit. "I think the boss must really like you boys. He had to call in some favors for this one. You're going riding."

Riding? Like horses? Or did he mean motorcycles?

Kevin and Seth looked at each other. Nothing the man did indicated he liked them, and Seth didn't want a treat. The cost of owing Winthrop was astronomical.

Erex led them out to the field where the archery contest had been held. All of the targets and the tent had been removed some time in the last two days, and the barbecue pit looked dormant.

Winthrop stood at the top of a newly-erected wooden tower. He was dressed in similar warm clothes.

A small group had gathered, including their fellow *guests*, Jeff and Todd. Kevin waved. Jeff smiled back and started to come over, but Winthrop cleared his throat and began speaking.

"My friends, today I have decided to provide a special entertainment. I spoke with my friend Torkelian." Winthrop took a puff from his stogie and blew out a stream of smoke.

A couple members of the crowd gasped while the rest appeared as clueless as Seth. *What kind of name is Torkelian?*

"He's coming, and he's bringing friends. There they are now." Winthrop pointed to the sky.

Seth squinted in the direction he pointed, the sun's rays

making it difficult to see, but off in the distance, five specks grew closer and larger. Seth gasped. They weren't airplanes or hang-gliders. Whatever they were, they had flapping wings. Soon, he was able to distinguish colors: gold, red, silver, purple, and green. Heads, legs, large wings. They must have been moving fast, and they had been spotted from really far away because they were getting larger rapidly.

Scales and a tail became clearer as the one in the lead let out a loud bellow. Seth's jaw dropped, even as every nerve screamed at him to flee. This… this thing. A monstrosity only possible in movies with high CGI budgets.

Only this was real. A real *dragon*.

Winthrop laughed. "Show off!"

A few people took several steps back, Jeff and Todd held onto each other, and one man screamed. Seth panted, his heart hammering. Kevin put his hand on Seth's shoulder and gripped hard.

The lead dragon, the red one, let out a burst of flame and bellowed again.

Winthrop shouted, "Stop, you're scaring my friends." Winthrop swatted at the air, smiling.

The dragon threw his (or was it a she?) head back, and a deep sound rumbled from within the enormous creature. It took Seth a moment to determine what the sound meant. The dragon was laughing. He swooped down to land beside the tower holding Winthrop. The ground shook from his feet's impact.

Suddenly, the two-story tower made sense. It wasn't just Winthrop's Napoleon complex. A leather saddle-like thing was strapped on the dragon just in front of his wings. Winthrop leaped aboard with surprising agility and pulled on straps from the saddle that connected to the loops on his belt. Other bands wrapped around him, forming a shoulder harness.

The dragon stalked aside, much more graceful on land than Seth would have expected of a beast the size of a house. As it moved, almost catlike, his red scales gleamed in the sunlight. He took a couple steps, spread his massive wings, and leaped skyward, soaring.

What the fuck? How could he rationalize this? Like every other experience, there had to be smoke and mirrors, but… The visceral feeling of coming face-to-face with an actual dragon could not be faked. His body was certain. He stood near an ancient predator. His reaction had been programmed in his very DNA.

These dragons were real. What did that mean for every other experience he had this week?

Erex tugged at the sleeve of Seth's jacket. "You and Kevin are next. Climb."

The little man led them to the large tower and scaled it with them, his short legs barely reaching each rung. In spite of that, he scrambled up quickly. Seth followed Kevin up the ladder, a mixture of fear, astonishment, and excitement filling him. A montage of past D&D games, *Dragons Riders of Pern*, and *Game of Thrones* played in his mind.

The purple dragon, gleaming in the light like a dark amethyst, swooped down, circled them once, and landed on its haunches, the tower swaying from the impact.

"This is Isarean. She will be your mount today."

A head, as long as Seth was tall, swung around to look at him, eyes faceted like a cut gemstone. Kevin's hand landed on Seth's shoulder, squeezing.

"She can speak, but the power of it might overwhelm you. Put your hand on one of her scales," Erex said.

Seth reached out, mesmerized, touching the sparkling, polished surface.

"Hello."

"What?" It wasn't a sound so much as being engulfed in sound. Like the rumble from the bass line in a song. Seth's whole body shook.

"Don't be rude. I said 'hello.' Or at least I communicated it to you. I'm Isarean."

"How are you doing that?" Kevin asked.

"I'm vibrating sound through my scales to your ear. It's somewhat tedious, but much more effective with you puny two-legs."

"Oh." Kevin's mouth hung open.

"Erex. Did you give me the morons?"

Erex patted her. "The boss said you would be the perfect mount for these boys."

"Terrific." A puff of smoke escaped her nostrils, warming the air. *"Just what I needed."*

Kevin shook himself. "We're not morons. We've just never seen anything like you. You're amazing, like a perfectly cut gem."

"Pretty words. Flattery helps. Climb aboard. I promised Cue… Mr. Winthrop I would bear you."

Seth ran his hand through his thick bangs. Cue? What did that mean?

"Seth, you sit in front. Kevin's taller," Erex ordered.

"Okay," Seth said.

Seth scrambled aboard the saddle with much less grace than Winthrop had, but then Winthrop appeared to have ridden a dragon before. His legs stretched in front of him, sliding into hook-like supports. It was more like sitting on a gently rocking sled. Straddling a being like Isarean would be impossible for all but skilled gymnasts. Kevin slid in behind him, hooking his legs around Seth's, and Erex leaped in front of them.

"Hey, I didn't agree to carry you, too, microdot."

"I'm just showing them how the straps and harnesses work. Okay?"

"I suppose."

Erex strung the straps through Seth's belt loops. These were much more heavy duty than on normal jeans. Then Erex slid the harness over his chest and buckled him in. It felt a bit like getting strapped into one of those roller coasters that turned upside down. His stomach flipped at the possibility.

Finally, Erex flicked the switches on his clothes and placed an oxygen mask over his face. "It gets really cold up there, and the air's too thin. It's hard to breathe." He assisted Kevin with strapping in and then leaped to the tower. "It'll be easier if you wrap your arms around Seth."

That's when Seth realized just how close together they were. Kevin's pelvis was snugged right up to his ass. Close enough that he could even feel the quickly hardening lump between Kevin's legs. What was that all about?

Seth's back was flush against Kevin's torso. There was a grip for Seth to rest his hands on, but the only choice Kevin had in the tight quarters was to wrap his arms around Seth's chest and lean his chin on Seth's shoulder.

The sensation of Kevin wrapped around him created a reaction between his own legs. His traitorous prick was ready for another round.

"Ready, boys?" Isarean rumbled.

"I'm ready." Kevin called out by Seth's ear.

"Me, too," Seth said.

Isarean took a few steps to move away from the tower, and then her grape-colored wings flared to the sides, their iridescence shimmering in the golden sunlight, and leaped.

Seth's stomach tried to stay behind as Isarean took them into the air. At first, she flew in long lazy circles with Torkelian just ahead and to the left of her. A holding pattern of sorts while the other dragons landed and loaded their chosen passengers. He shuffled around to test the straps but found he was securely held to the saddle.

Neat, cultivated blocks of land like a patchwork quilt decorated the landscape in shades of brown and light green as far as Seth could see. Cows, horses, and other farm animals grazed pastureland, and every so often a farm house could be seen with smoke curling up from the chimney. Upstate New York was known for being rural, but Seth hadn't realized to what extent.

He studied the purple scales beneath him as Isarean's wings pumped. Simply magnificent. What had Isarean called Winthrop earlier... Cue?

What does she know about him?

"Now, Seth. No pumping Isarean for information. That would be cheating." Winthrop's voice almost sounded light, but there was an edge to it that set Seth's pulse skittering.

Torkelian bellowed a roar, and the dragons fell into a V formation reminiscent of geese, with Torkelian and Winthrop in the lead.

Seth had been in airplanes before, so the height wasn't too surprising. But the whipping wind in his face made him appreciate the self-heating clothes he wore. A shiver still passed through him.

"I got you," Kevin yelled over the wind.

It was true. Kevin holding him made him feel safe, like this wasn't the most bizarre experience ever.

Seth laughed and let go, at least metaphorically. He was riding a goddamn dragon, and it felt glorious.

"Time for some fun now." Isarean's words passed through Seth's body. *"Hang on."*

Seth grabbed the handle, and Kevin pulled Seth closer as Isarean flapped her wings, bringing them higher and higher before she swooped down in a deep dive. Seth's stomach plunged like the big drops on a roller coaster, and a yell escaped his mouth, but one tempered with laughter.

She wasn't going to hurt them. Winthrop would not have gone to all of this effort to kill them when he had so many easier opportunities. At least, he hoped that was true.

Seth held on tight, leaning back into Kevin's arms as Isarean spiraled up through the clouds and then flipped on her back, hanging them upside down. The blood rushed to Seth's head as Kevin's arm's tightened around him. Muted laughter, from the oxygen mask, flowed past Seth's ear.

Isarean dove and looped over in a figure eight pattern.

"Yeah!" Seth whooped, punching a fist in the air.

Seth placed a hand on Kevin's thigh. Kevin cradled him in the crook of his legs, allowing Seth to feel his friend's arousal grind against him.

Kevin spoke into Seth's ear. "This is amazing! I never imagined..."

Seth turned, his mouth so close to Kevin's lips, they would have touched if not for the clear plastic masks. Kevin's breath came in quick pants. It had to be the adrenaline rush.

"I'm glad I'm doing this with you... I mean... riding this dragon. Not the other stuff," Seth said.

Kevin's face fell for a moment and then went blank.

What? Was Kevin even upset about riding the dragon?

"Yeah, me, too. You'd never believe me if I told you about this after."

When Isarean finally landed, Seth practically fell out of the saddle when the straps were released. His legs shook from gripping so hard that they could barely hold his weight.

Kevin tumbled next to him, but turned to Isarean, placing a hand on a scale. "Thanks for that. The ride was amazing."

Seth laid his hand next to Kevin's. "I will treasure this for the rest of my life."

Isarean's huge neck bent so that she could see them, the gem facets of her eyes sparkling in the sun. *"Maybe you two-legs aren't so bad. Glad you didn't vomit. Messy. I'm happy you had fun."* She pivoted away and leaped in the air. The wind from her wings knocked them back a step.

Seth took his time climbing down the tower, hooking his elbow on each rung, his hands too raw to get a firm grip. As it was, he fell the last five feet, landing in a heap on the ground. But it was a good kind of tired and sore. Wonderful and satisfying. Like hot and heavy sex.

Kevin's cheeks were bright red from the cool wind, and his eyes gleamed like the dragon's scales. It had been a hell of a ride.

Winthrop walked up to them, back straight, not a hair out of place. "You boys have no stamina. You look wrecked."

"Sorry, Maynard." Kevin stood with his hands on his knees. "That was thrilling, but I'm beat."

"So much for youth… I guess I should let you rest while I play with some of my other… guests. Plus, I have lots of *fun* planned for you tomorrow. You'll need to be ready for action."

CHAPTER TWENTY-ONE

Tuesday, April 4, 4:32 P.M.

Back in the room, Seth, windblown and sweaty, peeled off his clothes down to his underwear, wanting to collapse. He rummaged through the dresser for something comfortable to wear.

Kevin coughed from behind him. Seth turned to see him studying his hands, his cheeks flushed like Mars.

"I'm going to use the tub," Kevin mumbled.

What had Kevin's color up? Exhaustion clouded Seth's mind. Soaking in warmth sounded wonderful, but then images of Kevin, naked, just like this morning, chased around his memory. Would he ever stop seeing that? It was such a lovely picture, but it made him feel like a pervert. He schooled his voice to a cheerful tone.

"Good idea. I'll go next."

"We could, you know, share. It's huge." Kevin focused over Seth's shoulder, his lower lip between his teeth. He huffed a breath and headed for the bathroom.

What?

Sure, the tub was ginormous, but Kevin should mind. Shouldn't he? On the other hand, they were both guys. This didn't mean anything. They showered in the group locker room all the time. Kevin probably thought it was saving water.

The sound of water running echoed from the bathroom, and Seth paused at the threshold. Kevin had stripped off his clothes and was examining a circular tin while waiting for the water to fill.

"You in?" Kevin asked.

"Sure." He vowed to keep his eyes above the waist. He turned away and stripped off his underwear.

"You mind if I put this stuff in?" Kevin held up the round container. "It's supposed to be soothing."

Seth peeked at the orange label, *Ortigia Miele di Neroli.* "Go ahead."

As the water filled, Kevin poured in a helping of the crystal sand then climbed into the tub. He settled in the bottom with a hiss and then a long breath. "Ah."

Seth tried to avert his gaze and not watch Kevin's delectable cock, nestled between his muscular legs. Seth climbed in and leaned back against the opposite side of the tub, closing his eyes. His mind spun with images of dragons, famous basketball players suddenly in their prime, and achieving his dream to actually be in space.

"Seth?"

Seth's eyes fluttered open, fixing on his friend's face.

"I'm sore. Um, down there. Is…is that normal?" Kevin ducked his head and wouldn't look at Seth.

Seth didn't know whether to smile at how adorable Kevin looked, all unsure, or feel bad that he caused it. "It's normal. I'm sorry. I didn't mean to hurt you."

"It's okay. I just wanted to make sure nothing was wrong. I don't think that crazy ride helped, but this bath does."

Seth gulped. The ride would have made it worse. However, the soothing water seemed to loosen his tongue. "I kinda like that soreness afterwards, feeling well fucked." As soon as he said it, he wished he could call it back. Duh, gay guy likes gay sex.

"I can see that." Was the red on Kevin's face from the warm water? "It does have a certain… satisfaction to it."

Awwwkard. How was Seth supposed to reply to that? Maybe ask if Kevin would do it with a girl wearing a strap-on? It wasn't any of his business, and truthfully, he didn't want to know. The image of Kevin with some girl, any girl, any one… Seth suppressed a grimace. He never had liked seeing Kevin with others, but now it was exponentially worse.

Kevin's mine.

But he wasn't, and he never would be. Seth's heart barely had any defenses left. It knew who he wanted, craved, needed even.

When did I start to need him?

The situation was intolerable.

"I'm going to catch up on some reading for school." Seth pulled himself out of the water, dried off, and headed for the bedroom.

"You study too much. I'm going to stay and soak a little while longer," Kevin called after him.

Seth dressed quickly and nibbled from a tray of assorted cheeses, crackers, veggies, and dips that had been delivered while they bathed. He grabbed his smartphone and slipped into bed, calling up some reading he needed to do on the eReader app.

It was a while before Kevin came out. Seth kept reading, not that he was absorbing anything. His eyes went over the words, but they refused to resolve into anything coherent. Maybe he should take another walk. Anything to get away for a bit and grieve in private for the relationship he could never have, but his body was just too exhausted and his heart sore.

Finally, around eight o'clock, he gave up and turned off his reading light. He went to sleep, hoping he could escape for a few hours into dreams.

* * *

"You thought this meant something?" Kevin sneered at him across their dorm room.

"No, of course not. You're straight. It was just sex."

"Bullshit, dude. You want this ass." Kevin slapped his own ass and shook it at him. "It's prime, grade A, and you're right, completely straight. What is it with gay guys lusting after straight guys? It's fucking disgusting."

"I'm not. I don't." Seth's hands came up in front of him, shielding him.

"Liar." Kevin walked over to the mirror and grabbed his comb, touching up his hair. "I'm going out tonight with a couple girls I met, and I'm gonna fuck them until dawn. Get this gay stink off of me."

"I..."

"You don't want me to go, but I'm not yours."

Kevin walked closer and stood behind Seth. He leaned in and started planting kisses on Seth's neck, soft, gentle, and, oh, so arousing.

"What are you doing, man?"

"What does it look like, Einstein?"

"What about the girls?"

* * *

Seth opened his eyes. Just a dream… But the kisses on his neck continued.

What?

Seth lay under the blankets of the bed with his back to Kevin, who was nestled up against him, his erection pressing Seth's buttocks. Kevin kissed Seth's neck with gentle pecks and licks, sending arousal coursing through Seth and waking his cock, which stood up and took notice.

Seth turned his head to look Kevin in the eye, but Kevin's were closed. He just kept kissing whatever was in front of him like…

Holy shit, he's asleep.

Their lips joined, and Kevin's tongue poked inside, sending the most amazing sensations whipping through Seth.

This is wrong. He doesn't know what he's doing.

Kevin's arm came over him, pulling on his waist, until Seth's ass was right against Kevin's thrusting hips. Kevin moaned, and Seth wanted this to go on forever. His cock, now fully hard, was ready for action, ready for anything.

"Kev?"

Kevin whispered against his mouth, "Ung, just kiss me."

What was Kevin dreaming? Who did he think he was kissing?

"Kev, s'me Seth."

"Less talking, more making out." Kevin kept dotting his

back with kisses.

Sensation rippled through him from each contact, making him pulse with want. "Kev, this feels great and all, but…."

"Just shut up. Let it happen."

Seth flipped to face Kevin and shook him. "Wake up!"

Kevin's eyes shot open. "What? I'm awake."

"You were kissing me."

"I know. I woke up and we were kissing and…I just went with it." Kevin shrugged.

Seth's mind tried to process that, but all that would compute was *Duh*. "What?"

"I went with it. I…is that a problem?" Kevin sounded so casual, like this was what they did, although his face was unreadable in the dark room.

Seth blinked several times. "What?"

"Can you pick another word?" Kevin's voice hardened.

"Why would you keep kissing if you knew it was me?" That was the real question.

"Um… I…it's not like we haven't been all week. It just seemed okay. For all I knew, Winthrop ordered you to."

And there it was. This all came down to Kevin trying to do what he needed to do to get through the challenge.

"He didn't," Seth said.

"Oh, okay then." Kevin's voice sounded a little higher than normal. He flipped over to face away from Seth. "Good. I'll just… go back to sleep."

"I understand. G'night."

"G'night." Was that hurt in Kevin's voice?

Seth rolled over and tried to sleep, but couldn't. He kept replaying the conversation over and over in his mind. He had spared Kevin, right?

CHAPTER
TWENTY-TWO

Wednesday, April 5, 7:56 am

Seth crawled out of bed, feeling strung out and exhausted. He had barely slept, his eyes stung, and his heart ached. What the fuck was he supposed to do with all of this?

Kevin was already up, dressed, shoving a croissant into his mouth, and doing something on his computer.

Seth stumbled to the bathroom, did his business, and showered. Having received no orders, he dressed in jeans and a T-shirt, and walked over to Kevin. "Kev, I …" The room competed with the surface of Mercury for highest temperature.

"No worries, man. It's cool."

If it was cool, why wasn't Kevin turning around to look at him? Why did he feel as if he disappointed Kevin somehow? Shouldn't Kevin be relieved to have one less embarrassing memory?

There was nothing more Seth wanted to do than continue their middle of the night tryst, but he couldn't live with himself if he forced himself on Kevin.

A knock sounded at the door, and Erex came in. "Come on, boys. We're taking a little trip."

Back to yet another elevator. Could the house really have this many elevators, or was something else going on? In a world where people rode dragons, anything seemed possible. Seth gave up trying to apply the laws of the real world to this place. He was like the scientists positing dark matter to account for five-sixths of the matter in the universe. They had never observed it, but it explained the data. Winthrop's home ran on laws that were outside of Seth's experience.

They traveled up to the fourth floor this time, which was fun considering it was a three-story building. The door opened to the roof. Seth squinted against the bright sun. A helicopter sat in the middle of a painted circle, blades already spun up.

Erex yelled over the noise of the rotor, "Come on, that's our ride."

Kevin and Seth ducked their heads as they ran with Erex. Seth's bushy mane whipped at his face, and his T-shirt rippled around him. After they strapped into seats, the helicopter lifted in a smooth motion. So much less exciting than yesterday's amazing ride. As they crossed the border for Winthrop's property, an electric tingle passed up Seth's body.

After about an hour, they came to a populated area, a city. Tall buildings filled the skyline. He knew New York well enough to know this wasn't it. What other cities were close enough? Did that even matter? A man who could send them to space in half an hour or instantaneously to the Caribbean could have flown them anywhere in an hour. For all he knew, this was Tokyo.

He had his first hint when they approached a building near water... big water, the ocean. This wasn't the blue-green waters of the Caribbean but the darker waters Seth associated with his home state of Connecticut.

The helicopter veered toward a brick building by the harbor and set down on its helipad. The blades spun down, and Erex led them to a door on the roof.

"Where are we?" Kevin asked.

Erex smirked. "On a roof."

"Thanks, Erex. Not helpful," Kevin replied.

Why does Kevin try? They never answer.

Seth shivered as a cool, misty wind blew past.

They took a staircase down one flight, arriving at a single door.

Erex knocked in a rhythmic pattern: tap, knock, tap, knock, tap, knock, and then entered.

An elegant foyer greeted them, decorated in beige. A mirror hung on the wall across from the door with a hallway leading to the left and right. Erex lead them to the right to a tastefully designed sitting area. A dining area opened to the left.

Winthrop sat on the loveseat, his bulk making it look like a large chair. Seth stifled a laugh. The loveseat wasn't on some crazy platform. "Thanks for coming, gentlemen. Please, have a seat." Winthrop gestured to two single chairs across from him and inhaled a puff from his cigar.

Seth sank into the soft, maroon chenille chair. So comfortable. On the coffee table in front of the seats were two envelopes.

"I've decided to make you an offer, gentlemen. After this week is done, I want both of you to come work for me."

Kevin answered before Seth could form a coherent thought. "We haven't finished school."

"Not a problem. Part of my compensation package is to

pay your way through the rest of school. That includes medical school for you, Kevin, and, Seth, if you want an advanced degree, say a PhD, well, you got it."

Holy shit!

All week, Seth stood on a foundation of quicksand. Nothing made sense. None of the usual rules applied. How could he even consider extending his stay in Winthrop's magical mystery world? There had to be some catch.

Kevin opened his mouth to speak.

Winthrop held up his hand. "I'll answer all your questions. But first, Rosa?"

An older woman about an inch shorter than Winthrop, in a black and white maid's uniform, stepped forward. "Yes, Mr. Winthrop?" she said with some kind of accent, perhaps Spanish.

"Give the boys a tour of their signing bonus."

"Yes, Mr. Winthrop. Please follow me." She gestured around them. "This is the main living room."

Seth glanced over at Kevin, who shrugged and stood, following her.

"Through these doors is the terrace that overlooks Boston Harbor. It's a bit cold out there right now, although we could turn on the gas fireplace out there to warm it up if you like."

A waterfront apartment with a view. *Holy crap.*

"That won't be necessary," Kevin said.

"This is the dining room, and through here is the kitchen."

The large space had a center island with a built-in stove and generous gleaming granite counters.

Seth had never done much cooking, but Kevin studied the room with eyes as wide as the moon.

"Look, double ovens. Do you know how many cookies I could bake at Christmas time?" Kevin asked.

"Dude, how are you not as big as a house?"

"Exercise, asshole." Kevin punched Seth in the arm.

"I'll be available to prepare breakfast and dinner for you as needed," Rosa stood with her hands clasped in front of her. "This is the laundry room, and through here is my room." A room large enough to hold a bed and a three-quarter bathroom was neat and tidy. Pictures of children, presumably family, hung on the walls. "This way, please."

Her room. As in she's a live-in maid? *No way.*

Out of the kitchen and down the hall, they passed an elevator inside the apartment and a small guest half-bathroom.

The apartment had its own elevator. Seth laughed and pointed it out to Kevin.

"Maynard would accept nothing less," Kevin said.

For a moment, this felt normal. He and Kevin looking at an apartment, planning a life together. Seth wished it could be real with all of his might.

Next, she showed them a sitting room with a foldout sofa bed. "This is a guest bedroom with attached bathroom." A brick fireplace stood on the left wall.

Seth pictured his parents visiting. Staying in this room.

Then they entered the master suite. The huge king-size bed stood against the left wall. A door on each side led to enormous walk in closets with a chair, full-length mirror, and dresser.

This wasn't an apartment for two friends, it was designed for a couple. *Oh, my stars...*

"This is the dressing space."

Another door on the left led to a giant bathroom with a whirlpool tub and an oversized shower.

Just like at the mansion. Winthrop imagines us bathing together.

Across from the bed was a large fireplace surrounded by a white marble mantle with a large screen TV mounted above it.

"This fireplace is a fully functional wood fireplace, as is the one in the sitting room next door. Very cozy for those long winter nights."

Romance. This suite was designed for two lovers.

Unlike the maid's room, this room looked empty and unlived in.

We could hang Kevin's autographed photo of Eli Manning to the right of the fireplace.

They could display their various family photos on the mantel. A homey image filled Seth's mind.

As she led them back down the hall to find Winthrop, Seth steeled himself. He could dream about it all he wanted, but this was all impossible.

"Sit." Winthrop gestured to the chairs again.

What are we, dogs?

"So what do you think of the place?"

Seth looked at Kevin, who shrugged, and then turned to Winthrop. "It's nice. What did you mean, signing bonus?"

"It's for you. Both of you. If you accept my offer."

"Why? We live in Ithaca." Kevin asked.

"Shortsighted." Winthrop shook his head. "You have a little over a year until you graduate with your class. Kevin here is dreaming of Harvard Medical School. With his grades and my influence, he's already been accepted. Seth, MIT is excited to meet you. I know it's on your shortlist of choices. I didn't even have to endow a chair. It seems some research you did was quite exceptional, and they would be pleased if you did your graduate studies with them."

MIT? It was his first choice, if he could get in. He only considered the others because MIT was a stretch.

Living here. Going to his dream school. Kevin at a top medical school. The two of them together. Life like a clear night, the stars out in their multitude and never a cloud. Too bad those stars were about to implode. Winthrop was one sick bastard. Seth couldn't even begin to fathom what the fucktard would want for all of this.

"Here's the deal. You get this apartment, full ride for the rest of your schooling. After graduate school, you come work for me. Seth, you get a lab, funding and resources, people. You build the team, and you go explore space. Who knows, maybe I'll build a hotel on Mars."

Seth stared at the man. He was an undergrad. It would take him years after grad school to work up to a lab of his own.

"Kevin, you will be on my medical staff. They take care of my employees. I find it's cheaper to hire my own than deal with a broken system like medical insurance. Every member of the medical staff is given access to labs to do research. I know you're fascinated by artificial limbs. I can arrange for you to meet Dr. Hugh Herr and get a lab set up to aid in his research."

Seth looked over at Kevin. His eyes sparkled, and his breath quickened. A secret dream that Winthrop had once again ferreted out?

"The best part, you two get to be together. I'll see to it."

Seth crashed in his mind. "We *get* to be together?"

"Of course. I've seen the way you two are with each other. Even before this week. Now I'm certain. You two are completely in love."

A volcano of emotion welled up in Seth. Winthrop's notions had already hurt Kevin so much. "Excuse me. I don't know what delusional world you're living in. This whole week has been some strictly concocted fantasy for your entertainment. Kevin and I are friends, not lovers. This, all of this, is some sick plan of yours to keep us under your thumb. The apartment is probably filled with cameras so you can watch all of the sex you imagine we'll have. Keep the fantasy going."

Winthrop's nostrils flared, and he shook his lit cigar at them. "Watch your tongue, boy. You still owe me one more day."

Seth inhaled and schooled his expression to calm. "With all due respect. I'll meet your needs until the end of the deal we made, but I'm not interested in anything further."

"Kevin, what about you?" Winthrop asked.

Kevin stared at Seth. His mouth started to move then stopped. He seemed lost in thought, then he nodded to himself and plastered a smile on his face, although it didn't reach his eyes. "This is a very generous offer, but Seth's right. We're just friends. We'll go our separate ways after college."

A knife pierced Seth's heart and twisted. Separate after college, permanent heart amputation.

"Besides, I don't want to be a family doctor. I'm going to study sports medicine and become an orthopedic surgeon. Maybe work with athletes. I want to get into Harvard on my own merits."

"I think you boys are making a huge, shortsighted mistake. On so many levels. I've seen you together."

Kevin shrugged. "We did what you asked. Nothing more."

"We'll see about that. I have one more challenge left for you tonight. Erex, take them back to the mansion. Let them select their costumes and get ready. Tonight is a masquerade ball. When the masks come off at midnight, we'll see what is revealed."

CHAPTER
TWENTY-THREE

The whump-whump of the propeller blades as they rode back to the mansion in the helicopter was loud enough to make conversation difficult. The situation they were in made it impossible.

Stupid, stupid, stupid.

Seth should have played along and not angered Winthrop. Or at least did what Kevin had done and declined politely. But really, what the fuck was up with the crazy man? Everything he offered was a dream come true, a PhD from MIT, a lab of his own for real space exploration, and Kevin, all on a silver platter.

Would Kevin have accepted if he had? Would he have agreed to be Seth's fuck toy to get a free ride? No, that was unfair. Kevin had more strength and integrity than that. A week was one thing, but living together in a one-bedroom gilded cage was so not his style.

He wanted to reach out and squeeze Kevin's hand, do something to wipe the miserable look off his best friend's face, but he didn't know how. Would Kevin interpret it as Seth coming on to him?

Winthrop had said they had one last challenge, and then he was done with them. But what would be left of Seth's heart? The walls were down, the red, beating organ exposed. He could have had everything if he agreed to Winthrop's proposal. No, he would never *have* Kevin. Not really, not in the way that counted.

He would never have the man's heart. They weren't *soul mates*. Kevin would find a girl. It was just that simple.

So one more challenge, in costumes. Great. One more round of make-believe. A fitting finale to a whole week that felt like one big masquerade.

After about an hour, they crossed in to Winthrop's land, and sparkles crawled over Seth's skin. The helicopter landed on the roof of the mansion, and Erex led them to the elevator, pushing the button for the second floor. They walked down a hallway and turned into yet another impossible room.

Racks and racks of clothing and costumes filled the gymnasium-sized space. At one end of the aisles, several women worked at sewing machines. Beside them stood a three-way mirror with a circular fitting platform in the middle. A man wearing a Julius Caesar costume perched on it while a woman knelt and placed pins.

"The boss keeps costumes in stock." Erex gestured to the aisles of garments. "He likes to throw masquerades and hates it if anyone has a low-quality costume, so everyone just comes here to get one that is up to *his* standard. If we don't have it, the girls can make it. What would you boys like to be?"

Seth turned to Kevin. "Any thoughts?"

Kevin shook his head. "Too many." Kevin's voice lowered to a whisper. "Look at the choices."

Seth smiled. Kevin loved Halloween. They both did. Last year, they had dressed as zombie basketball players with elaborate makeup. "Could we just browse?" Seth asked Erex.

"Sure. Each row is labeled." Erex pointed to the sign for the first row. "I'll come back to check on you later."

Seth and Kevin looked at the signs above the rows.

Kevin pointed to a row labeled 'Sci-Fi movies.' "Let's try this one."

Uniforms and other outfits filled the space, from *Alien* to *Star Wars*, *Terminator* to *Men in Black*, it seemed like every major motion picture was represented. There was an entire section devoted to *Star Trek* that contained uniforms from classic Trek movies, Next Generation movies, and the latest ones that rebooted the series. Uniforms from the original TV series and all the spin-offs were there as well. Seth decided not to quibble that these weren't movies. Each uniform came with a bag of accessories, including communicators, tricorders, and phasers.

"We could go as Kirk and Spock?" Seth held out the classic gold and blue shirts.

Kevin lifted an eyebrow. "I'd have to be Spock, wouldn't I?"

"Why you?"

"Your hair is too bushy."

Seth imagined a mop-haired Spock and snorted a laugh. "Okay, let's keep looking."

Another aisle was labeled 'Superheroes' and had every comic book hero imaginable, including Superman, Batman, Wonder Woman, the X-Men, and the Avengers. They had costumes that looked like they came straight from the movie set and also ones from every era of the comic book's art, and TV costumes as well. A blond guy examined the Tick's distinctive blue suit.

Next, they turned down an aisle labeled 'Medieval.' Suits of chainmail and plate mail stood in a line.

Kevin lifted up a mail shirt to examine it and fumbled, almost dropping it. "Damn, this is heavy."

They passed by a myriad of assorted gowns intended for women dressing in the medieval period.

The rows went on and on.

They turned down a row labeled TV shows, and Kevin stopped in front of a bunch of costumes for *Supernatural.*

"We could go as Sam and Dean."

Seth loved *Supernatural.* Sam and Dean, the main characters, were both smoking hot. He even read some fan fiction about the duo, but he thought Dean and the angel character, Castiel, would make a better couple. Right in front of him was Castiel's trench coat, Bobby's baseball cap, and Dean's signature leather jacket.

"Okay, but you're Dean."

"Awesome," Kevin said in Dean's signature sarcastic tone.

"Nice." Seth pushed him on the arm. "True to character."

They grabbed the clothes and headed up the aisle to the seamstresses.

The girl at the sewing machine looked to be about sixteen years old and had brown hair with orange tips. "Sam and Dean. Cool."

"What's a pretty girl like you doing here?" Kevin asked in a husky voice.

Seth's cheeks heated. Kevin couldn't resist flirting. How was Seth supposed to deal with all this?

"Charmer. Follow me, boys." She led them to a changing

room and brought in two artists.

"Sam and Dean have tattoos. We'll just paint them on," the girl said. "Mr. Winthrop insists on authenticity when possible. Shirts off."

Seth averted his eyes as Kevin's shirt came over his head. He would have thought that after having sex for a week with the guy, Seth wouldn't be so drawn to his lean muscular chest, wide shoulders, and six-pack abs. But that was not to be. Instead, he was even more attracted.

A young man wearing a tank top that showed off his completely inked arms approached Seth, while a girl wearing a white dress and white boots went to Kevin. The two artists painted the anti-possession pentagram design in painstaking detail on the left pectoral muscle toward the center just like in the show.

After that, the costumes were easy. Genius, really, they would be comfortable all night. Seth wore fitted jeans and a brown T-shirt with a tan windbreaker. A stylist came in and brushed his mop to resemble Sam.

Kevin also wore a T-shirt and jeans, with the signature leather coat over it. His short hair matched Dean's close enough that the stylist sprayed some product and declared it done.

Erex arrived and smiled at them from behind an eye patch. "Sam and Dean. So good of you to join us. I bet you'll find several vampires, werewolves, and other creatures tonight, but no killing."

Seth grinned at Erex the pirate. He even appeared to have a genuine peg leg. These people took costumes seriously.

Erex led them back to their room where a lunch tray had been set out.

"I'll pick you up at six o'clock. Don't ruin the costumes." Erex left.

Seth looked down at the ratty clothes. What constituted wrecking?

"Were you tempted today?" Kevin's expression rivaled top poker players.

"Tempted? By what?"

"The job offer. He was going to pay you to follow your dreams." Kevin's eyes bore down on him.

"Maybe." Seth tried to keep his gaze steady. "But what would I have to do in return? Winthrop doesn't do things that don't benefit him in some way."

"You have a good point. He's a cold bastard." A glare of pure hatred crossed Kevin's face. Seth guessed it really had been awful for Kevin this week, doing things his body wasn't made for.

Seth couldn't help wondering. "Were you?"

"What?"

"Tempted?"

"Maybe." Kevin studied his hands. "For like a minute. He dangled... Harvard."

A twinge tightened in Seth's belly. "I know you want to go to Harvard. You don't need him to get there."

Kevin shrugged. "It's a dream. He claims I have the grades, but it's such a long shot." Kevin's body drooped.

"You'll do it. You can do anything." *Way to sound infatuated...*

"What about you? Isn't MIT high on your list?" Kevin asked.

"MIT would be sweet. I could stay at Cornell or head to Caltech. There are a few others. It depends on where I get in."

"It would be cool if we went somewhere together." Kevin widened his eyes. "We could still be roommates."

A week ago, Seth would have jumped at that. Now, he

could barely imagine sharing a room for the rest of the year, much less several more. Being so close to Kevin and not being able to touch him was getting harder and harder.

"Yeah, maybe."

The frown that crossed Kevin's face was there and gone. Seth almost thought he imagined it.

Seth's mouth spoke before he thought about it. "We have time before we need to decide anything."

* * *

When Erex arrived at six, they were ready. He handed them each a long, fake knife to complete their costumes. Seth studied the wicked, jagged blade with runes carved in the side, glad it was made of something soft. Then Erex gave them wallets with fake FBI credentials and a vial of liquid.

"Holy Water. Blessed by an actual god."

Seth laughed and pocketed the fake credentials and vial.

Erex stared at Seth for a moment before gesturing for them to follow him to the elevator. This time, it had symbols on the buttons instead of numbers. Erex pressed the button that had a white bubbly thing that looked like a cloud on it. The elevator ascended, again passing way more than the three floors—or even four if you counted the roof—that could possibly exist in the mansion. It was becoming so commonplace that Seth barely even considered how it was happening.

When the elevator opened, so did Seth's mouth. In front of him was a floor that was fluffy white, like cotton, or Cumulus clouds on a warm day. There were no walls, just blue sky all around and above them. Seth expected it would be cold, but it was temperate, so he assumed this must be another illusion. At least until he looked around and saw strategically placed wood burning fire pits, giving the air a pleasant smoky smell. A tent ceiling held up by 4 poles at the corners sat about fifty yards away housing a buffet, a band, and a dance floor.

But the amazing part was the people. There were perhaps a hundred dressed in every costume imaginable. There were a group of zombies, a Green Lantern, Boba Fett, and someone donning a steampunk outfit. Several different Presidents of the United States, including Washington, Lincoln, and JFK, stood chatting together. No Jackie or Marilyn in sight.

Someone had braved the chainmail shirt and dressed as a Knight Templar. He conversed with Mork from Ork, who seemed to have lost Mindy.

That's when Seth realized that, once again, there were no women in the room. Not even the attendants at the buffet or members of the band.

Seth and Kevin made their way to the buffet. Several people greeted them along the way. "Hello Sam, hello Dean." Jeeze, these people really knew their *Supernatural*.

Walking on the white fluffy stuff disconcerted Seth. His feet sank in perhaps a quarter of an inch but never really hit solid ground. More like some physical force, friction perhaps, prevented him from sinking. He had never experienced anything like it. Once he lifted a foot, the fluff returned to its original position, a pristine white as if it had never been touched.

Kevin and Seth found seats at a square table for two just outside the tent near the raised platform at the right. A huge chair was situated on the platform. It looked almost big enough to be a love seat. Constructed of a red stone that resembled marble, it had a white cushion and a heart-shaped pillow backrest. The back of the chair rose a good ten feet and was carved with Greek letters, hearts, and bows and arrows. The circular arms of the chair were fronted with cherubs holding bows and arrows as well.

He loves his tacky thrones.

Winthrop arrived in their midst on a golden palanquin with red accents and red poles. Four seven-foot-tall people dressed as completely convincing Cyclops, carried it on their shoulders while Winthrop reclined.

But it was Winthrop's costume that really shocked Seth. The man was wearing a white diaper with a huge gold baby pin. A white sash with gold accents crossed his dark chest hair and huge paunch. On his back was a pair of small wings, red with gold-tipped accents. He had a gold band around his arm with heart-shaped stones, and he carried a small bow and arrow. The arrow heads were shaped like hearts.

Oh, my God, Winthrop is dressed as Cupid.

Seth couldn't believe his eyes. The man was embarrassing himself. The costume left far too little to the imagination, showing off rolls of fat on Winthrop's body. The little diaper was utterly ridiculous.

Still, the guests applauded as the palanquin was set down in front of the throne, and Winthrop stood with the help of the Cyclops. He turned, facing the crowd, and pretended to look around, targeting the arrow.

When his eyes fell on Seth and Kevin, he pulled back and released the fake bow as if to shoot them, his eyes gleaming. For a moment, Seth wished Cupid was real. Maybe if Kevin were shot with his arrow, his friend could love a man.

Winthrop sat with a flourish, and servants scurried around him, bringing food, wine, and a cigar.

Seth focused on the food in front of him but found he had little appetite. At some time during the night, they would have one more challenge. He wondered what Winthrop had in store and dreaded it because he had a feeling it would be amazing and riddle him with guilt.

"Sam, Dean." A husky voice spoke from above them.

Seth looked up, amazed that someone else came dressed in a *Supernatural* costume. "Castiel?" A man he hadn't met before stood behind them, dressed in the angel Castiel's signature trench coat.

"Of course, were you expecting the Easter Bunny? Although why anyone would think my father would want to be celebrated by a rabbit that laid eggs are somewhat confusing."

Seth was impressed. This guy took his character seriously with dialog reminiscent of his character in the show.

Kevin spoke, "Would you like to join us? It gives our costumes more mojo."

"Actually, I came to ask Sam to dance."

Seth drew back. Why would this man want to dance with him?

Kevin looked up at Castiel with wide eyes. "Cass, say it isn't so. I always thought you and I had something special."

Now Kevin spoke like Dean from *Supernatural* fan fiction? Could this night get any stranger? Of course, it could. When Winthrop involved himself, up was down, black was purple with pink polka-dots, and marshmallows could speak.

Cass shrugged. "Perhaps, in the show. But I can't resist. Your costume partner is adorable."

Kevin frowned up at the angel look-alike, but Seth thought perhaps this was a good idea. A way to start rebuilding those walls. He stood and followed Castiel to the crowded dance floor.

The notes of *Imagine Dragons'* 'Radioactive' filled the space. The dance started innocently enough. Two gay guys losing themselves to the music. Cass's hands landing on his hips surprised him even though they faced each other as they moved in the sinuous rhythm. It felt wrong somehow with Kevin's gaze on them.

Seth considered excusing himself as Cass pressed closer

and closer.

Wrong, this was wrong. His nerves screamed. But this was reality. Here was an attractive man who was actually interested in him. He needed to let go of the fantasy that Kevin was or ever would be his partner. He stayed and lifted his hands above his head, swaying in time to the music.

Seth turned his back and let the guy grind into his ass. There was no mistaking the bulge in the man's pants. Castiel liked what he was doing, a lot, and Seth wasn't surprised by that. He'd hooked up like this in clubs before. It all felt pretty standard.

What wasn't standard was his complete lack of response. He knew he was screwed. Somewhere along the week, his body decided it belonged to Kevin, even though Kevin didn't want it.

He redoubled his efforts, willing his body to react. He remembered earlier in the week, teaching Kevin to dance like this. How they both had responded. Was there any chance Kevin could have interest in him? He doubted it, even as he wanted to believe.

His eyes fell closed, he imagined it was Kevin behind him, and he could feel that extra shimmy in his hips and the beginning of a response in his flaccid member, just from the fantasy. Oh, he was so fucked.

A tap on his shoulder startled his eyes open.

Kevin's face made granite look soft. "Cass, I'm cutting in."

"Really? I didn't think this was your thing," Cass said.

Kevin's eyes narrowed as he stared Cass down. "It doesn't matter what you think. Back away."

What the fuck? Why was Kevin acting like this? Why would he care?

The Castiel look-alike shrugged. "You okay, Sam?"

It took Seth a moment to realize the guy meant him. His heart raced, and his face heated. "It's cool."

"Maybe we'll dance again later."

Catching the belligerent look on Kevin's face, Seth was pretty sure he wouldn't be dancing with the man in the angel costume again.

Kevin slotted in behind him and picked up the sway of the music. It was easy for Seth to lose himself in it now. To lean into the man and grind. Kevin's scent surrounded him as his hands shifted up and down. Damn, he learned the moves fast.

At the end of the dance, Erex was waiting for them and led them off the dance floor to Winthrop.

Winthrop focused on Kevin. "You didn't seem to appreciate my little gift."

"Excuse me? What gift?" Kevin's eyebrows climbed.

"So polite. I sent Castiel to complement your Sam and Dean. I figured the three of you would go off and… I believe the term for kill is… gank something. In fact, I remember them taking on some mythological gods. Perhaps you would come after me." He held his hand to his chest in an exaggerated gesture. "I am Cupid, after all."

Seth fought the urge to laugh in the man's face. He was the most disgusting, ridiculous excuse for a Cupid that could be imagined. However, he was impressed that Winthrop knew anything about *Supernatural*. The show didn't seem like his sort of thing.

Kevin's voice was gruff. "Castiel didn't seem to know his part. In the show, he helps Sam and Dean. He doesn't take Sam from Dean."

"I noticed that." Winthrop smirked. "Sam and Dean are inseparable."

Kevin frowned. "You and Cass should remember that."

Seth was confused. Were they still talking about the show or something else?

"Well, this is a marvelous segue into the final challenge, boys." Winthrop snapped his fingers, and everything around them, the party, the people in costumes, everything but the clouds and Winthrop, disappeared. Where music surrounded them before, now only silence.

"Where did… how… what?" Seth stuttered.

"Doesn't matter. It's safe for you to trust that you are somewhere quite alone for your final challenge." Another finger snap, and a bed made of the same cottony stuff as the floor rose. Next to it, a table appeared with a tray of chocolate-dipped strawberries, a bottle of champagne on ice, and two champagne flutes. "I wasn't sure if you boys had enough to eat. Mustn't let you get hungry. You'll need your stamina. So here's a little snack."

"Enough with the food. What's the challenge?" Kevin asked.

"So impatient. One thing is crystal clear to me. You boys are in love. I think you've been in love for a long time. It's not for me to say what's been holding you back, but it's time for that to end. Tonight, you will tell each other the truth about your feelings. Both of you. From the heart. I mean it, boys, no bullshit. You know the consequences for failure."

How would Winthrop know if it was bullshit? Why would he do this? Ask Seth to take his already bleeding heart and rip it out and present it to Kevin. What was Kevin going to do? He couldn't have real feelings for Seth. Could he?

Seth glanced at Kevin and met his eyes. The man was white as the clouds around him, panting slightly.

"After you have a lovely heart-to-heart, I expect you to consummate your revelations by making love. I'll even be generous. I don't care who tops. You can choose. Lube and condoms are right," another snap, "there." A bottle of lube and a strip of condoms appeared on a bump in the clouds next to the bed. "Good night, boys. Make it good. You've come so far, I would hate for it to all fall apart now. *Au revoir.*"

And before their eyes, Winthrop vanished.

CHAPTER TWENTY-FOUR

Wednesday, April 5 11:49 P.M.

Seth stared for several moments at the spot Winthrop had occupied.

Impossible.

Everything was impossible, and Seth was beyond trying to explain. Here he was in the clouds in a room with a bed made of the fluffy white substance.

And he had to tell Kevin how he felt.

Could he do that? What was Kevin going to do? Seth knew the answer. Kevin was going to say whatever he thought Winthrop wanted to hear.

What did Winthrop have on Kevin? What were the stakes for his friend if he failed? They had to be significant and horrible given what Kevin had been forced to do. Certainly Winthrop had Seth and his family by the short hairs. He hadn't

239

come this far to lose everything, their house, his education, his father's job.

Seth was lucky in a way. All he had to do to meet Winthrop's challenge was tell the truth since that coincided with what Winthrop believed in his usually deranged imagination. It would be embarrassing since Kevin couldn't feel the same way, but he would have plausible deniability later. He could say he was just doing what he had to do.

It might even be a relief for Seth to say the words out loud. God knew they circled around in his mind far too often.

Kevin walked over to the table and took the bottle of champagne. He fumbled with it a bit before the cork popped off, a dribble of the bubbly liquid spilling out. He filled the two glasses, replaced the bottle in the ice, and lifted his flute with a shaking hand.

Seth reached for the other glass. Maybe liquid courage would be a good idea right now. Reminding himself that telling the truth was easy, doing it was another matter as tiny stars went supernova in his belly.

Kevin held up his glass, and Seth stepped forward and clinked his to Kevin's.

"What are we toasting?" Seth asked.

Kevin shrugged. "To us?"

Seth could see the wisdom in that toast. Winthrop wanted declarations of love. "To us." He took a sip of the bitter liquid, the bubbles tickling his nose. Champagne wasn't really his thing.

Kevin put down his glass and picked up a strawberry. The edges were a perfect red, while the rest was coated in creamy chocolate. He lifted it toward Seth's lips.

As the strawberry came toward him, Seth's heart thudded. He searched Kevin's face for a clue about the sweet and romantic gesture and met his eyes. When he opened his lips and bit down on the strawberry, the moment became intimate and erotic. Especially the way Kevin's eyes followed his mouth, his pupils dilated.

At the same time, confusion pelted him like a meteor shower. Why would Kevin react to this?

The flavor of chocolate and sweet, juicy strawberry caressed his tongue. Kevin's mouth dropped open a bit, and he dragged in a breath when Seth licked a stray dribble from the corner of his lips.

Seth discarded his glass and grabbed a strawberry of his own, bringing it to Kevin's lips. The way the man opened his mouth and engulfed the strawberry brought the most pornographic memories to mind. He thought of the day they sixty-nined. Remembered the feel of those full lips wrapped around his cock. That certainly got his prick's attention.

Kevin swallowed, his Adam's apple bobbing. He looked Seth directly in the eyes and reached out, taking Seth's hand.

"Seth Griffin. For the last three years, you have been my best friend. You're my go to guy. The person I can trust more than anyone. But I have kept something from you. A secret inside. I think I kept it from myself. But I can't keep it any longer. Seth, I love you. I think I have for a long time now. This week just made me face myself and the truth about how I feel."

The soft look in Kevin's eyes made him appear so sincere. Seth's heart melted just a little. He wanted to believe so badly. Could Kevin really fake this just to entertain their host? It was like that day in space, seeing the Earth for the first time, a whole new perspective. One filled with infinite possibilities and wonder.

Seth's words tumbled out of his mouth. "Kevin Fields. I've wanted you from the moment we met, but I settled for less because you don't go for guys. Friendship with someone as amazing as you was enough." Fear tried to grab Seth, tightening his stomach, but he pushed the feeling aside. "Or so I told myself because it was all I could have. I couldn't have the love I really wanted. And I did want it, and I do want it. I love you. This week has shown me what we could be like together. I've never felt this way about anyone else. No one makes me feel the way you do."

Kevin stepped forward and wrapped his arms around Seth and pulled him into a passionate embrace, joining their lips, claiming Seth.

Seth couldn't think, his brain refused to consider all the amazing things he heard and all the truths he just said. Possible? Impossible? This whole week was impossible, but every moment had happened.

His cock plumped, and need zinged through every nerve in his body from Kevin's kisses. From his best friend's embrace. From the way Kevin's hands caressed up and down his back. All of it.

Was there something here? It felt so real, so right, like they just...*fit*.

The scent of Kevin's leather jacket and that unique spice that was just Kevin swirled around him, making him giddy. Seth shifted his hands under the leather and pushed the jacket off Kevin's back. Suddenly, he needed skin, all of it, now.

Seth yanked Kevin's T-shirt off and stripped his own. He pulled Kevin close, their chests rubbing together, just right.

"I need you." Kevin moaned. "I love you so much."

"Right back at'cha."

Tugging the button on Seth's jeans, Kevin's hand trembled as he eased the zipper down, his hand so close to Seth's trapped erection.

Kevin's eyes met Seth's as he reached in and slowly shimmied the pants and briefs down Seth's legs, sinking to his knees, freeing Seth's shaft, which bobbed forward.

This feels so real. I want to believe...

Kevin engulfed the purple head of Seth's swollen prick, licking, eliciting little mewls from Seth.

Seth placed a hand on Kevin's head to steady himself and watch his cock disappear into Kevin's mouth. He resisted the urge to thrust, but it was hard, so hard. He ached to plant his hands on his lover's head and thrust, but he didn't want to hurt Kevin.

Kevin pulled off. "Do it, fuck my mouth. Use me."

Seth didn't know where this was coming from, but he couldn't refuse an invitation like that. His left hand joined his right on Kevin's head, and he plunged forward, in and out, into that hot, wet channel.

Kevin wasn't idle either. His tongue swirled around the head and flattened around the base.

Seth's orgasm started to build, growing larger and larger, to astronomical proportions. Kevin said he loved him. Wanted him. Needed him.

He pulled out of Kevin's mouth with a pop, Kevin chasing after, trying to regain his prize.

"No, I don't want to come like that. Not today. I want you to fuck me."

Kevin smiled up at him, lips saliva slick and swollen from sucking. Eyes smoldering, pupils blown out. "Hell, yeah."

Kevin stood and led him to the bed, laying him down on the white, cottony surface. Then he slid off his own jeans slowly, eyes blazing, until they were both naked together.

Seth reached out a hand, and Kevin climbed onto the bed, positioning himself alongside Seth.

Kevin grabbed the lube and squeezed some onto his fingers.

Seth bent his legs and let one knee fall to the side. Then

Kevin's fingers were there, right there, on his pucker, pressing gently.

This wasn't Seth's first time bottoming, but he knew Kevin had never prepared anyone before. So he placed one foot flat and used the leverage to thrust himself onto Kevin's finger.

Kevin jumped and looked up at Seth.

"You can go a little harder. I won't break." Seth pulled Kevin's mouth to his, kissing him with all of the love he felt.

Kevin obliged even as their tongues dueled, pushing in and out, making sensitized nerves fire in his tight passage, sending pleasure winging through him.

"Add another finger," Seth said.

Kevin lifted his head and watched as he pushed in two fingers, spreading them apart just as Seth had done. Kevin was a quick study.

"Yeah, like that, do another."

Kevin added a third. "How do I find your sweet spot?"

"You can't miss it. Just go a bit deeper."

The first time Kevin hit it, Seth's entire body jolted with pleasure, but he knew what he really wanted. "I'm ready now." He grabbed a condom off the fluffy side table and ripped it open. He took his time rolling it down Kevin's thick length, making it part of the foreplay.

Kevin removed his hand and poured lube over his cock. Seth rubbed it in, coating Kevin and causing him to moan.

Kevin gazed at Seth, a question in his eyes.

Seth lifted his legs in the air and spread them. Kevin looked another moment before he moved in between Seth's legs and draped them over his shoulders. Kevin lined up his prick with Seth's hole and pushed forward.

"Oh." Seth moaned with the stretch of the first penetration.

So good. He loved the openly aroused look on Kevin's face as his cock pushed inside, inch by inch.

Once Kevin was fully seated, he paused and met Seth's gaze. Kevin's eyes twinkled like stars on a warm summer evening. *Impossible. Impossible.* But the evidence in front of him told a different story. One of love and longing.

"Please, just move."

Kevin slowly slid his hips out and thrust forward, rubbing Seth's sweet spot. "Fuck, yeah."

After that, Kevin built a slow, steady rhythm, pulling out and thrusting forward deep inside Seth. So deep that he had to be nudging Seth's heart. Things couldn't go back to the way they were, to just friendship. They had changed too much.

"I love you," Seth cried out as Kevin smacked his prostate over and over.

"I love you, too." Kevin leaned in between Seth's legs and took Seth's lips, thrusting his tongue in a wet, hungry kiss.

Seth clutched Kevin's shoulder tight enough to leave marks. He wanted to believe Kevin, needed to. He knew he couldn't stand watching the man go off with a woman again. It would tear him up inside.

He rocked his ass, meeting Kevin's thrusts as the orgasm built inside him. Kevin's cock was a perfect fit. It hit every nerve, stroked every hot spot, and the release was looking to be epic in proportion.

"Can't hold off much longer." Kevin whimpered. "Come with me now."

That was all it took. Seth let go, his cock spurting strings of hot jizz across his and Kevin's abdomens, painting them. As his channel clutched, tightened, Kevin stilled and threw his head back, his cock expanding and contracting.

Kevin flopped over, smearing the sticky spunk between them, holding Seth close. "That was... amazing." Then he kissed Seth, gently, tenderly.

So sweet, it made Seth want to cry from the beauty.

Kevin pulled out with a hiss and rolled to his side, removing and tying off the condom. From somewhere, he had a wash cloth and gently wiped Seth clean and then collapsed next to him.

They held each other. Seth had never felt so sated and happy as he drifted off to sleep.

CHAPTER TWENTY-FIVE

Thursday, April 6, 7:47 am

Seth woke alone in their room at Winthrop's mansion, the sheets cool and empty beside him. How had he gotten there? He frowned, got out of bed, and shuffled over to check the bathroom. Kevin was nowhere to be seen.

After last night, Seth had expected to wake up in Kevin's arms. Instead, his lover? friend? his clothes, the desk his computer had sat on, every sign that he had ever been in the room, was gone.

Seth's stomach clenched.

The items that had been provided for Seth had vanished as well. All that remained was what he had brought with him. His clothes had been laundered and folded. Had everything been an illusion or a dream? The room wobbled.

Pausing before turning on the shower, he shook his head. Where the hell was Kevin? Was he okay?

He called Kevin on his cell phone, but it went straight to voicemail. "Hey, Kev, it's Seth. Um… Hoping everything's all right."

Seth dressed, packed his computer, and sat on the bed to wait, his chest tight.

Erex arrived a few minutes later. Before Seth could react, Erex walked over to Seth and placed a metal device on the side of his neck. Ants seemed to crawl under his skin and then a needlelike prick. Who knew Erex could move so fast?

"There, no more secret messages from Mr. Winthrop. Follow me."

Seth rubbed his neck over the residual sting. Were his thoughts finally his own?

Back up a staircase this time, just one flight, through the main entrance to the front yard. Two limos were parked in the large circular driveway. Kevin ran across the lawn toward a boy and a girl.

It's his youngest brother and sister.

It all became clear. Winthrop had Kevin's brother and sister. They were only eight and ten years old. Kevin mentioned they were supposed to be on some unexpected retreat. Winthrop…

Kevin would have done *anything* to keep them safe.

And he *had* done anything. Including pretending to be gay and to love Seth. Tears prickled at the corners of Seth's eyes. He was so happy they were safe, but he couldn't bear to look at their joy. He didn't know why Winthrop had done all this. Maybe the man really was just a sick bastard.

But something had changed inside of Seth. He couldn't just be Kevin's friend and nothing more. Kevin was straight. He wouldn't be able to stand the sight of Seth.

Winthrop appeared at his side as if by magic. Seth didn't even blink. The bastard, wearing a shit-eating grin, handed him a manila envelope.

"It's all there: the mortgage, the credit cards, the student loans. They're all paid in full. Your family is debt free." Winthrop brushed at his lapel.

Seth pulled the documents out and scanned them quickly. Everything signed and official. Nausea twisted his stomach. The urge to bend over and vomit almost overwhelmed him.

Kevin had done this to save his brother and sister. Seth had done this for money. *This is what a whore must feel like.*

Winthrop gestured to the first limo. "Erex will take you back to school now."

Seth dashed toward the fancy car as fast as he could to get away from here. How he was going to face Kevin?

Fiddling with the strap on his backpack, Seth stared as Erex got in and told the driver where to go.

Seth couldn't go back to the way things were. He couldn't. He had come too far with Kevin to watch him date women again.

He had to move. He would call Cornell housing as soon as he was back on campus and arrange for a different dorm room. Maybe by next season, he would have had enough time to grieve, or he would have to quit the basketball team senior year. Right now, he was too raw.

At least they didn't have any classes together. He would never have to see Kevin. That rubbed him like sandpaper, too.

To pass the time, which seemed much longer than the limo ride out, he opened the packet again and was shocked at what he found. Not only were his loans paid off, but so was his tuition for the rest of his undergrad education. Why would Winthrop have done that? The paperwork even said that he had fulfilled all of his obligations to Winthrop, and it detailed how no further requests could be made of Seth in exchange for this.

He shook his head. His life would be easier and so would his family's. But his heart ached.

Erex glanced up from the *American Girl* magazine he was reading. "We have all of the clothes you used this week in suitcases in the trunk. Mr. Winthrop says they are yours to keep. He hopes you'll think back on this week fondly."

Seth shuddered. "Not likely."

The comment was enough to stifle any further conversation.

During the endless ride back, Erex opened a full picnic basket containing turkey sandwiches, potato salad, pickles, and brownies for lunch. Seth tried to eat but found his stomach rejected the notion of anything as mundane as food. He figured he had consumed enough calories this week to last a month.

When the limo pulled up in front of Dickson Hall, it was after five o'clock in the evening. How had the trip taken so long? One last impossibility in a week where dragons were real and Kevin could love a man.

He would have to wait until morning to call the housing office when they opened.

Dragging the luggage behind him, he pulled out his key and opened his dorm room. He looked at Kevin's side and his friend's favorite poster. The room was filled with the man's scent. Tears sprung to Seth's eyes. He threw himself on the bed and lay there, dreading when Kevin would come home.

Eventually, sleep claimed him, but disturbing images of Kevin having sex with the many girls he had dated filled his dreams.

He woke the next morning to the sound of a key in the lock.

CHAPTER TWENTY-SIX

Friday, April 5, 7:12 am

Light peeked in through the curtain covering the window. Seth blinked, squinting his eyes at the dorm room door as it opened. He scrubbed his hand across his face and pushed his hair back only to have it flop forward again. Somehow, the night had passed, and Kevin was returning. Seth sat up, still in the same clothes from yesterday, and put on his glasses.

Kevin entered and turned to him, his eyes red and tired, but a sweet smile graced his face. "Hey. You took off before I could talk to you."

Seth turned away, unable to meet Kevin's eyes. "I figured it would be better that way."

"What? Why?" Was that panic in Kevin's voice?

"I'm going to make this easy for you. As soon as the housing office opens, I'm going to arrange to move out. You did what you had to do to save your brother and sister. You

251

don't need the reminder. You'll move on, live your life, find that perfect wife, and have a family."

Silence.

Then Kevin's hand was on Seth's cheek, turning him until their eyes met. A soft smile graced his face. "Do I have any say in all that?"

Seth's mouth dropped open. "What?"

Kevin shook his head, chuckling. "Again with the what. Seth, listen very carefully." He paused. "Are you listening?"

Seth nodded. What could Kevin possibly say? It couldn't be…

Kevin stared right into Seth's eyes. "I'm gay."

Seth tried to pull away, but Kevin's hand on his shoulder kept him steady. "What? No. You date girls."

"I'm gay."

Seth wanted to believe, but people didn't just change, no matter how much he wanted them to. "Maybe this week confused you."

"I've never been confused, just in denial. I'm gay. Not curious, not bi-sexual, but gay. I've always been gay."

"What? But what about Lola and Lisa and Laine and…"

Kevin's lips turned up at the corner, and his eyes softened. "I thought I could change myself. I thought if I kept dating women, one would stick. But they never did. There was never a spark."

Seth's heart raced faster than light speed. "Why? Why do that to yourself?"

"You know my family is religious. I grew up in Indiana. Around there, when a guy really wanted to insult you, he called you a fag. I didn't want to be gay."

Seth could sympathize. He knew many people were still on the wrong side of this issue. He had been lucky, growing up in a liberal family. His parents had understood when he told them he was gay.

"I came out to my parents last night. Winthrop flew them in so I could escort my brother and sister to them. They didn't even know he had them. "

Seth's mental capacity went super nova. "What? You came out? Why?"

"Why do you think, numbnut? I told you yesterday. I love you. You said you loved me, too. Winthrop could freakin' hear our thoughts. He wouldn't let us lie. Did you find a way around that?" His voice dropped to almost a whisper. "Are you saying you don't have feelings for me?"

Kevin gazed at Seth from under his lashes, biting his lower lip. *So open, so vulnerable.*

Seth stood. A spark ignited inside him. This was real. Now. The spark grew, filling his heart with a blazing joy. They were free. No acting any more. No crazy threats hanging over their heads. Kevin had come out for him.

"I… I love you so much, Kevin Fields. So much, I was going to move out because I couldn't stand to see you with anyone else, but I wanted you to be happy."

Kevin shook his head, a wry smiled on his face. "I will be. If you say we can be together."

"I… yes. I want that more than anything."

Seth stepped into Kevin's outstretched arms. What started as a nightmare culminated in the fulfillment of his wildest dreams.

"Why didn't you tell me? This week? I thought I was torturing you. I felt dirty inside."

Kevin shrugged. "I'm sorry. You didn't seem to really care about me. The job offer, I thought you refused it because you didn't want to be a couple."

"Stupid. I didn't want to trap you."

Kevin's arms tightened around Seth. "Well, next time, try using your words, asshole."

Seth held on to Kevin, surrounded by his warmth. "Okay. How about, 'So you came out for me?'"

Kevin's arms tightened around Seth's waist, pulling him close. "No, I came out for *me*. Even if this doesn't work with us, but I know it will. I needed to tell my family the truth. I needed to stop living a lie." Kevin frowned, his lip quivering.

Seth's arms and legs shook. Kevin's dad tolerated Seth being gay, but had cornered Seth on a couple of occasions to lecture him or offer to pray for him. "How did they take it?"

"Dad's not speaking to me. Mom cried, but we talked all night. I think she'll support me. My brother and sister just rolled their eyes, like *duh*. Apparently, Winthrop told them I was in love with you and made them watch *Glee* or some shit. I was so worried about what he was doing to them, but they had the best week of their lives. You know his mansion, it's crazier than Disney World. They want to go back. Winthrop invented the whole retreat thing. My parents never even knew anything was wrong."

"He was going to evict my family, make me leave school, take my dad's job. When I found out you did it to save your brother and sister from Winthrop, I felt like such a whore, deflowering the straight guy for money."

Kevin reached up and smoothed Seth's bangs behind his ear. "You're not a whore, and I'm not straight. That's why I never had a steady girl. I could never connect with any of them."

"I just thought you were a womanizer."

"Asshole." Kevin slotted their lips together.

Seth melted against him. Somehow, all the planets had aligned in a way that was physically impossible but completely perfect.

As Kevin's tongue slipped into his mouth, Seth gripped him tightly, trying to convey his excitement for their future together. One filled with friendship, passion, and love.

EPILOGUE

Erex stood with his boss, Maynard Frederick Winthrop IV, in front of a fifty-inch monitor in a large room filled with little people seated at computers. Todd, Jeff, and Vincent surrounded him. They all watched Seth and Kevin embrace.

"Will they live happily ever after now?" Erex asked.

"Of course. They have some rocky times ahead. Kevin's family is not pleased, but the fact that both of their college educations are fully paid for means that his family can't ruin his life."

The little man looked up at Winthrop, his eyes wide. "May I ask a question, my Lord?"

"Of course, Erex. I'm not a monster."

"Why did you bring me in from the field and have me do all this?" Erex gestured to himself and his three-piece suit.

Winthrop walked over to Erex and ruffled his hair. "I know you would have preferred not to be thrown into this head first, but I needed to see how you handled yourself. Just one moment…" Winthrop snapped his fingers, and almost everyone in the room changed.

Gone was the bald, obese, short body. In its place was his real physique—young, thin, muscular. Still only five-feet four inches, but with gleaming tan skin and a radiant smile. The suit was gone, too, replaced by a Greek style toga, a quiver of arrows graced his back between enormous white-feathered wings.

Next to him, Erex had changed as well. Still small, but more cherubic than human. He, too, had wings and a bow and arrows. The three humans remained the same.

"Ah, that's better. It feels so good to remove the costume."

"I prefer you in this form, my Lord Eros."

"I do as well. To answer your question. Who shot the arrow that pierced Seth and Kevin's hearts?" Cupid asked.

Erex's skin crawled like he was back in the tight suit. He studied his bare feet. "Me, my Lord."

"Erex, look at me."

Erex tilted his head back and beheld his sovereign.

"I'm not angry at you. It's not your fault they fought what fate intended for them. Humans are quite stupid. To cope with their utter idiocy, they make up rules and proclamations. They claim authority no one has given them. This makes them act contrary to their own best interests."

Erex let out the breath he held. "That's crazy."

"True. God tried to tell them in his book. Over and over, he said love one another. But God also gave humans free will, which they often use to screw up." Cupid's face hardened into angry lines. "These two boys were going to miss out on happiness because Kevin couldn't accept himself. I couldn't let that happen. So, I intervened. Some of the others say it was a bit extreme, but it was the jolt the two of them needed to get things moving."

"Well, it certainly worked, my Lord." Erex paused for a moment. "Will I return to the field now?"

"No. You did such an excellent job assisting in this, I've decided you're going to help with other cases."

"Thank you, my Lord! It's an honor to serve."

"Todd, Jeff, your designs for the sets for Seth and Kevin were excellent. I'd like the two of you to stay on to help with other cases. It's nice letting someone else worry about the details. I never would have considered using feathers for a headboard."

Jeff took Todd's hand. The two met each other's eyes and nodded. "It's a privilege. Besides, it's amazing watching you conjure something we imagined."

"Vincent, excellent acting as usual. Are you sure you don't want to audition for some movies? You had Seth and Kevin convinced you were in mortal danger."

Vincent grinned. "Nope, I'm happy to be part of the team."

Erex laughed. "I thought Seth was going to pass out when Fluffy fake punched you."

"Fluffy may be an ogre, but he's just a big softie," Vincent replied.

"Are all of our interventions because humans consider homosexuality to be wrong?" Erex asked.

"No, humans are endlessly inventive when coming up with ways to make themselves miserable. We shall continue to fix that. One couple at a time."

Cupid looked at the screen once more as the embrace between Kevin and Seth became more passionate. "We've seen enough. Cut the feed." He gestured to the cherubic technician in front of him.

The screen went blank.

"Come, gentlemen, we have plans to make."
"Of course, my Lord. Lead the way."

ABOUT THE AUTHOR

Kathryn Sparrow has had stories spinning around in her head her whole life and finally decided it was time to write them down. After working twenty years in the software industry, she has left the engineering world to be a chauffeur mom (because she doesn't really get to stay-at-home.) She lives with her fantastic, geek husband and her two adorable, sometimes infuriating daughters, who are too smart for their mommy's own good. If she had spare time, she would spend it knitting, crocheting, cross-stitching, and doing any other handicrafts that catch her fancy.

Find more about the author at the following places:

Main Web site: http://www.kathrynsparrow.com/

Twitter: https://twitter.com/KSparrowAuthor

www.ingramcontent.com/pod-product-compliance
Lightning Source LLC
Chambersburg PA
CBHW020907160726
47993CB00005B/1850